ULTIMATE SPANKING

A COLLECTION OF
TWENTY EROTIC STORIES

EDITED BY

MIRANDA FORBES

Published by Accent Press Ltd – 2010

ISBN 9781907016127

Printed and bound in the UK

Cover design by
Red Dot Design

Contents

The Spanking Man
by Monica Belle

He had to be one of the least attractive men in the bar and he'd just threatened to spank me. No, he'd managed to imply that I might enjoy a spanking, which was worse, as if I might ever, ever, ever want him to lay me across his lap, pull down my jeans and panties and smack my bare bottom. It was unthinkable, impossible, totally inappropriate. Not that he was ever going to get to do it, not in a million years, but even for him to dare to think that I might be interested was too much. I mean, he had to be fifty if he was a day, and he was balding and thick-set, with a slimy grin painted onto a round red face that rose from a squat body on a short, thick neck. And he'd offered to spank me. Me! Tamara Chertsey, a twenty-year-old student, less than half his age, taller than he was and a size ten in my skinny jeans.

It was the skinny jeans that were the problem. They clung to my cheeks as if they'd been painted on, and while I do like to show off, that was not for the benefit of people like him. I always hate it when older men grab an eyeful of what they shouldn't be looking at, and I never cease to be amazed that some of them proposition me, as if I could possibly be interested. But to imply that I might enjoy a spanking really took the prize.

As I'd passed him his drinks and his change he'd said "Spank you very much" instead of "Thank you very much", and winked. I thought I'd misheard him. I wanted to have misheard him, but there was no mistaking the implication of that oily wink. My reaction showed in my face, and I realised that with a piece of truly breathtaking arrogance he'd misread my outrage for a pleased reaction. Or perhaps shock mixed with a secret thrill, because his grin had immediately grown broader and dirtier.

Before I could think of what to say he'd taken his drinks and started back to his table. I wanted to chase after him. Tell him what a filthy old pervert he was. Point out how utterly impossible it was that a girl like me might be interested in him in any way whatsoever. But most of all to tell him that I did not, under any circumstances, want him to spank me. Of course I couldn't, because he was hideous, and even if he wasn't it would have been hideously embarrassing in front of everybody else in the bar. And he was so arrogant he'd probably have taken my protests as further proof of interest.

So he left me seething with embarrassment. And furious with him, but equally furious with myself, for not reacting quickly enough and because I could not get what he'd said out of my head. It was just too offensive; even the basic suggestion that I might enjoy having my bottom smacked was a gross affront to my dignity, and to female dignity in general, let alone that he might be the man to do it to me. A set of images had begun to form in my head, in much the same way as I sometimes think of the most inappropriate thing at the most serious moment, like deliberately wetting myself in the middle of an exam.

At first the images were simple: standing shy and embarrassed as I admitted to him that I'd like it; draping myself across his lap with my bottom raised for his attention; having my jeans and knickers taken down to get me bare; and last, and worst, being spanked.

I sneaked a double shot of over-proof vodka in the hope that the awful pictures would go away, but that only made it worse, adding yet more humiliating details: such as getting it in the bar in front of other people; being made to repeat myself so that everybody could hear as I asked to be punished; and having my thighs pulled apart for him to see if I was wet. I was. Very wet. And by the end of the evening there was no denying that I was ready for a good, hard fucking.

Which was exactly what I got. Not from him, obviously, but from my boyfriend, Connor, when I got back to the hall. He'd been in the middle of an essay and was astonished by how horny I was, when I normally came back from work tired and ready for sleep. When he told me to wait a bit, I got down under the desk and sucked his cock, which soon had his attention. I offered myself to him, kneeling on his bed with my jeans and knickers pulled down, my top and bra up over my tits and my bum stuck up, which was the closest I could bear to come to my awful fantasy. He took full advantage, taking me by the hips for a rough, hard fuck while I played with myself. But even as I came I was biting my lip, determined not to admit to what was going through my head, which was the image of him giving me the same treatment but with my bottom hot and red from spanking.

The moment I'd come I was filled with guilt and shame for my fantasy, even though I'd been imagining Connor doing the spanking and not the awful man from the bar. I felt as if I'd betrayed not only myself, but every woman on the planet by giving myself an orgasm over something so impossibly degrading. But, despite my every effort to get rid of them, I still didn't stop thinking about it, nor could I hold back the ever-more dreadful fantasies evolving in my mind.

Logically I knew that the experience would be as painful as it was shameful, thoroughly unpleasant from start to finish and not sexy at all. Unfortunately, I've never been very good at making myself accept logical explanations, and the same terrifying thoughts about being spanked stayed lodged in my head day after day, until by the end of the week I could picture the entire scenario of how it would be, like a scene out of some grotesque film, half horror, half porno.

I didn't know his name, but I thought of him as the Spanking Man and would imagine myself going over to where he'd been seated with two equally repulsive friends, not to give him a piece of my mind, but to admit he'd been right. And then I would ask, very politely, if he'd mind spanking me. He'd respond with his slimy grin and a knowing chuckle, pointing out that he was busy talking to his friends but agreeing to give me what I needed as long as I did exactly as I was told and didn't talk back. He'd tell me my knickers would be coming down, that I was to be spanked on my bare bottom, right there and then, in the middle of the bar, in front of my boss, my workmates, friends from uni' and a good fifty random strangers. I'd protest, but I'd give in, standing there like an idiot as I unfastened my jeans to make it easier for him to get me stripped. People would see, conversations slowly dying all around me as they realised they were about to witness a bare-bottom spanking, my bare-bottom spanking. The music would stop, only to start again, no longer pop but something catchy and a bit silly to accentuate the ridiculous, humiliating situation I was in. He'd pat his legs and down I'd go, my eyes tight shut and my hands braced against the floor, my hair a curtain around my face, my bottom lifted. He'd fiddle with the zip of my jeans, drawing it slowly down, his fat, moist fingers pressing into my flesh. There would be a bubble of shame growing in my throat as my exposure continued, my jeans tugged down off my hips to get my knickers showing, tight across my cheeks, but not for long. He'd pull them down, casually, as if baring a young woman's bottom in public were the most natural thing in the world. He'd touch me up, enjoying the feel of my flesh and the shape of my bum. Maybe even pulling my cheeks apart to inspect my anus and the rear view of my pussy. Maybe even sticking a finger up me to see if I was wet. I would be, and he and his friends would laugh to see my excitement. He'd spank me, his fat little hand rising and falling on my bare bottom to make my cheeks bounce and set my legs kicking in my pain and frustration as I was punished. I'd be sobbing, tears streaming from my eyes, but the state of my pussy would tell a very different story, wet and ready between my open thighs, and I'd be ready for the final humiliation, being made to suck his cock to say thank you for my punishment.

To make it worse I seemed to have dredged the whole thing up from some dark corner of my subconscious mind, including that final, awful detail. Certainly I'd never done anything of the sort. In fact I'd never been spanked in my entire life, and on the rare occasions when I'd come across references to it, the idea had always filled me with the same horrified fascination as a car crash. Yet I'd never been indifferent to it, that much I had to admit, and eventually I came to realising that there was a little kink in my psyche which the Spanking Man had managed to trigger.

I could have killed him, cheerfully, but the damage was done and as time passed and my fantasies grew ever more vivid, and the urge to play with myself over them stronger, I realised that there was only one thing to be done. Fantasy and reality are very different things, as everybody knows, or should know, and it occurred to me that the only way to get rid of my unspeakable desires was to have somebody do it for real and so teach myself what a horrible experience it really was.

When I first thought of the idea as a solution, I rejected it immediately, laughing at myself in a way that came uncomfortably close to hysterics. And yet the more I thought about it, the more I grew certain that it was the only way out. The only question was: who was going to spank me?

Connor was out of the question. He was great as a boyfriend, but in a rough, super-masculine sort of way. I'd spent ages training him to respect me, explaining what should have been obvious, such as the fact that just because I like it hard and from behind doesn't mean he can treat me as his personal fuck dolly; or that he should boast to his mates at the rugby club about how hot I am in bed. The thought of how he'd react to a request for a spanking was enough to set me blushing hot, because I'd not only get it, and hard, but my secret would be around the entire university within days.

I couldn't ask any of my other male friends either, for similar reasons, because it would be unfaithful to Connor and because they were sure to want to fuck me afterwards, and that was out of the question. Yet the idea of asking another woman to do it was more embarrassing still: not only would I have to explain why I wanted a spanking, but whoever I went to was sure to conclude that I was a closet lesbian. What I needed was an older, sensible man. Somebody who would do it to me, and be sufficiently awed by what I was allowing him to do so that he'd respect my limits. He'd have to be a stranger as well, in order to make sure the story didn't get out. And he'd have to be attractive, naturally. I thought of the internet, but if there's one rule that should never be broken about meeting up with people you only know online, it's not to go alone. But to take a friend with me would be nearly as bad as asking her to do the spanking herself.

Really I was only making excuses, and I knew it, because there was one other possibility, which I kept coming back to: my own uncle. It was an appalling thought, and yet we'd always been close. He was a lot younger than Dad: handsome, single, and one of the few people I could really talk to, even to the point of going to him with questions about sex that I was too embarrassed to put to my parents. Better still, if I explained my problem he might just be able to find a solution that didn't involve putting me across his knee. Finally, he was very, very gay.

I tried to postpone the inevitable, telling myself I was being silly, that my wild fantasies would go away eventually. They didn't, and only got worse, keeping me in a state of almost permanent arousal that grew so strong in the middle of my month that it was all I could do to keep my fingers out of my underwear. Connor loved it, although I never told him what was making me like that, but it was starting to affect my work. In the end circumstances caught up with me. Uncle James picked me up at the end of term.

He quite often came to visit, because he only lived fifty miles away, much closer than my parents. When he rang to offer a lift, I accepted without a second thought, telling myself that I didn't have to tell him. And if I chose to, then I'd only ask his advice rather than suggesting a trip across his knee. Even that was going to be pretty embarrassing, and when the day came I found myself silent and uncommunicative, responding to his happy conversation with monosyllables or not at all. He noticed this attitude before we were even out of town.

'What's eating you, Tamara? Don't tell me you've flunked your prelims?'

'No, no, nothing like that.'

'What is it then?'

'I ...'

And then it just came out: the whole story, from my encounter with the Spanking Man to my decision to ask him to show me what it was really like.

He laughed.

'It's not funny, Uncle James!'

'No. I'm sorry. But you do realise that your desires aren't all that unusual. A lot of girls like to be spanked.'

'Oh come on, Uncle James, that's just male fantasy!'

He shrugged. We'd had similar discussions before, on other sex-related topics, and I knew he was happy to leave me in what he called my ignorance. For a while we sat in silence before he spoke again.

'And you really want me to try and spank your fantasies out of you?'

'Yes. I know I can trust you.'

He nodded, accepting his due before going on, his voice doubtful. 'I'm not really sure it's a good idea, Tamara. What would your parents say?'

'They're not going to know!'

'That's not the issue. I'm your uncle.'

'Exactly. With anybody else it would be sexual. I have to, Uncle James. I really do. And surely it's better for me to come to you than somebody else?'

'Would you go to somebody else?'

'I ... I'm not sure. Yes, I think so.'

He didn't answer, leaving me burning with embarrassment. We'd been about to pull on to the motorway from a roundabout, but he went past the slip road, taking the next exit instead, a lane that led off into the countryside.

'Where are we going?'

Again he didn't answer, but my stomach had contracted into a tight knot. I was about to be spanked. I stayed quiet, biting my lip and telling myself I could back out if I wanted to, as we followed the road, first between high, green hedges and then in among stands of tall, grey-barked poplar by the river.

7

He stopped the car on the verge, where some thick bushes fringed the plantation, got out and came round to open my door for me. I joined him, suddenly unable to speak but taking his hand as he offered it to me, his eyes fixed to mine.

'Are you really sure you want this, Tamara?'

All I could manage was a nod. He responded in kind, his voice once more light-hearted as he spoke again. 'Come on then, but if you change your mind, just say.'

He had a firm grip on my hand and led me in among the bushes. I was shaking badly, hot with embarrassment and apprehension, because although I knew I was safe with him, I also knew it was going to hurt. That it had to hurt, or I wouldn't be able to get rid of my fantasies. That was what I wanted, what I needed, but that didn't make it any easier when he sat down on a low branch and looked up at me, not speaking, but his eyes once more offered the chance to back away from the insane situation I'd got myself into. I'd folded my arms across my chest, protecting myself and I looked down, unable to meet those level grey eyes.

He drew a faint sigh. 'I suppose you'd better come across my knee then.'

My response was a weak nod, but I couldn't make myself do it and just stood there fidgeting until at last he took pity on me. Reaching for my hand once more, he drew me gently down into that impossibly undignified pose I'd come to think of as the spanking position. I braced my hands and feet the way I'd imagined myself doing so many times, thankful that my long hair meant I couldn't see much as I lifted my bottom. He took me gently around my waist, another detail I'd imagined many a time, and which wrung a sob from my lips. His hand settled on my bottom, sending a sharp stab of humiliation through me. So strong I was immediately choking back the tears, and yet something was fundamentally wrong. In my imagination I was always bare-bottomed, and any other way simply wasn't going to work. My voice was a croak as I spoke up.

'I … you… please could you turn up my skirt, Uncle James, and … and take down my knickers?'

He hesitated. His hand rested across my bottom. Then gave

8

me a sudden, hard smack and it had begun.

It did sting, making me kick and wriggle across his lap, but he wasn't doing it all that hard and it didn't hurt anything like as much as I'd expected. Being covered didn't help either.

'No, really, Uncle James. I need to be bare bottom, and … and you can do it harder.'

I heard him swallow. 'Tammy, if you asked that of anybody but me …'

His words had trailed off as he took hold of the hem of my skirt. I shut my eyes tight, my whole being focussed on my burning shame as my skirt was turned up over my bottom and tucked into my waistband along with the tail of my blouse. With my knickers on show, Uncle James hesitated once more and I found myself wondering if he was having second thoughts about pulling them down, to give me time to contemplate the indignity of my position before I was bared. Or was he simply trying to not to laugh because the pair I'd chosen that morning were pink and patterned with little yellow ducks. Only when he took hold of them did I know they were really coming down, and I'd begun to shake uncontrollably as he spoke once more.

'Completely bare?'

My answer was a sob, but it was supposed to be a yes and he took it as one.

'OK, if you insist. I suppose I'd better pop your knickers down.'

Even as he spoke he'd done it, peeling the tiny scrap of cotton down over my bum cheeks, and not just a little way either, but all the way, turning them inside out around my thighs.

I felt the cool air on my pussy and knew I was showing from behind, my bum hole too, because my bottom was well raised and my cheeks were fully open. That was as it should be, as it always was in my imagination: every rude detail bare for the inspection of the man who was spanking me, and for anybody who happened to be looking on.

It was then that the real shame hit me, even before the spanking had begun: a choking sense of humiliation so strong it

9

was a physical pain and made far, far worse an instant later as he began to actually spank me.

Then it really hurt: powerful, stinging slaps delivered full across my cheeks to set my flesh bouncing and my legs kicking wildly in my half-lowered panties. I couldn't speak, but only yelp and gasp, with my hair tossing in my pain and my hands thumping on the soil beneath my face.

I'd asked for it and I got it: a hard, bare-bottom spanking across a man's lap. Every bit as painful and humiliating as I'd imagined, only it wasn't horrible at all. For the first few smacks I thought it was going to be, but then the most extraordinary sensation had begun to well up inside me. My feelings of exposure, the heat of my smacked cheeks and a new sensation of utter helplessness all coming together to create the most delicious sense of arousal I had ever experienced short of orgasm itself. I realised what I'd done immediately. Uncle James was right. At the realisation of how completely I'd betrayed myself, I burst into tears and he stopped immediately. But it was too late. Some girls do like being spanked, and I was one of them.

After that there was no stopping me. I introduced Connor to the pleasures of punishing me and he took to it like a duck to water. But even that wasn't enough, and when Uncle James came to visit me he'd take me into the woods and I'd have my bottom smacked before we went for lunch. I loved every second of it, and yet I never lost that lingering sense of resentment for the Spanking Man.

It was nearly a year before I saw him again, not in the bar, but walking along the towpath by the canal. There were other people about but nobody close, providing me with the perfect opportunity to tell him what I thought of him, and I'd put a lot of thought into my words.

'Do you recognise me?'

He looked surprised.

'Um … no. I'm afraid not. Should I?'

'Yes, you should. I'm a student and I work in the Cricketer's during the evenings. About a year ago you made an inappropriate comment to me.'

'I assure you I did not.'

'Oh yes you did, you little pervert. Instead of saying "Thank you very much" you said "Spank you very much", and if you think that spanking women is –'

'I'm sorry, but I said no such thing. As a matter of fact I'm against all forms of corporal punishment, and would never make such an inappropriate remark in any case. You must have misheard me.'

I tried one last, feeble sally .'But you winked at me!'

'Perhaps, in a friendly way, but I can assure you …'

He carried on, but I wasn't listening. There was no guilt in his face, no sly glint in his eyes, just honest outrage. He was telling the truth. My mouth came slowly open as the reality of the situation sank in. I'd spent months agonising over what I'd thought he wanted to do to me, and he didn't. I'd had myself spanked by my own uncle, and I needn't have. I'd got myself hooked on a dirty slutty kink, and I had only myself to blame. There was no Spanking Man, only a spanked girl, me.

Perfect Bound
by Shanna Germain

It's the librarian look that gets them. They walk into my little erotic bookstore expecting – what? – I don't really know. Not me. Not this tall woman behind the checkout counter in her twin set, glasses hanging by their silver chain, swinging into that laced space between her breasts each time she moves. They're not expecting this dark pile of hair, these swept-to-the side bangs that half-hide my dark eyes. Or the long black skirt, slit so that it seems to promise a glimpse of thigh, of more, if only they could see behind the counter. They're not expecting this cliché, this proverbial boy's wet dream. Not expecting me.

I can tell by the way they move their eyes toward me, and then away, like I'm just another book on the shelf. I've seen boys look at porn with the same denial of fervour.

Take this boy. Not a boy, really. Twenty-five if he's a day. Tight black jeans over his skinny legs and ass. Torn grey T-shirt that says *Getting Lucky in Nebraska*. A small silver piercing rests just under his thin, pale lips. He'd be emo – I keep up on these things, make it my job to know – if not for the naturally blonde hair.

He's been here before, but only to browse. Today, it's different. He's looking for something. I wonder which of his friends clued him in. He circles around the checkout counter for a while, picking up books and looking at them without looking at them. Opening them wherever the pages fall. Cracking spines. Smudging ink with his thumb.

I keep doing the thing that I'm doing. It looks like paperwork, but really it's just little squiggles on paper, something that lets me keep my eyes busy. Something that lets me lick the end of the pencil, tongue the lead just a little.

He makes smaller circles, like a cub playing at predator. Instinctual. Clumsy. Big feet and his smell on the wind.

I look up from my squiggles and tuck my pencil into my hair.

'Can I help you find something?' I have my dark red lipstick on. The colour that says *open me. Take a peek inside.*

'Oh, just looking,' he says. Looking as he says it. Brave boy. Big blue eyes.

I lick my teeth, show the flash of white against the dark. I reach into my hair for my pencil, pull out one long, loose curl that falls down against my neck.

'Well, if you don't need anything …'

'Wait.'

'Yes?'

He lowers his eyes and picks up a book from the counter in front of me. It's the *Art of Spanking*. Milo Manara. The boy's palm covers the illustration on the front cover. He flips the book sideways and runs his finger down the spine.

Now comes the break point. Will he ask, or will he leave here with only a book to tide him – and me – over?

The boy swallows. I can hear the sound as loud as if it was my own throat. He slides the book across the counter toward me. His fingers tap-tap the book's cover.

'I hear you specialize in … binding,' he says. 'Printing.'

The word he's looking for is imprinting, but I let it slide. 'I do. Do you have something you need … bound?' I give him back the pause he's given me. The emphasis.

'Please,' he says. Something so soft in his voice, so painful in his need. Even his body sags with the letting go, the asking. His shoulders soften.

I reach across the counter, touch one of his fingers as it covers the book. 'Something in particular?'

He bites his bottom lip, making an indent in the pink curves. There is a space of time, two or three seconds where he can still back out. Buy the book instead. I wait.

'Me,' he says, finally. 'Me.'

13

I smile at him with my dark lips and my white teeth. I pull the pencil from my hair, and the barrette with it, and a layer of dark curls falls down around my face.

'Flip the sign then,' I say. 'I charge by the hour.'

He shakes his head, and his hair shifts across his brow. 'I don't ...'

'You can come in and sort books.' I think of how many boys I already have sorting books. And dusting. I have a pretty dark-haired boy who does my books – in the monetary sense – and one who does my taxes. 'Or something.' I point at the door with my pencil. 'Flip the sign.'

While the boy – I'll have to ask his name at some point – flips the sign in the door from *Open* to *Shut*, I open the drawer in front of me. It's filled with rows of old typewriter ribbon. I have a man who buys them for me wherever he can find them – auction houses, garage sales, estates. He sends them to me by the boxload. I pay him for his costs and shipping and I bind him and bend him over my knee whenever he comes into town.

I like the ones on spools, with nylon ribbons. Black. No lift-off tape or coloured ink. And they have to be truly old. Not just replicas. A bit of ink gets on my fingers as I find the one I want.

The boy is back. I shake loose the rest of my curls with ink-smudged fingers. His eyes follow the movement. I take the typewriter ribbon in one hand and the book he's chosen in the other.

'C'mon back,' I say.

The chair in the back room is the one I like best. It's antique, I think, with an ornate back and a red velvet cushion as a seat cover. Taller than most chairs today and no arms – that's the important part.

I sit. When I cross my legs, the fabric of the skirt slides open. His eyes follow that movement too.

'Have you done this before?' I ask.

'N-no. No.'

'You understand what happens here? You understand that once we start, we don't stop?'

'Yes.' Surer this time.

I unspool the end of the typewriter ribbon so that it falls to the floor like curls.

'What's your name?'

'Stephen, with a p-h.'

'Well, Stephen with a p-h, how did you get here?'

'I just live around the –'

I sigh. Boys. Sometimes they're the perfect thing in the world. Other times …

'No, who told you about me?'

He sticks his thumbs in his belt loops. 'My friend Anthony.'

Of course. Anthony. He's one of my window washers. Pretty, pretty boy with cocoa skin and a piercing fetish. Comes by once a week or so. I have a brief delightful image of getting the two of them together, under my thumb, so to speak. Getting ahead of myself though. We'll have to see how this session goes first.

'Get undressed.'

This is the moment when some boys hesitate. Some ask questions. Some go home. Stephen with a ph just starts to undo his belt. All of his nervous energy is transformed into the process of taking off his clothes. He does it carefully, the belt through its buckle and the slide out of his jeans. I'm not a sub, but, if I was, that movement, that sound, would be enough to get me wet. I wonder if he knows this, if he's played that way before or if it's just something that comes naturally to some people.

I unspool the black ribbon all the way while he undresses. By the time I'm done, the ribbon covers the floor around me and he's standing before me. All lean white body. Only his chest and cock have any colour in them, rosy red, both.

'Come closer.' I shift my legs again, let the skirt's slit slide higher.

I'm tempted to start at his cock – it juts out at me, asking to be touched – but I'm afraid it will send him over the edge too soon. Instead, I wind the ribbon around his thin waist, replacing his studded belt with this thin black line. Around and around his waist, just below his belly button, down toward the brown hairs that rise up his belly, down toward the place where

15

his torso meets his thighs. I work around his cock, never touching it, pretending it isn't there between us.

When his waist is wrapped, I snip a short piece of ribbon off and reach to his wrists. I put them in front of his body, loop them together and tie them off.

He is so obedient that I wonder if he's paying attention, if he really understands what's happening. His eyes are closed, and the tip of his tongue plays softly at the corner of his lips. I run the sharp edge of my nail up between his thighs, and he takes a sharp, quick inhale. Fully here then. That's good.

I cup his balls in my palm. They feel full and solid, like living Ben-Wa balls in there. I roll them softly, watching his cock pop each time the pad of my thumb hits the underside. He's a sigher, sending soft exhales of air, so quiet that they're hardly hearable. I wonder what he'll sound like when I really get started. Will he stay quiet? Or can I break the noise from him?

I make the first loop of ribbon around his balls, and he opens his eyes. The wet pink of his tongue finds the corner of his lips again. I wrap him all the way up, from the soft curves of his balls to the wide base and finally all the way to the small flared tip. There's so much ribbon that I have to double-wrap in places.

When I let go, he looks down at himself. No words. His cock jumps again; the head is shiny and slick. I know it won't be long before he starts leaking onto the ribbon, before he wets it enough that it will mark his body with its ink. I wear black skirts for a reason.

'Lay down.' I'd pat my lap, but he's already moving. He puts his bound hands over his head, without me having to tell him, and then he lays himself across my legs.

He weighs less than I expected and I didn't expect much. His cock presses into my thighs. And he's got a great ass, full and curved, despite his lean build. The black ribbon around his waist accentuates the white globes of his cheeks. I run my palm across the pale skin, finger the space between his cheeks. I can't hear his sighs, but I can feel them, in the push of his ribs and belly against my legs.

I draw back my hand and lower it on the fleshy part. Not hard. Just testing. A little smack, a little pink against that pale. And again. Still no sound. No movement from him. His cock doesn't change against my lap. Either he's in over his head, or he's ready for more. Sometimes it's hard to tell the difference.

I cup the curve of his ass in my palm again. I love that place, the curve of skin and muscle. Those little dimples that only boys seem to have. His body relaxes against mine. Sighs into relief. That's my cue to start again, my hand coming down hard and fast, so fast that my palm stings. He wiggles, pressing his cock harder into my thigh, trying to escape the blows, trying to move closer to them. Above his head, his bound hands close on the air.

When I stop, his breathing – not sighs now, but something heavier, louder – fills the room. I press my finger to one of the pink marks on his skin. He clenches his ass and lets out his first words.

'Holy fucking shit.' His voice is filled with both awe and discomfort.

'Oh, Stephen with a p-h,' I have to laugh a little. 'We've only just begun.'

I put one hand on the back of his neck, bend him just a little so that his ass rises higher, his cock presses harder. I start at the rounded bottom of his ass, covering the pink marks that are already there. His skin is warming up, or my palm is. With each stroke, he shudders just a little. He tries to give his feet a hold on the floor, but I have him bent so that he can't quite reach.

The skirt material is thin enough that I can feel the edges of the typewriter ribbon that I've wrapped around him. I know it's chafing him now, rubbing against his skin in a way that is both pleasure and pain. I open my legs a little beneath him, creating a hollow for his cock between my legs. He rubs into the space, tries to settle himself into a rhythm.

I spank the back of his legs, the inside of his cheeks, slow and steady. The sound of my palm against his flesh, the way he wiggles under my blows – is it so bad to say how much I love it? How much I live for moments like these, for boys like these? If I were to slide one finger beneath my skirt right now, I know how wet I'd be, how open. But that's for later. I don't want to fuck this boy, I just want to do this, raise my hand to him again and again. I want to imagine him later, when I'm alone, his pinkened skin and his ribbon-wrapped cock. His quiet, submissive desire. I want to see him sorting books later in his skinny black jeans and remember this moment, him squirming and sighing across me.

The book he chose earlier is next to the chair, and I lean over and pick it up. Hard cover. An art book, so it's heavy and wide. Not as much noise and sting as a soft cover, but a lot of heavy pain. I crack it against the side of his ass first. He inhales sharply, and raises his head to try and look at me.

I push his head back down and grab the ribbon at his waist to hold him steady. Already, the ink has marked his flesh, imprinted his struggles on his skin. They're beautiful, long black strips of ink filled with potential for words and stories. Desire made visible.

The book makes a flat sound against his skin. Nothing like the sharp slap of my palm, but strong in its own way. His sighs get louder, turn to low moans, and then, finally, to soft words. *Gods* and *oohs* and *fucks* that slide out of his mouth as though he can't help himself. I don't think he can.

Finally that word that I wait for, the soft whisper. *Please.* I pretend I don't hear it – the book is loud against his flesh, getting louder, getting faster. His back is all muscle and tension as he tries to get comfortable, tries to guess where the book might land next. *Please*, he says it again, even as he's trying to get loose. His cock makes my skirt wet, his string of *please, please, please*, makes the rest of me wetter.

I drop the book. I need to get closer to this again, back to the sound of my hand on his ass. Back to marking his skin with the sting of a slap. I'm faster with my hand, more precise.

This time, when his feet dig for a hold, I let him have it. For a second, he's off-balance, surprised to find himself with any leverage at all. And then he's fucking my lap, rubbing cock and ribbon against me. He rises up to meet my hand, lowers himself to meet my lap. He does all the work now, and I let him, focusing on placement and speed.

His *please*s turn to *fuck-fuck-fuck*s and I know he's going to come. I wish I could see his cock, wrapped and rubbed a little raw, as he lets go, but it's enough that I can imagine it. It's enough that I can see his ass clench tight under my hand. I tighten my grip on the ribbon, use it to help his momentum. I up my spanks, faster and harder, meeting his ass each time it rises, and then giving a sharp hit on his downstroke.

Soon, he comes the way boys do: loud and quick, and drenching the front of my skirt. The room smells instantly like sex and sweat and cum. While his body shivers and pumps, I softly stroke the sore places on his skin. Small bruises – from the book, likely – are beginning to show through the pink. He's going to feel this every time he sits down for the next week, maybe longer.

He lays across my lap for a long time while I stroke his skin back into the memory of softness. After a while, my thighs start to ache. The rest of me is already aching for my fingers, the memory of him behind my closed eyes. Later, I tell myself. Wait. Keep this pleasure.

'Stephen, it's time to get up,' I say.

'Oh, oh yeah.' When he slides off of me, his grin is all boyish, but not flustered or embarrassed. Not any more. Chest and cock still jut, still pink, with more power now, not less.

I brush a hand over the front of my skirt where the fabric is wet. My fingers come away ink-stained.

'Here, let me cut that off you.' Careful with the scissors, I cut through the ribbon at his wrists and waist first, and then slice against the softening skin of his cock. He doesn't flinch, not even when the scissors touch his skin. 'There you go.'

I gather up the ribbon that has fallen from his body. I'll use this later, remembering. I admire my handiwork across his body – black ink, pink handprints. I wonder what he'll think of later, after, when he undresses and sees the marks I've left on him.

'What about you?' he asks.

'Tuesday afternoons,' I say. 'You can wash windows.' Him and Anthony. I think they'll work well together.

'No, I mean, what about *you*.' He actually points in the general direction of my skirt, which makes me want to laugh. Someone is training these boys well, long before they come to me.

'You're off the hook for now,' I say. 'Next time.'

He actually looks a little sad. 'Oh, okay.'

I pick up his book. 'I'll wrap this up for you to take home. Come on out when you're ready.'

By the time he comes out, I've tucked my hair back up in its up-do. I've reapplied my lipstick. I have my pencil between my lips, the taste of lead in my mouth. My glasses are tucked between my breasts. He's looking and not-looking at me again.

I slide the book across the counter to him. 'I hope you enjoy this,' I say. 'It's been bound quite beautifully.'

His face actually goes pink, from the cheeks on up. The reminder of the colour sends a small shiver through me.

'Oh, and flip the sign on your way out, will you?' I watch him walk out, memories of that ass beneath my hand. When the door shuts, I lean over and start making squiggles on my paper. I'm expecting the dark-haired boy who does my books any minute now.

Advantage Headmaster
by Philippa Johnson

The shadows were lengthening across the sweeping lawn in front of James Bendrick's office. A light breeze drifted in through the open window, as did the distant *chock chock* of tennis balls from the main court behind the schoolhouse, where the annual inter-school tennis tournament was in progress. His establishment – a private girls' boarding school – nearly always walked away with the top prizes. Trophy cabinets were full of the results of previous years' hard work. Something was troubling Bendrick though: the usual whoops, cheers and occasional applause were interspersed with strange catcalls and wolf whistling.

He reached forward to a bank of switches close to his desk, and a large flat-screen TV flickered into life. Adjusting the remote control, he quickly found what he was looking for: the camera covering the school's centre court showing the final match in progress.

On court was Nina Birch, Bendrick's personal choice for head girl. Tall, blonde, athletic: she was the perfect choice. Her shapely hips and prominent firm breasts were flattered by the tight white T-shirt and her short tennis skirt barely covered her ample derrière.

In addition to being head girl, Nina was the deserved captain of the school's elite tennis squad. As Bendrick contemplated the spectacle of Birch bending forward to retrieve a tennis ball, he inhaled sharply: rather than seeing her buttocks neatly framed by the regulation crisp white knickers, edged with lace, Birch appeared to be entirely naked beneath

21

the microskirt. A good thing, he mused, he was able to access an instant replay. He did so and slowed down the action to get a better look. When Birch bent right forward to retrieve the ball, the space between her thighs glowed white. She had on the tiniest thong; the back strap concealed by her muscular buttocks. The bending forward coincided with another chorus of catcalls from a group of sixth-form boys from a nearby school. So that was it: he would have to deal with Nina after the match. His tongue ran over his lips, savouring his evening's entertainment.

One Hour Later

Bendrick was roused from his perusal of the evening paper by a faint knock at his door.

'Come!'

Nina Birch stepped into the room still clad in her tennis attire, sporting a rosy glow, flushed with success and, Bendrick thought, a slightly mischievous smile playing around her lips.

'Good match, Nina?' he enquired nonchalantly.

'Oh yes, sir. We won again and it was all decided by the final match,' she said breathlessly.

'I'm sorry I couldn't come to watch, you know how I take a personal interest in my tennis girls.'

'Indeed, sir, I think you missed a treat today,' she smirked imperceptibly.

'Good job I had the CCTV installed this year, then. It was almost as good as being there.'

'Oh … I … didn't realise you could watch the match, sir,' she began to stammer as the colour drained visibly from her cheeks.

Bendrick went on, barely acknowledging her nervous interruption.

'It was the demented cheering of those sixth-form boys from St Stephen's that alerted me,' he said.

He took a tennis ball from one of his desk drawers and tossed it so that it landed in the middle of the Persian rug that occupied the centre of his vast office.

'Now, bend over and retrieve that ball.'

Nina knew better than to argue: she stepped forward and reached down with her right hand. As she did so, her pleated white skirt rode over her fleshy posterior. She straightened briskly and the hem came to rest a couple of inches below the crease twixt buttock and thigh. She turned to face him, her hands folded neatly before her.

'Since when do you girls decide what undergarments to wear?' he thundered.

'As you know well, the senior girls in my establishment have their underwear personally selected by me. Thongs may well be appropriate, especially if you're coming here for some personal attention. Sometimes even for a night out when wearing a tight-fitting skirt or skin-tight trousers. But *never* on the tennis court.'

'Well, the boys were certainly enjoying it,' she said with a smile.

'Enough! You know you're making things worse for yourself, Nina. In two weeks you will leave this school and go to university. I want you to be an asset to this place, and in the next two weeks I intend to drive that lesson home forcefully. I'm sure you know what I mean.'

Birch looked down at the floor. As head girl she was more than used to the headmaster's attention. A summons to his study induced in her a curious, nervous excitement. She found a session with Bendrick would often leave her glowing and expectant; a feeling she would often recall while exploring herself under the duvet at night.

And, as head girl, it was her duty to discipline the other senior girls; a duty she had grown to relish. She had progressed from lightly spanking the others over their school mini-skirts to full-blown, bare-bottom thrashings using the crop, wooden paddle and, occasionally, the cane Bendrick had presented to her after she was elected head girl by the senior staff.

'What you have done is so serious that a mere thrashing, even a severe caning, will not, I think, do the trick. I'm going to push you beyond your limits, introduce you to pain and sensations in other parts of your body. This will be an experience you will never in your entire life forget. And when we've finished this evening, it will be repeated, daily, until you leave the school.'

'First, you will fetch the large, leather punishment bench from my outer office and you will arrange yourself in the customary manner.'

Barely half a minute later, Birch was draped across the large punishment stool. Her knees were on a padded ledge just above floor level while her torso was splayed horizontally across the expanse of black leather. Bendrick had the authority to strap girls to the bench, though it was something he seldom chose to do because it was his belief that girls must submit voluntarily if they were to grow up into respectable young women.

'Knees apart!' he barked.

The punishment bench was constructed so that its occupant was forced to thrust back her rear in order to remain comfortable. Even at this angle, the string between Nina's buttocks was almost invisible. Bendrick moved swiftly behind her, grabbed the top of her miniscule thong and tugged it swiftly upwards.

She gasped in pain and surprise as the string bit into the crease of her bottom.

'Dental floss for the buttocks, eh?' sneered Bendrick. He gave the string several sharp tugs and Birch squirmed, straining to retain her dignity.

Abruptly, he let the garment go and it twanged painfully back into place. She knew better than to cry out in pain; a sharp intake of breath was all that could be heard. Then silence.

Without warning, the slaps started to rain down on Nina's exposed behind. These were not the almost playful slaps he often delivered to warm a girl up; his arm swung back and the palm of his hand landed with full force on the firm, rounded cheeks of her youthful behind. Her face was buried in the leather and she emitted small grunts with each resounding slap. Later, several of her friends told her they could hear the spanking across the lawn in the schoolhouse. Bendrick had pointedly left the window open in order to make an example of her.

Her cheeks began to redden; changing from light pink

through scarlet to a deep, angry purple. When Bendrick was satisfied that her rear was covered in its entirety, he began to aim the slaps lower. This was a new sensation to Birch; school punishments were normally restricted to a girl's bottom, very occasionally the palm of the hand was also thrashed. She twitched and squirmed as her thighs and the backs of her legs began to sting and burn. Still, though, she knew better than to cry out in pain.

After five minutes or so, Bendrick was satisfied that his initial attack had had its desired effect. Birch was subdued, breathing heavily and fighting back tears.

'Stand-up, Nina, and come over to my desk,' he ordered.

As if nothing had happened, Nina got up from the punishment stool, smoothed her white skirt over the smarting skin and stepped forward. She was motioned to come around the side of the desk, standing next to the headmaster, avoiding eye contact.

'Now lift that skirt so that I can have a good look at your choice of undergarment,' he coaxed.

Nina lifted the hem of her pleated tennis skirt and held it at waist level. The front of the thong was almost as skimpy as the non-existent back: a film of diaphanous fabric showed off her shaven mound to perfection. The sides were of intricate lacework and a small embroidered heart was placed directly over the top of the start of her labial crevice.

'Very pretty, I'm sure. In fact, you must tell me where you bought it because it's an ideal punishment garment. It leaves nothing, or almost nothing, to the imagination.'

'Erm … it's from Agent Provocateur, sir,' she whispered.

'Reassuringly expensive, eh?'

She opened her mouth to reply but was caught off-guard as she felt Bendrick's finger gently tugging at the side of her knickers. She knew that he took a close interest in his girls, but never before had he so blatantly invaded her feminine intimacy.

Holding the flimsy garment to one side, he gently brushed his fingers against her labia. She shuddered with fear and excitement. Her outer lips were perfectly smooth, freshly

25

shaven that very morning.

The shaving of pubic hair was mandatory for all girls and the results were checked on a daily basis by Matron. Nina and the others strongly suspected that this was a duty to which Matron had no objection, as she would often linger in her inspections of her favourites. The girls would line up outside the dormitories, skirts held to their waists, while Matron would pass along the line, sliding her long fingers into each girl's white school knickers in turn. A girl who did well was rewarded by a finger gently circling her clit, sometimes even entering the moistness of her vagina.

'Good girl,' Matron would say. 'Now off you go and have your breakfast.'

Those who tried to skimp on their morning shave would first be subjected to a full inspection. This involved lowering her knickers to her knees, spreading her legs so that her underwear was taught, bending over and grabbing her ankles. This allowed Matron a full view of the offending genitalia including the anus and bottom crack.

She would first pass along the line, slapping here and pinching there before entering her office to retrieve a small flogger. She would then pass down the line in the opposite direction, flicking out mercilessly at the exposed buttocks and into the girls' most intimate folds. Once satisfied that the recalcitrant girls were all burning to their inner cores, they would be told to straighten up, place their knickers in a laundry basket at the end of the corridor, and report to Nurse Midgley for waxing. They would, of course, miss breakfast and were obliged to spend the rest of the day minus their undergarments. This policy was designed to encourage the girls to maintain exacting standards of intimate hygiene. The penalties for not doing so ensured that it worked.

Back in the study, Bendrick began a more thorough examination of Nina's intimate contours. 'Lie down on my desk and place your feet so that they almost touch your buttocks,' he said firmly.

Nina lay on her back and stared up at the ornate ceiling. She felt strong hands pulling the sides of the thong and she

26

obligingly lifted her buttocks off the leather-topped desk to assist with its removal.

He parted her knees with his hand and, extending two fingers, entered her vaginal cavity. As he did so, the tip of his thumb brushed lightly against the tip of her clitoris. It was all Nina could do not to scream with pleasure and anticipation. Her breathing became deeper and her pupils started to dilate.

He began to move his fingers in and out and she responded with tiny thrusts of her hips. Her cunt began to moisten and her head moved rhythmically from side to side. Sensing her growing excitement, he used the little finger of his right hand to circle the bud of her anus. This at first tightened instinctively, but Nina was far too well trained to deny access to a superior. She allowed her sphincter to relax and, moistened by her own wetness, the finger began to explore.

Nina's face was flushed with ecstasy and, calculating his moment exactly, Bendrick abruptly abandoned his stimulation of the writhing 18-year-old. He took a thin leather strap from his desk drawer and brought it down swiftly across her splayed labia. Without a thought for decorum, Nina shrieked and closed her legs instinctively.

'Get those legs open!' he barked.

The strap hissed through the air once again and landed, this time vertically, on her splayed pussy. Her clit began to sting and she screamed at the top of her voice.

'Get used to it, Nina, if you relax a little I can even bring you off this way.'

He brought his hand up to his shoulder preparing to strike again. Nina fought to control her breathing and readied herself for the next slice. It landed on her clit and she bucked involuntarily. Then another and another and another in exactly the same spot. And with each new impact another thrust of the pelvis upwards. A few more strokes and her entire genitalia was ablaze. It was certainly painful, but there was something else as well – a growing excitement, a building pressure, a longing for release.

'You're nearly there,' he whispered. 'Just breathe through the pain and try to ride it.'

The strokes became even more intense and she surprised herself by raising her hips ready to receive the next.

'Now countdown from twenty to one,' he ordered.

'Twenty … ah! Nineteen … ow! Eighteen … oh, Headmaster!'

Nina was only aware of the pain, the boiling excitement and the need to concentrate on counting backwards. Each swish of the strap became more intense and landed on top the previous strike, intensifying the sensation.

She was down to ten, her breathing more rapid and her eyes closed and she felt her climax mounting.

'Nine!' she screamed. 'Eight … oh God … seven …ah! Six, oh oh oh … Five! Four … Christ! I'm … I'm … coming. Three! Please, I … can't. Two! Fuck! One!'

Nina was enveloped by strange and unfamiliar sensations that seemed to pulse from her toes to her head. She writhed uncontrollably on the desk as wave upon wave rippled through her body.

Bendrick padded across the Persian rug and opened his walnut cocktail cabinet. He withdrew his ice bucket and returned it to the desk across which Nina still lay. With a pair of silver tongs, he retrieved an ice cube and began to rub it over her swollen pussy lips. The sensation was a sweet release from the stinging torment of his strap. She uttered little sighs of contentment as the cold substance drew the heat from her throbbing cunt.

'That's just the beginning, Nina,' he said. 'Now we'll progress to the next stage of your correction.'

Nina was ordered back to her dormitory to retrieve her regulation tennis underwear. She was reminded that any delay would result in even more severe punishment.

She left the study, her tiny skirt flapping against her inflamed bottom and thighs. Clasping her hands to her buttocks, she could feel the heat radiating from beneath the skirt.

A few moments later she returned to Bendrick's office. He took the knickers from her and asked her why she had seen fit not to wear them on the tennis court.

'Well, some of my friends said I wouldn't dare wear that thong on court,' she said feebly.

'Well now you will wear them, and to very good effect,' he sneered. 'But first, I want you to dip them in the ice bucket and wring them out before you put them on.'

Nina did as she was told. The water stung her hand as she immersed her school tennis knickers. She bent forward and put them on, flinching at the unfamiliar sensation of having her nether regions clad in something so cold and wet.

'Now kneel on my desk, and remember to keep your knees as far apart as possible,' he instructed.

Next she was told to lean forward and rest her chin on the backs of her hands. Behind her, she heard Bendrick opening his punishment cabinet.

He returned with a small, round wooden paddle. Without warning, it struck her right cheek and made a satisfying *splatting* sound. She thought she would be unable to endure any further blows, but he soon silenced her by telling her that her next punishment would be in front of the entire school on the last day of term unless she bore this one with fortitude.

Blow after blow after blow landed on her moistened and smarting posterior. Wearing a pair of saturated knickers gave her a peculiar sensation and reminded her of her vulnerability. She began to move her hips slowly from side to side. Once the Headmaster considered that his wooden paddle had had the desired effect, he paused and ran his hand over her exposed flesh.

'I think we'll have these off now,' he suggested.

Without hesitating, Birch leapt from the desk and pulled off the sodden knickers, placing them on the desk.

'Now, it's time for the frog position.'

Birch knew exactly what he meant. He strode over to the leather Chesterfield sofa on the other side of the room. Birch followed behind, and as soon as the headmaster was comfortable on the couch she turned her back to him, squatted on all fours and placed her legs either side of his hips. Her head rested on her hands at the edge of the Persian rug. He had the perfect view of her exposed bottom, her parted labia and her rectal orifice.

He slapped a small leather paddle against the palm of his hand. He began, slowly, striking her cheeks and deliciously parted thighs and she twitched with each hit of the paddle. 'I think you particularly enjoy this position Nina, don't you?' he said.

'Yes sir, I know it allows you to see everything, and if you're happy then I'm happy,' she replied.

'Good girl!'

He patted her thighs and, once again, started to circle her anus with his forefinger. She expected him to explore her rectum, but instead of doing so he picked up a small, rubber flogger – a Spartacus Leather 10-inch Pink Thong Whip – from the sofa, and began flicking it so that its stinging tips landed at the entrance to her back passage. Her buttocks moved up and down with every fresh sting. Soon, the sphincter was winking in time with his intimate attentions.

Then he moved lower, ensuring that the ends of the flogger landed between her parted labia and roused her clitoris from its slumbers.

'Nina, one thing you will learn when you leave the school is to make sure that your man is satisfied,' he said. 'What pleases your man will ultimately please you.'

'Now lie on your back with your head and this satin cushion and place your bottom on my lap with your legs drawn up to your chest,' he commanded.

Soon, her pink inner labia were on display with her swollen and equally pink outer labia. He reached down and began to stroke her pussy. But soon the strokes became less gentle and he started to pinch and squeeze. His hand was cupped and he paused before landing some not so gentle slaps on her fleshy mound. She gasped in pain but didn't dare close her thighs.

'Nina, you are both very good and very, very bad,' he smiled.

'Now remove your T-shirt – I assume you're not wearing a bra as usual – and come back to stand in front of me.'

She sprang from his lap and pulled the tennis shirt over her head. She was standing in the centre of the Persian rug, dressed only in her tiny tennis skirt, white sports shoes and knee-length socks.

'Stay exactly where you are, bend over and place the palms of your hands on the rug,' he ordered.

'And I'm sure I don't need to tell you to open your legs as wide as you can.'

Obligingly, Birch reached forward and spread her feet so that her legs made a wide V-shape. He picked up a crop from the top of his desk and stationed himself behind her and to her left.

She expected the end of the leather to start stinging her buttocks, perhaps even her thighs. Instead, he rested it on the carpet and brought it up swiftly so that it struck her already smarting cunt. She almost leapt into the air with the shock of the impact.

'Hold your position,' he commanded. She dared not do otherwise. He brought the crop up again and again and always managed to find the delicate fold between her outer labia with each hit. Then he swung the crop back and started to cover her buttocks and inner thighs with short, sharp, stinging slaps that made her draw breath.

'Just remember, you have two more weeks here and we can repeat this all day and every day unless you co-operate fully.'

Next, he ordered her to stand, feet together, in the centre of the rug with her hands clasped behind her back. The effect was to push forward her ample and superbly rounded breasts.

Bendrick circled around her and came to rest in front of her only a few inches from her face. He reached out his right hand and, with one swift and calculated movement, pulled and twisted her left nipple cruelly. It was all she could do not to leap back and scream. Instead, she inhaled sharply and bit her lip. Abruptly he let go of the nipple, drew back his hand and gave her left breast a hard smack on the side.

'You're lucky I don't have any nipple clamps,' he said. 'Mind you, if I place an order tonight they'll be here in a couple of days. In fact I think I will do that very thing.'

He reached forward with his left hand and weighed her right breast in his palm. Just as she was beginning to enjoy the sensation, he drew his thumbnail across the centre of the nipple digging it in sharply.

He turned back to his desk and retrieved the crop.

'Now make sure you hold your position,' he instructed.

He raised the crop and began inflicting sharp little stings all over Nina's prominent, firm breasts. Soon little pink patches appeared everywhere the crop had visited. She stood stiffly to attention, never flinching and never protesting.

Then he took up the small rubber flogger and began directing well-aimed strikes at her already proud nipples. They began to change colour from a rosy pink to a darker, angrier hue.

When he decided that she had taken almost all she could before breaking down and abandoning her customary poise, the punishment was over. For that day at least.

Birch would be a difficult act to follow; there was barely a girl in the lower sixth who came close to her in terms of ability, beauty and the natural inclination to submit. Moreover, she was equally adept at keeping order among her peers and was accorded unquestioned respect by the other pupils.

Bendrick turned to her and smiled enigmatically.

'And the next time that you and your team mates decide to choose your own underwear, I'll thrash the lot of you over the tennis net in front of the spectators.'

Nina blushed at the thought of such public humiliation. Giving the boys a cheap thrill by wearing a g-string was one thing, having one's nether regions exposed to all and sundry was something else entirely.

Now put these damp knickers on and get yourself back to the dorm for a good hot shower.'

Nina walked demurely to the headmaster's study door and looked back over her shoulder.

'Oh, and, Nina?'

'Yes, sir?'

'I expect you to dish out suitable discipline to the rest of the tennis team. I'm sure this was your idea, but that doesn't mean the rest of them were blameless. Make sure they learn their lesson, will you?'

Nina smiled. 'Of course, sir, you know you can rely on me.'

With that, she closed the door quietly behind her and began contemplating the next few hours that she would spend in the company of five young ladies in need of a firm hand.

Anatomy of a Brat
by Poppy St Vincent

I have been burned.

My burns were not delivered by a card shark or by a flamethrower. I have been burned by the sun. It is only a little burn and it was not my fault. It is my skin's fault because my skin is silly. It believes I am a vampire and thinks I should stay indoors whenever there is enough daylight to see where I am walking. I do not think that a tiny bit of sun should turn anyone's arms such an unnatural shade of crimson. It is the deepest red my skin ever can achieve. It matches my mood. I am furious.

I am furious because my burn stings horribly. I am furious because it is so unfair I should have to lather up like a clown in white goo to go outside. I am furious because I would never have got burned if Dan were not staying with us.

Dan makes me laugh and smile, and flirts in the sweetest way. Dan was with me all morning and I did not want to look silly in front of him. I wanted to be like a normal girl. Dan was there the whole time and saw no problem at all with my using a factor of cream that you would have made me throw away as useless rubbish.

I am furious because you were right when you told me to use factor three million before you left this morning. I am furious because I was in a sulk with you for going away and so I may have used a lower factor than even I thought I needed just to make a point. I do not know quite what point. I am too angry to remember. I am just furious.

I have rubbed baby lotion over my burns twice. I now smell

good and am really quite slippery. I think of you trying to hold me like this and almost smile. I have done all I could to make it better. But it hurts so much I can't stand it and I am furious all over again.

And now you are home and are horrified at what I have done to myself. I try to tell you it was not me it was the sun and my useless genetic makeup. I offer you the phone number of my parents. It is their fault, but you ignore my help without so much as a pause.

It is all so unfair and I am so grumpy I think my only option is to squeeze my eyes tight shut while I am scolded. I ignore as much as I can. The way you talk means I get to ignore about one word in twenty but that is fine by me.

I am irritated by my own carelessness but I can't admit this. And I hate knowing that from now on you will check whether I actually use sun cream, so my very realistic aim of getting a tan becomes far less likely.

I feel two feet tall when you talk to me that way. Your being right makes everything twenty times worse but I swallow my strop. I know that arguing with you is ill-advised and can work an evil magic: the kind of magic where a telling off grows and mutates into something terrible and memorable, the kind of thing that hurts my bottom.

I wonder if Dan's being here saved me from a spanking. I can't believe you have not noticed my mood. I know your embarrassment threshold is much, much higher than mine. You would not hesitate to tell me off when Dan is with us, but it is less likely I think. I am all yours. I love this.

Dan knows about us. He knew you long before I did. You and he live the same way, and his girlfriends get much the same treatment I do. He spanks them and treats them with the same adoring bossiness you do. You are so alike in this, I wonder you are not brothers. You and I have talked about how you would not hesitate to spank me in front of him. This is the reason I am normally so good in Dan's presence.

I know Dan is safe and honourable. I know you trust him, even with me. I am always only the tiniest bit of a brat around Dan. I know exactly what he will let me get away with and I can play him to my heart's content. It is not like that with you. I can't control you at all.

You have finished scolding me. I know I must continue to not let you see my rage. I take what I can get and walk away the moment you allow me to.

I head away from you and seek out Dan. He will cheer me up and say nice things. He has to be kind because that is what he does. I need to feel spoiled after being dressed down so thoroughly. I wish to be soothed and to have nice things said to me. I want to feel happy and not feel told off.

I find him in the den watching something appallingly dull on the TV. It may be some form of sport, or a film with war or cowboys. I look but I see no pretty dresses and decide the TV is irrelevant and that I may interrupt with impunity. I bounce next to him on the sofa and smile hopefully. I like chatting to him. He will make me smile. Endlessly patient, he does just that, at least until he spies my burned arms.

Dan sighs in a way that is irritatingly reminiscent of you and asks if you have seen what I managed to do to myself. I tell him you have indeed seen and have told me all I need to hear on the matter. I thank him and request a change of subject. I want gossip on his latest girlfriend and not a rehash of a telling off that was unnecessary in the first place.

Dan looks at me with narrowed brown eyes, his head slightly cocked. He listens like you listen. It feels like a preliminary hearing. Apparently the double jeopardy rule does not apply to me.

I sit, I listen, and I try to look like I am good. I don't squirm like I do when you tell me off. But he talks and I feel resentful and embarrassed.

I like Dan to think well of me, I like him to not see the bad parts. I want him to be nice to me. I want to get my own way with him, like I can't with you. So I try hard to smile and be compliant or something that looks like compliance, but I have just sat through being told off once and I am not prepared to be good twice in a row. I do not want to be told off by Dan at all. I can't see why I should accept any of this. I feel stupid and search for a response other than anger. I can't find one.

The moment Dan starts to suggest that I need more after-sun lotion I take my moment with both hands. I can glimpse freedom and start to scuttle away. I have not yet made it off the sofa before his final sentence.

He tells me to put on some moisturiser. He does not ask, he does not suggest. He uses the tone of a man who expects to be obeyed. He tells me that I am 'going to'. There is no request and no room for manoeuvre – just a bloody order.

Do you know the moment when it is all too much? I am cornered and fed up. How much is a girl supposed to take?

Although Dan is someone I adore and I think is wonderful and I would sooner cut off my own hair than hurt him, I just can't take one more moment of not getting my own way. I do not respond politely as I might. I do not thank him for his concern. I do what feels most satisfying: I stand up and walk out. The devil then takes hold of me and I realise this is my one chance. I have been told off and dismissed. If you were to do that I would retreat and count myself lucky not to be tipped over your lap. But this is not you.

I mutter, just loud enough to be heard, the rudest thing I can think of. It feels so good to let it out, so satisfying to be able to express myself like that. As I leave, I hold the door behind me in both hands and slam it shut as hard as I can. It is childish, I know, but it helps me. I storm away feeling I have scrabbled back a bit of the self-respect I lost a few moments before. I won't be spoken to like that. Dan will know he has upset me and he will say sorry.

I walk away faster than feels natural, dodging the guilt close on my heels.

It is but a moment before I see you standing a few feet away in the corridor. Your head is tilted to one side and you look at me as though I were a thing of particular interest, a specimen in a bell jar perhaps. I stop. The word *thwarted* bobs into my head and I try to ignore it. My mood of righteous indignation walks past me and leaves.

You are silent. I decide to be silent too. It may help. I wonder how excellent your hearing is. It would not have to be very excellent to hear the door slam, but the expletive I hissed out a moment earlier may well have escaped your notice. I am not the slightest bit sorry. I know you will know this. I just hope you will not find out what I am not sorry for.

I try the ancient ninja invisibility trick. I squeeze my eyes shut. I can't see you therefore you can't see me. For some reason this does not work. I open my eyes and you still are looking at me. I flick my eyes towards the front door; it looks much more welcoming than you. You say just two words.

'Stay there.'

I used up all my bravery on the door slam and the passionate wording at my exit, so I stay where I am told to and watch you open the door I used so much energy to shut. In the silence of my hot whirring head I use every profanity I can think of while I strain to hear the conversation within. It is a problem with masculine voices that they sound a bit vague and threatening when heard through a wall. Silly as it may be I do not dare move even a step. I feel sick. My arms hurt, I remind myself I am a victim in all this.

I worry about what you two are saying. I realise in my clenched brain that Dan is the one man in the world you would allow to spank me. You told me this once. I stand imagining my escape, wondering about asylum and where the nearest cathedral is and if they still grant sanctuary.

I also realise that if I had used those words to you … I can't even think that sentence. It had not occurred to me you might be a bit irked if I used them in your house, to your friend. Dan will not tell you. He couldn't. It was between him and me. It is none of your business.

The door opens, softly as if to mock my previous slam. I feel so, so stupid. I have one-sixth the strength of either of you. I realise that slamming the door made me look idiotic.

You don't have to say anything. You look at me with raised brows and move to the side to make room for me to pass. I walk with silent steps. I am showing you that I can be good now. I can be quiet. Quiet isn't something you ask of me and I offer it as testimony of my goodness.

I want a hug. My hand brushes your stomach as I walk by, my hand up, half reaching out. I stand at your side, close enough to feel my skirt rest on your leg. I want to hold your hand but content myself with standing just behind you. I feel the warmth of my arm burn reflect off your clothes. I wonder if I could claim brain fever as the cause of all this badness.

I can't be mad with you because I want you to hide me. Like a shy child at a party I want to cling to you for comfort. I understand that you are part of what I should be hiding from, but this feels so unfamiliar I want it to be just you and me. I know I have been rude and bad tempered. I know that my rage scared me and made me do things I hate. I know I am desperately unhappy that I have been so unkind, but I want you to make it better. I want you to hold me. I want you to make me safe.

But it is not just you and I. There are three of us. Dan is here and you two are united in this. I realise you know everything I have said and done. I realise, with slow and mounting horror, that you knew when you scolded me I needed to act like this. This is what you do. You let me behave as I must and only when I have done what I need to do you come and get me.

This is you coming to get me. You knew all along.

I can't let Dan see me cower. I will not let him see me submit. I let go of my physical need for you and move one surreptitious step away. I raise my head and glare out of the window. I can't stop myself; I need to do this too. I wonder if you know this like you know everything else. I want to reclaim self-respect. I want to be treated nicely. I want all of this silliness to stop. I catch Dan's eyes and raise my eyebrows in silent challenge.

You speak to me in a tone that makes me lower my eyes and want to crawl into your arms and away from you all at once. But I will not and I cannot crumble like that. I will not submit in front of Dan. Inside I am ashen, but I cannot show this to you. I just can't.

You remind me what you expect of me, how you love me and that I should hold myself accountable to the highest standards of behaviour. I think how wonderful if I could hold myself accountable rather than suffer the ignominy of having

39

you do it for me. I do not say this. You tell me how I let myself down and how I let you down. I cannot imagine how I find defiance after those words but I do. It is silent defiance and imperceptible to most men, but you are not them.

You allow me time for a response, a chance to tell you what happened. If this were only you and I, then I would stammer and stutter out a true version of events, already repentant, already wanting forgiveness. I wish, I wish, I wish I could.

I can't.

There are two roads in front of me, two choices. I always submit to you but this time I have to go all Robert Frost, don't I?

'Well maybe,' I start and inject as much sarcasm into my voice as I can muster, 'I got a bit annoyed because you had just spoken to me and I listened to you and maybe –' getting into the spirit of it '– I was in pain and did not need to be told yet again what I already knew. I just wanted some sympathy.'

I am warming to my theme now. I know how much you hate to see me in pain.

'It really hurts, it really does.'

All intolerance is gone from my voice. I appeal to your concern and let my pain stand for my defence.

'So I am sorry –' I try to sound it, I really do, '– if I was a bit sharp, but it hurt and it still does and I don't know why you both have to be so mean about it.'

I gave it my best shot and I cannot believe it won't alter the outcome. I know I can't sway you, but it has to work on Dan. I do not want to look at you because I have no chance to change your mind, but Dan is a whole new ball game. Dan can change your mind for me. It will all work out.

Or not.

You don't speak to me. You turn me around very gently, taking care not to touch my burn. You place me in the corner, as though I belong there, as though this is normal, which it might be if it were just the two of us.

'You can do better than that, little girl. Why don't you think about it?' You speak so softly in my ear that it sounds like a caress. I remember fifty times a day how much I love you and this is one of those times. 'But you know not to stand in the corner like that, don't you?'

My breathing gets deeper. You absolutely cannot mean this. My hands shake and I whisper to you that I just can't. Your hands are a familiar touch when you help me. My skirt is unzipped and coaxed down my legs and I step out of it, like a child at bedtime. You lift my hands and place them on my head. You take my tee shirt and fold it halfway up my back and then gently, terribly you roll down my panties and leave them underneath my bottom, resting in a neat line at the tops of my thighs.

Anger leaves me. It betrays me because it can go when I am destined to stay here.

You talk together in relaxed voices, with no concern for my plight. You are not discussing me so much as talking as old friends, light banter flowing with shared references that amuse you both.

I flitter between relief and humiliation at being ignored. If I had the slightest ability to do so I would turn around and be enraged, but I embody futility.

There are clicks and then the brief fizz of beer bottles opening. It sounds like any friends meeting on a warm day.

I pretend I am not here. I don't think about the total ignominy. I try not to visualise my yellow tee shirt over the pale white of my back and how my round bottom sticks out, speaking for me, telling of my disgrace.

I try not to imagine the clash of my red arms against the sun-brightened blonde of my hair. I feel the line of my parting under my hands and remember with horror that I did my hair in pigtails this morning. It amuses you to see my hair like that and it was so hot outside and it seemed cute at the time. Now it mocks me, another sign of my forlorn position. The parting is neat and straight and reminds me of the line down the centre of my bottom as it faces the room.

I hear my name in murmured conversation once or twice but you do not sound like I want you to sound. You sound amused, relaxed, no rush and no concern. I want you to sound worried about me and to think you might be pushing me too far. I inwardly plead for you to come and get me and cover me and say sorry and kiss me.

You say my name and unbidden I respond. I respond in a secret way, signs of my desire, hidden between my clenched, closed legs. But you merely ask if I have anything to say to you both. Still facing the wall, I can only nod.

You tell me to turn around and lower my arms, and I turn on one heel. I keep still, grateful you positioned my panties to allow me a semblance of modesty at the front. You ask me what I want to say. I mumble an apology to you and to Dan. I am almost crying, not with repentance but with resentment.

When you do not ask me to extend my meagre apology, when you let it rest on the air, when you allow it to speak for itself, it is then I realise you are going to allow Dan to spank me.

I feel I am falling and I scrabble for a hold, for a way to understand this. I know that when all this is passed I will lie awake for hours feeling guilty about the way I spoke to Dan. I know he has become a receptacle for all the rage I feel over not being able to control you. I know, and I hate this, that until Dan spanks me I will use him to hide from you.

I understand the two of you have discussed this, without asking me, without warning me. I understand how necessary it is and how much I have to lose and gain. I just want you to stride in and come and save me. I am yours, all yours. All this is about your hands and your eyes and, my heart sinks when I realise, your decisions.

This is so horrible. The inequality between you and me is overwhelming. Now faced with the both of you I crumble into obedience, into submission, and you both know it.

Without a word you come to collect me. You know I cannot walk to Dan on my own, and it occurs to neither of us that any of this need be expressed in words. I hold onto you and you place me to his right as he sits on the sofa.

I do not know how to let go of you. You guide me forward over his knee. Your hands offer terrible comfort while you move my legs and arms to where you wish them to be. You leave me then, but I feel you close, in a supervisory role. But you are with me so I am home still. This is all you; you are in charge of every moment.

Over an unfamiliar lap – a new kind of awkward – I wait for the lecture. My head hangs; I feel at odds and I don't want to cling to him like I would to you. I worry about his hand on my bottom.

Dan tells me how he cares for me, that he considers me a friend and wants me to be safe and well and happy. He tells me that the language I used is not only beneath me, but also how unkind it is to speak to a friend that way. I say nothing. I know he is right. I am furious and indignant that he feels he can say these things to me. If he thinks he can speak to me like this then I think it is acceptable to swear at him. I resolve to never, ever be open or friendly with him again. I almost hate him. But that thought makes me sad, so I ignore it.

He starts to spank and I do what I can to keep still, to keep my legs together, not to kick too much. His hand is flat against me, his arm holding me steady as I arch away from him. His pattern and his grip are unfamiliar, a stranger's touch. I am aware of my nudity in a way that makes me try to pull inward and away from him. I feel his fingers forming a cup around the curve of my bottom. I hear the noise of the impact and my shouting out the scene of my humiliation. I try to stay still, to not react. He does not spank with your strength or your deep knowledge of me, but the fact that he is not you makes it so much harder to bear. He concentrates at the base of my cheeks and then, at your suggestion, peppers my thighs with sharp stinging swats that make me try to kick him away, and cry out for him to stop. Again at your behest he redoubles his efforts. I do not know any more where his hand strikes me; I cannot distinguish one slap from the next. I stop fighting. I accept the pain.

He stops. His hand rests on my burning bottom. The lightest pressure is unbearable but I accept it. I do not say a word. I open my eyes and see tendrils of my hair hanging in front of me, damp with energy and heat. I listen to you talk to him and to his replies.

I breathe. Slowly I come back to myself. I remember how

and why this happened. A tiny spark of indignation reignites. I say nothing but I feel the tension in my back when I try to peel away from Dan without moving, as though I can pull myself inward and leave my body where it is.

I wait, feigning patience. If I try to get my own way now I will lose. My bottom burns, my face is bright red with the shame, my arms are red with burn from the sun. My bottom is pink though, a deep pink. It is not red. I know this because I listen to you two discuss its colour.

I am allowed up. This permission is hard to take. I stand stiffly with compressed emotion. I don't rub my bottom. You have never told me not to rub my bottom, but I do not think I could cope with another order. I will stay still. I will seem to accept every word.

You tell Dan how you know I have not had enough. You notice all the signs I think you will never see: a tilt of my head; the evasiveness of my eyes that shows concern with not being caught, or rather a yearning not to do wrong when you can see it; and my breathing a little more evenly than is normal while I strive for control over myself. You point out the tension in my hands, the way my shoulders push down and back. You notice it all.

I could spit with rage as you describe all of this to Dan. I am angry that you have known this all along. I am angry that you never told me, so that I could drop the pretence or find new ways to hide my feelings. More than anything I am angry at your light tone. I feel stupid and small. You know so much and I am so safe with you. I want you. But I am enraged with you; such an impotent anger. I let this emotion roll over and smother the others.

I flash a glance at you, one where I do not hide how I feel. You catch it and offer it to Dan as one last piece of evidence. I have not said a word and still you have read me like a score sheet. Not one note escapes you.

You tell me to stand behind the sofa. I know the position I have to adopt. I concentrate on my breathing and keep even my eyes still in the hope I might disappear somehow, but an image jars in my head. The vision of the sofa's paleness clashing with the hot, dark, angry pink of my bottom will not leave me. I smile a furious, defensive smile when I realise how little camouflage I have. Just as you instruct, I place myself over the back of the sofa, moving forward so my feet dangle off the floor and I lean forward, resting my arms on the seat. I am unbalanced, steadied only by your firm hand on my back.

Dan moves to the side so he can see what you do. He does not move to see me, but to see what happens to me. I grip the cushion tightly and stare at my fingers when I think the word *punishment*. That word is almost impossible to bear.

Before you lift your hand I know you have won. The position I am in, the way I obeyed you without question, the way the whole room stills for you, waits for your next move, tells me you have won.

Out of the corner of my eye I see a familiar movement of your arm and hear the slide of leather through denim and I know you are taking your belt off. It is not just that you have won, but now I am sorry too. You don't need to do one thing more. I tell you this and I mean it, I mean every word.

You comment on what I say, not to me but to Dan. I want you to take me more seriously than this. I want you to listen to me, to let what I say alter your course. I feel so powerless, so helpless, so observed, but without one tiny element of control. You see every part of me, you understand me so completely you can ignore what I say. You know my lies where I do not.

You push my back down and position my bottom to your liking. From the first stroke of the belt I realise how much my bum already hurts. Your belt flicks burning ribbons onto my already swollen cheeks. I bite my lip and tense all the muscles in my back and my stomach. I will not call out. I will not ask you to stop. I will not … and I forget the rest.

I kick, my legs splay in an acknowledgement of my total lack of dignity and I cry out 'No'. I make sounds, and buck and writhe. I push my arms and try to move away, to move towards you. I exist only to make this stop. I beg you to stop.

You stop. For one moment I feel my heart lurch and I think you stopped because I asked. You say nothing. You wait for me to compose myself. I do not know whether to curse you or myself when I do just as you wish. I settle. I wait. I submit.

I do not know how many more times you cross my cheeks with leather. I do not know because I have given up now. I acquiesce to every line, every stripe. The pain is total, more than I think I can bear but your actions tell me you think this is what I must have. I accept it because you think it. I pant with the pain and with the ease into submission. I make noise but it is for me, not a message to you.

At some point you stop. It takes several seconds for me to realise this. You ask if I have anything to say to Dan. I thought this could not get any worse but that is always when you are at your best.

I look up and stutter an apology. I mean it. He smiles and I smile back at the end. I feel ashamed of being mean. I have no rage for the first time in hours. I understand now, finally, why you did this.

You saw me lash out at myself, you saw my horror when I spoke unkindly to a man I adore. You saw my rage, my unhappiness and my confusion. You came to fetch me. Every act was a loving act.

I have no idea about anything else in the world. I am not what I thought I am. I am what you say I am. And you say I am loved.

I am loved.

Master and Commander
by Sadie Wolf

There's no need to bother with any of those paddles and whips you get in sex shops. Far better to use what comes naturally, what is to hand, so to speak.

The hand of a strong man can deliver a spanking that can make a grown woman cry and if more is required then he can grab something that's to hand like the remote control, a wooden spoon, a fish slice or a shoe.

Best of all and really the only piece of equipment required, he can take off his belt and use that. A leather belt is the original and best, and for those who want to take it that extra bit further, there's always the buckle end.

So you see there really is no need at all to waste money on expensive black leather paddles with the word 'Bitch' embossed upon them, even if at first glance they do look quite tempting. (Sadie Wolf on Spanking 2009)

Is there anything more romantic than the idea of living on a narrow boat? And is there anything more exciting than the anticipation of a first date with someone you really, really like? Especially when that someone is a man who has already told you, over the course of several long and intimate telephone calls, that his favourite *thing* is giving oral sex and that he has a *rule* of always making the woman come first.

Rebecca put her bag and coat and the directions on the passenger seat and started the engine. In two hours time she would be with him. She was to drive to the nearby village and he would come and meet her and take her to his boat.

47

Her friend Jill – his sister – had introduced them in an obvious but very welcome set-up. Rebecca had never been out with a friend's brother before, and she had been a little worried about the etiquette of the situation. What had she said and done that Jill knew about and that he may not approve of, and would his sister feel duty-bound to tell him? Jill reassured her that she would not be passing any information in either direction, and when Rebecca expressed reservations about sharing *how it was going* because she was dating her brother, Jill dismissed her concerns. 'Say what you like, he may be my brother, but he's a man and men can be a nightmare,' which immediately got them back on normal girl-girl footing.

Mark, on the other hand, was not so relaxed, saying right at the start, 'Don't tell my sister any of my secrets will you?' She'd thought he was joking at first, but quickly realised that he wasn't. 'You have been warned,' he added sternly.

This sternness was sexy; in the past she had gone out with *new men* or 'metrosexuals' as they seem to be called nowadays; all serious writer-types, stringy students, men who wouldn't know how to be stern if their life depended on it. These types never lasted long as boyfriends; they were simply not substantial enough for her. She never felt as if she could lean on them; never felt that they were strong enough to hold her.

More recently, she had tried a different tack and dated a few older guys, thinking that they would be stronger and more powerful than men her own age. But, again, she had been disappointed. Her most recent string of dates with a man had been promising at first; he was fifteen years older than her, had lived an interesting life, knew lots of people and seemed confident and comfortable in his own skin. But there the positive points ended.

The more time she spent with him, the more cloying and fussy she found him. He worried over minor details like car parking, planned their every date with military precision, and as for the sex … He seemed to think he was being chivalrous, but it just came over as overly-intimate, almost like going to have a chat at the doctors. All talk and no sexual desire. He asked practical questions out of context, taking the thrill out of everything. Actual sex was pedestrian, over-friendly rather than passionate; like making out with the human equivalent of a Golden Retriever. And when she had tried to communicate her needs and desires, it had gone spectacularly wrong.

She had tried to initiate a little light spanking session by doing something mildly annoying to get a rise out of him, then acting like a naughty schoolgirl and lying across his lap. He still did not take the hint, so in the end she had actually *asked* him to spank her. Horrified, he had jumped up as if he had been burned and looked at her as if she had just confessed to killing a member of his family. She had felt humiliated; he had actually called her a 'dirty little pervert' and not in a nice way, and that had been the end of that.

By the time she had met Mark, she was fast giving up hope of ever meeting anyone. But when he walked into the bar and sat down with her, she just *knew*, somehow. She could *feel* the strength rolling off him.

A couple of weeks after their initial meeting, and well into the long phone call stage, Jill called Rebecca and invited her out for a drink after work. Rebecca gave her an update and Jill looked almost as excited as Rebecca felt.

'And what's more, he's invited me to go and stay for the weekend!'

'On the boat?'

'Yes, on the boat.'

'Wow, you are privileged. I can't remember the last time he invited a woman onto his boat.'

After two more drinks and no food, Rebecca was feeling decidedly inebriated, and could almost feel her tongue loosening. Talk returned to the topic of the weekend on the boat.

'Seriously, he seems really into you. He never talked about what happened, but he had a really rough time with his wife. It was a very nasty divorce and I think it's taken him a while to get over it. Sounds like you might just be the one to put a smile back on his face.'

Rebecca felt a glow of pride and, in a rush of gratitude, found herself confiding in Jill. She told herself the story of Mark's divorce, which he'd told her all about, was her information to share, even though as she spoke the words out loud she knew that it wasn't. The look on Jill's face told her that she'd made a very big mistake.

'She cheated on him? With Paul, his best friend! Oh my God, how could she do that! I always knew she was a bitch, but God, I never realised. Poor Mark, I can't believe he never told any of us!'

'He said he felt too ashamed ... hardly wanted to admit it to himself. You won't tell him that I told you will you? I think he only told *me* because I told him how Steve used to cheat on me, and it kind of came out, he doesn't want anyone to know.'

'I'm sorry, Rebecca, I'll keep quiet for now, but I don't know if I'll be able to keep it to myself for ever. You know, you really shouldn't have told me.'

Rebecca spent the next hours and days in a terrible state of wired anxiety. She wanted to call Jill and beg her not to say anything, but she sensed that would only make things worse. She thought about confessing to Mark, but the thought terrified her. She both longed for and dreaded his texts and phone calls, wondering if her world would come crashing down at any moment. In the meantime they chatted on the phone as usual and as the end of the week arrived she began to think she had got away with it. Surely, if Jill was going to tell him, she would have done it before she went to stay with him for the weekend?

She pulled up in the little car park beside the village hall as per Mark's directions. It was a beautifully sunny, hot day and there seemed to be some kind of fete on. Tourists and young families with buggies were all over the road and the grass verges. She got out of the car and stretched. Her blouse had stuck to her back in the heat and she loosened it to let the air onto her body. She brushed her hair in the car window and checked her make-up in the mirror. She saw a silver car pull up – it was him.

He got out and walked over to her and picked up her bag without touching her.

'Good journey?'

'Yes thanks.'

He opened the passenger door of his car for her and closed it behind her. The journey took two minutes and neither of them said a word. He parked on a grassed area, opened the door for her and picked up her bag and started walking, through a gap in the hedge and down on to the towpath. Her skin prickled with fear.

The canal was pretty, with trees on either side; upon it there were swans and geese and beautiful narrow boats in traditional greens and blues, many with plants growing in pots on their roofs. His boat was beautiful, a faded dark blue. He stepped on first and handed her his arm. She followed him inside to the little living area. It smelled of fresh wood and was lined and panelled with pine. Outside through the little windows she could see the swans and geese on the water. He sat down on one of the bench seats and she did the same. She felt faint with terror. He looked at her.

'Well?'

'I'm sorry.'

Silence. He wasn't even looking at her any more.

'I really am sorry, I shouldn't have done it.'

'Then why did you?'

There was no answer to that. She didn't know why she'd done it, so she couldn't say.

'What can I do to make it up?'

'Nothing.'

Her face burned. She just wanted to get back into her car and drive home. But she couldn't leave it like this. She almost felt like crying when she thought back to her journey there, the sense of delicious anticipation, not just about the weekend but about the potential relationship ahead. They had talked on the phone about what they liked and he had said in a voice cracked with desire, 'Oh girl, you and I are going to have so much fun together,' and she had felt like nothing could be more perfect.

Why, oh why, had she done it? She was a fool! A fool, an idiot girl who deserved to be punished. *Deserved to be punished.*

So maybe, just maybe, there might be a way out of this mess. She didn't want to leave, and nor had he asked her to, but she couldn't spend the rest of the weekend there with him angry and not speaking to her, even though she was quite sure he would have no problem keeping it up. He'd left her in no doubt as to whether or not he took shit from anyone. He didn't

Anything was worth a try. Anything that might mean she wouldn't lose him.

He was looking out of the window as if she wasn't there. She took a deep breath and went and knelt down on the floor by his feet. She took his hand. It sat lifeless in hers. *Oh God.*

'Punish me.'

'What did you say?'

'Punish me. I don't know what else to do. I can't bear that I've made you angry. I want you to punish me enough so that you can forgive me.'

'If I punish you enough to make me forgive you, that's going to have to be one hell of a punishment. You've really pissed me off, Rebecca. I'm really fucking disappointed in you.'

'I know. I know you are, and I am really, really, so, so sorry.'

He looked at her and squeezed her hand for a fraction of a second.

'I know you are. But it's difficult for me to forgive something like that.'

'That's why I want you to punish me. So that you can.'

'Rebecca, I'd have to really hurt you, and I don't know if that's a good idea.'

'Please.'

He scowled, as if he were struggling with conflicting emotions. She held her breath and prayed. He sighed loudly, and then he stood up and drew the curtains.

'All right. Get up and get undressed.'

Shaking with a mixture of relief and terror, she undid her blouse, unzipped her jeans and took them off. Then removed her bra and knickers, as quickly and as unceremoniously as if she were getting ready for a swim.

He picked up an old wooden chair.

'Kneel down and hold on to the seat.'

She did as she was told, her knees on the hard wood floor of the boat, her forearms resting on the seat of the chair, her hands gripping the uprights at the back. She heard, rather than saw, him taking off his belt.

There was a loud crack, almost like an explosion, and then her body buckled in shock as he brought the belt down across her buttocks. For a second it was like jumping into cold water, the breath was knocked out of her body, and then a split second later the pain ripped through her and she screamed. The pain seemed to build in intensity and to be going on for too long, and then just as she thought that he brought the belt down again, layering a new pain on top of the first one. It was too much for her and she screamed and tried to stand. He pushed her roughly back down on to the chair by her shoulders and then with one hand firmly in her shoulder blades he slapped her hard around the side of her face.

'Just shut the fuck up. People can hear you.'

He let go of her and leaned back, and this time when the belt hit her she pressed her mouth against the seat of the chair and stifled her scream, so that it just came out as a sort of stifled sob. And she managed, somehow, to hold herself still.

It was a huge effort of will. She did it by reminding herself of how he had looked when she had arrived, and how this was the only way back, the only way to gain his forgiveness.

Again and again he brought his belt down on her, until it felt as if her whole body had gone into a state of shock. It was almost as if she were having an out of body experience and looking down on herself from the ceiling. Almost, except that she could feel everything: each new blow took a split second to arrive, like thunder after a flash of lightning, and each new burst of pain layered upon and accentuated the pain from previous blows.

She felt that he was working up and down her buttocks but also layering blows on top of blows, so that the whole area burned and burned with pain. In her mind she imagined what it looked like: red marks, wheals. She wondered if there was blood and how badly it would bruise. In front of her eyes was the back of the chair, and she kept her eyes fixed on the wooden spindles, the pattern of the grain, the faint dusting of sawdust, the little marks and nicks in the wood. Outside she could hear people walking along the towpath, the low voices of adults talking and the sound of children running and laughing. They were only feet away but the sounds seemed to come from another world.

She was sobbing freely now; she had managed to stop screaming after each blow. Her face and the seat of the chair were wet with tears and her body felt battered and exhausted. She slumped more heavily against the chair, every last bit of resistance gone out of her.

She felt the tiniest let-up, the tiniest easing in the intensity of the blows. Heard him exhale as if he too was exhausted, and then it stopped. She didn't quite dare believe it at first; she thought it might just be a longer than usual pause, or a break between whacks, but he had really stopped.

She heard and felt him straighten up behind her, and stand back. She imagined him surveying his handiwork and she hoped that he was pleased. She also felt the first glimmers of pride. Pride in herself for holding still by will alone when she had not been restrained, pride in herself for containing her screams without the assistance of a gag.

'Sit up.'

She carefully unfolded her body and sat up on her knees, so that her bottom didn't touch her heels. She felt raw and tender and bruised. She didn't dare meet his eye, so her gaze focussed on his thighs, on his work jeans. How she wanted to cling to him, but she didn't move; she waited. He moved over to the snug and sat down on the low seat that also doubled as a little bed. He rested back on the cushions. He was only four or five feet away from her but it felt like a million miles.

'Come here and suck me off.' She heard the ragged catch of desire in his voice and her heart leapt. Everything hurt as she crawled over to him, but inside she was overflowing with joy and happiness. She kept her eyes on his jeans and with trembling hands that fumbled and slipped she found the button and undid it and unzipped his jeans. She eased them down along with his underwear; he didn't move or help her so that she was only able to ease his clothing down just enough to get his cock out.

It was the first time she had seen it: it was thick and rock hard and surrounded by dark, almost black hair. She took it in her mouth with infinite gentleness and licked her tongue around him, then took him deep into her mouth. She could taste the come on the end of his cock already, and soon he abandoned his nonchalant pose and grabbed hold of her hair and the back of her head and pushed her down harder and further onto him. He pushed his hips up towards her and swore under his breath and she knew then that everything was going to be okay: she had survived.

'Jesus, Rebecca, you're going to drive me fucking crazy, you know that,' he murmured. And with a groan that almost sounded like he was in physical pain, he came into her mouth. She swallowed his come and then half lay, half sat, resting her head beside him until he moved over and made room and pulled her up onto the seat beside him, where he wrapped his arms around her and they slept.

She was still wet when she woke up. She had been in too much pain and then been so grateful and relieved about sucking his cock that she hadn't really noticed how aroused she had been. But between her legs, she was sticky and soaking wet. Her bottom still stung, but it only really hurt if she moved.

He opened his eyes and looked at her, and she was relieved beyond belief to see that he looked at her with desire and affection, not disappointment and disgust. He drew her to him and kissed her deeply. She felt her entire being melting in a pool of love and submission.

He pulled back and looked at her seriously. 'I don't ever want to have to do that again, do you understand? I want to be with a woman who's not going to piss me off in the first place. This isn't a game, you know. Although ...' he shifted slightly and looked down at her bottom, 'you took that really well, and I have to say, there's nothing sexier than a woman with a well-spanked arse.' He kissed the top of her head. 'But seriously, I hope you've learned your lesson. I'm not into loads of drama. I want an easy life. A woman who'll do what she's told, when she's told, and I'm used to getting my own way.'

'I'm sorry, it won't ever happen again.'

'Good girl. You're forgiven.'

He kissed her again, and this time his hands stroked her shoulders and back, unlocking tiny tensions in her muscles so that her body relaxed into him. His hands travelled down and onto her bottom. She winced slightly as he caressed her bruises. And then her body relaxed once more as his fingers slipped between her legs, into the wetness. He gave a satisfied grunt as he pushed his fingers inside her, where she was burning. Her body told him how much his punishment had affected her.

'Mind you,' he said, as his fingers stroked upwards over her clit and she gasped, 'I didn't know you'd enjoy it quite so much.'

Perversion Process
by Rachel Kramer Bussel

Oliver is the one who turned me into a pervert, or, at least, that's what I like to say. Before I met him, I was definitely more on the vanilla side. I might have gotten a light spanking or two, had ice cubes shoved up my pussy, had a lover hold me down while he slammed his cock in and out of me, but Oliver took all of that to a new level. He meant business, and he showed me that in the backseat of his car after our first date. It had been a blind date, a set-up by my friend Christine.

'But what is it about him that I'll like?' I'd pestered her for the umpteenth time over margaritas, my voice sounding whinier as the night and the drinks went on. She'd shown me his photo and all but handed me his resume and, while he was cute, I couldn't really tell why she was so gung ho for me to meet him. Sometimes, though, I guess our friends know us better than we know ourselves, or maybe it was a lucky guess. I certainly hadn't confessed my kinky fantasies to her, or anyone else.

And I wasn't expecting Oliver to do more than try to cop a feel, maybe get up my skirt, so I agreed to come in for a nightcap. He brewed us both strong cups of tea, but, instead of placing them at his dining room table, he brought them both over to a large chair, rested them on the small table next to it, and told me to come sit on his lap. 'Like Santa?' I joked.

'Even better,' he said. So I did. I sat on his lap, even though my just-above-the-knee-length skirt meant my thighs would be bared to him. I shifted so I was straddling one of his legs, already feeling myself get wet. 'Here's your tea,' he said, handing me the glass. It was awkward, sitting like that and not acknowledging it. His whole body was so solid and firm beneath me, but I just politely twisted my head around and asked him more about running his own car dealership and his travels, while he asked me about being a fundraiser for a non-profit.

Then all of a sudden, he made me spill my tea. Well, maybe he didn't make me, but I wasn't expecting him to ask, 'How do you feel about spanking?'

'You mean, parents and kids?' I asked, stalling for time, not wanting to let on that the word had instantly conjured up images of my bottom bared for him, of my ankles and wrists bound, of him thrashing me with all kinds of implements, of him spanking me all over.

He took my hand and pressed deeply into my palm before pinching the skin there. My tea forgotten, he looked intently into my eyes and said, 'Serena, you know that's not the kind of spanking I'm talking about. Don't be coy; it doesn't suit you. I'm asking you how you're going to like it when I take you naked across my knee and spank that sweet ass of yours until you scream?' He stopped playing with my hand, letting it simply rest against his.

I swallowed hard, my face turning beet-red – I could feel it.

'I'd like that, Oliver. I'd like that a lot,' I said, unexpected tears rushing to my eyes. He wasn't talking about a playful, fun kind of spanking. He wasn't talking about playing bongos on my butt and then whipping out his cock, or giving me a good squeeze and slap while I writhed on top of him. Oliver was dead serious, like spanking was the only topic that mattered – and suddenly, it was.

'How much, Serena?' he said, inching closer, close enough so he could casually slip his hand down my skirt, toying with my thong by tugging it upward so it cut into my pussy lips, making me squirm. 'How much would you like it? What would you do for me in return?' He let my thong slap back against my skin, then dipped his fingers into the area approaching my crack.

'Whatever you want,' I whispered, my face hot, sure that

58

even though we were alone in his home, everyone in our small town was somehow listening in and now knew exactly how slutty and submissive and spankable I truly was.

'Whatever I want?' he asked, his voice suddenly rising into a tone that was light, almost festive. 'Even if I want to tape you being spanked and show it to all my friends so they can jerk off to you? Even if I want to blindfold you and gag you and use all my favorite toys on you? Even if I want to make you suck another man's cock while I spank you very, very hard? That would be okay?' His voice had returned to its previous fervour, and I could tell he was dying to touch me more intimately.

I thought about each potential scenario he'd just spun, visualizing them in my head. I thought about a camera being trained on me, recording the shifting of my ass from pale to pink, thought about him shoving a gag between my lips, thought about the effort of giving a blowjob while getting smacked where it counted. All of those would be more than okay. It suddenly hit me that Christine knew about each of our penchants for spanking, and that had been why she'd known we'd get along.

I nodded, letting a tear stream down my face. He stared at me intently, and I wasn't sure if Oliver would gently wipe or lick away the tear, or rip my clothes off and get us started on our spanking journey. What he did was this: he wrapped one hand gently around my throat, his thumb pressing against the tender point in the centre, and with his other hand, he slapped my face. Gently, at first, but enough to make me tremble, inside and out. My breath roared through my nose, then back out, and he slapped me again. 'You like to get spanked all over, don't you, Serena? Don't pretend,' he said, then slapped my face again. I couldn't deny it: the slaps made my pussy tight and wet, my cheek braced for the next blow, anticipating it even as I feared it, each sensation feeding off the other.

Then he pushed up my shirt, hardly glancing at the luxury push-up bra I'd purchased earlier in the day in his haste to peel down the cups. He then slapped my breasts in turn, while I sat there and took it. Okay, I didn't just sit there, and I didn't just take it. I liked it, craved it, wanted it. I hummed, then moaned in arousal as his hand struck each nipple directly, over and over again, before he leaned down and bit one while twisting the other. My pussy was starting to hurt, making me wonder if I was having the female equivalent of blue balls. It felt almost too good. When my hands threaded through his hair, urging him on, Oliver pulled up.

'Did I say you could put your hands on me? You don't touch me without permission, little girl, and you know that,' he said. No, technically I didn't know it, but I want to learn, wanted to be his student, his slut, his sub. 'Get up,' he snapped, then pulled me up by one nipple. My purple skirt rippled to my ankles. Out of his pocket, he drew a Swiss army knife, unleashing the blade. My eyes went wide, and I trembled this time with a touch of real fear. He smiled at me wickedly as he flashed the blade at me. 'Oh, you won't get this against your skin until you've earned it. I'm using this to get rid of your pesky clothes,' he said, before slicing through my blouse, then the $100 bra, then the long skirt, even though it was already almost off, followed by my black silk panties. Those were pretty much worthless by then anyway, soaked through as they were. My clothing fell to the floor, and I almost did too. He tossed the knife on the table, then turned me around. 'Raise your arms above your head,' he said, and I did, standing there in only my heels, necklace and earrings. 'Shut your eyes; I'll be right back.'

I wouldn't have considered ignoring his order. This was the best first date I'd ever been on, one that, even if we never hooked up again, had already given me practically endless fodder for future orgasms. I heard him return and tried to stand straighter, my calves feeling the strain of the position. First, he slipped a blindfold over my eyes, a blessed relief. I didn't want to see, only to feel. Then a collar that he fastened tightly around my neck, tugging on it and making my juices dribble down my thighs. But then he fastened cuffs to my arms, and must have climbed onto the chair to fasten them to the ceiling. I hadn't noticed a hook, but, then again, I hadn't been looking. The heels were the only thing saving this position from being truly uncomfortable, giving me just the needed height. 'Now you're ready,' he said, slipping his hand between my legs. I thought maybe he was going to offer me some relief: ram them deep into my core, let me clench around him rather than clench uselessly. But no. All I got was a light stroke, barely a tickle, against my wet sex. 'Spread your legs.'

I did, enough to feel the air greet my cunt lips. 'I take it you've been spanked before, Serena,' he said, pausing while I nodded and murmured something I hoped sounded like yes. 'Good, because I don't believe in going easy on bratty girls like you. Not only don't you deserve it easy, you won't like it. I know you. I know that you will rise to the occasion. Say 'orange' if you need me to slow down, 'red' if you want me to stop.' I nodded again. 'But, Serena? I'll be very disappointed if you have to safeword.' I swallowed, wondering just what he was planning to do to me. I didn't want to disappoint him, already, that early, didn't want to jinx what could be a very pleasant future. He leaned down and kissed me, then bit my lower lip, enough to make it sting. I tried to kiss him back, but he spat in my mouth, making me rush to swallow. 'Oh, and how could I forget?' he asked the air, before sliding clamps around my nipples and fastening them tight.

'Do you need to be gagged?' he asked me. It felt like a trick question. I'm a screamer, a loud one. Did he want to hear me scream? Did I? Or did he want me quiet and compliant?

'I don't think so,' I said, playing it safe, figuring he could always gag me later.

'Good. Now you're ready.' His voice was at once a bit scary and soothing, letting me know he did, indeed, plan to hurt me, but that he'd be there to take care of me afterward. I heard all that in his voice, and had trusted him from the moment we'd met, not because of Christine, but because of him. I'm good with people, can almost always tell at the start if they're trustworthy. I can't predict the future or if a relationship will last, but I can tell if someone is worthy of giving over my body, my mind, my soul, as I was about to do. I'd never been wrong.

He started hitting me with a paddle, not too hard, but enough to make me shake in my bonds. My toes curled downward in a desperate attempt to keep me in place as the smacks got harder. I wasn't sure which part of my perversion process I should be focusing on, since all the torments were working together: the bonds around my wrists, the blindfold keeping me from seeing, the collar tight on my throat, the metal pinching my nipples, the feet secured in place or the blows against my ass. He struck me harder, as if to let me know: my focus should be on my bottom. This was about getting spanked; the rest was just extra.

My instinct was to thrust my ass back at him, make it a better target, but I couldn't, not like this. He managed just fine, though, whacking me in the sweet spot where my cheeks met, then compounding the effect by raking his short nails along my tender, sore skin. Then his smacks increased in intensity as he brought volley after volley down against one cheek, followed by a barrage against the other. I'd been quiet up until then, absorbing the sweet pain into my body, focusing on the heat over the pain, focusing on how it made my pussy even wetter, so much so I was probably dripping onto the floor.

Then he started in with a flogger. Oliver didn't talk much while he did it, his heavy breathing speaking for him. This was work, of a sort, almost a sport; instead of table tennis, it was living room spanking. The soft suede of the flogger struck my back with a thud that reverberated through my body. I've long known my back is one of the most sensitive parts of my body, and Oliver made sure to see that it got its due before moving it to the front of me. The flogger only brushed against my tits, but that's all I needed to cry out, with the clamps seeming to get tighter as the flogger jostled them. 'Scream for me, Serena, let me hear that pretty voice. Tell me what you want,' he said in a rush as he then moved lower, flogging my pussy and making me squirm. My arms were getting tired, but the rest of me was wide awake.

'Aaaahhhh.' I let out a power yell, followed by biting my lip as he pinched my clit with his fingers, hard and then harder. How did he know I'd wanted this? How did he know my body could take this much? I had never been sure, going only by fantasy as I'd pressed my vibrator to my pussy and dreamed of

62

being overpowered, taken, spanked – used and abused.

Oliver finished off that round of erotic torture by twisting his fingers inside me, not enough to get me off, but enough to make me cry out once again. 'I need a kiss,' he said, pressing his lips softly to mine. His touch was soft, almost too much so, feather-light, utterly unexpected. I should have known that what would come next would rock my world, would make me scream louder than I had on the Cyclone roller coaster. Next time, I would know this was his m.o., but, that first time, I was clueless, blissfully so. He blew a breath against my lips, and when I puckered up again, I found something hard against them. No, not his cock, but a piece of wood. 'It's a cane,' he said. 'My favourite one. I'm only going to strike you ten times, but it's going to hurt, Serena. A lot. It's going to make you scream, and probably cry. It might make you hate me and never want to see me again, but that's a risk I have to take, because I need to hear what this does to you. Now, kiss it.'

I knew what caning was, at least, as much as my Internet research had yielded. I'd seen videos of men and women being caned, the bright red stripes across their skin, the looks of pain and pleasure yielding to one another in nanoseconds as their faces contorted. I wasn't totally sure I was ready, but I did what he said anyway. 'Okay,' I whispered. This date had already gone so much farther than I'd ever expected or hoped it could, I wasn't going to back down now.

He tapped the cane against my bottom at first, as if to get me used to its direction, its heft. It was heavy, solid, different from what had come before. I was ready … or so I thought. Because when the first stroke of the cane landed, I thought I was going to fall over. If my arms had been free, I'd have scrambled for purchase. As it was, I curled my fingers, twisted them as much as I could, prayed my legs stayed in place as tears gushed forth. The pain was exquisite, a whole other universe than the spankings that had come before. The next blow was quite similar, and built on the one before. The cane seemed inordinately powerful; after all, it was just a skinny stick, wasn't it? And yet, no, it wasn't, it was a weapon in his hands, not one of destruction, but instruction. He was teaching me, stinging, intense, soul-changing stroke after stroke. Oliver was teaching me what it would take to be his, and what I needed to know to own my own power. My mind went blank even as my body blazed, and by the end, I knew I'd crossed some irreversible line. I could never go back to my vanilla life, the random smacks, the small-time play.

Even as the tears streamed down my face while he tenderly unclamped, unbound, and decollared me before taking me into his arms, I knew he had given me a gift. I didn't just get through it, I'd gotten *It*; gotten the thrill of going somewhere else, of letting my body and, more importantly, my master, guide me. Maybe the reason no man had ever taken ownership of me like that was they knew I wouldn't let them; knew that as much as I might have looked like I was asking for it, there was a tiny part inside me that was holding back, selfishly storing my desire for myself, keeping it in reserve. With Oliver, I'd given him everything, risking him tossing it back at me, humiliating me.

He pulled me down onto the couch and soon I was riding him, his pants pushed down, his cock inside me. I was actually too spent to do much more than cling to him, and that was okay. He wrapped his arms around me and we held each other and hugged and fucked.

'I guess now I know how you feel about spanking,' he said later, laughing, as he fed me cheese and crackers and champagne, not minding when some of the sweet liquid spilled all over me. I waited until the next afternoon to call Christine and thank her — after Oliver had bought me my very own collar, one he later got personalized. Now I can't imagine having ever been anything other than a full-fledged pervert, and even have a tattoo that says 'His' to prove my loyalty. Spankings are a daily occurrence, and yes, we've tested out all those fantasies he mentioned that first night, and many more, though what the future holds, I don't know. That's for Oliver to decide, and me to bend over and obey.

Bitch
by Ashley Hind

Few people can be defined by a single word but I can: that word is *bitch*. It is all I am now. The title has been conferred upon me and I must live up to it if my heart's desire is to be gained. It makes no difference that I am still a partner and chief Arts Advisor for a London interior design firm, or that I am wealthy and beautiful. It is immaterial that I used to be confident and brimming with self-belief, and could trample over another's emotions to get what I wanted. For all my strength I had a weakness, and she used it. So everything I am I have to yield now, because I am full of her. She crams my thoughts and swells my heart and bubbles in my veins. I would shout her name from the rooftops, if only I knew it.

I am utterly obsessed by the female bottom, and that is my weakness. I have seduced hundreds of girls over the years in a vain quest to find the perfect example, becoming more particular and frustrated as my search continued. I love my own body to the point of narcissism. I have an effortless hourglass figure and my backside is delectable. It is full but shapely with a fine apple curve, the pale cheeks parted by a narrow but deep split that hides its secrets. The skin is pale and pristine and flawless. All traces of the jet black hairs in my crease and on my mound have been removed by electrolysis. It is almost perfect, only not quite full enough.

Antique mirrors line every wall and surface of my bedroom and cheval-glass stands cluster in the corners, all pointing towards my bed. There is not a single angle that is not covered, or a part of me that cannot be seen as I pose naked and fuck

65

myself. I despondently used to think that my own bottom would be as close as I would get to my ideal and that I would never get to experience the bliss of loving its equal. I had only ever seen a better one on a statue in a nearby gallery. I went there often to view its perfection and dream that the stone figure could become real flesh so that I could take her and make her mine. But better still *she* came, and she took me instead.

The statue I adore is of Erato, muse of love and erotic poetry. She stands with the cherub Eros clutching at her legs. He looks up at her, his face seemingly a mask of innocence. Yet you can see how tightly he pulls at her, and while she holds aloft an open book in one hand, the other hand is held across her chest, trying to keep her loose gown in place to cover her modesty. But mischievous Eros has already scored a victory, because she is unable to secure all of her gown and his downward pull has exposed her glorious bottom in all its white marble glory.

The artist has spared her the side dimples in the buttocks that afflict most Greek figures, and given her a very full rump indifferent to the forces of gravity. He somehow managed to give the impression of a deep cleft, scoring into the stone with absolute precision to leave a heavy shadow at the top where her cheeks met the base of her spine. But the crack itself was wonderfully narrow, the buttocks huddling together to keep the gap closed and secret. Their surface was creamy with an opaque shine and absolutely smooth, without a single blemish or imperfection in the marble.

One day I simply had to touch it. I had often felt the urge but had never before allowed myself. Her back arches slightly and her rump is pushed out invitingly, so I reached out and stroked it, just lightly, with the backs of my fingers. I was surprised when I found it cold. It was so life-like I had expected the warm give of real flesh. I tried to pull my hand away but it hovered above the surface and turned palm-in as if to grab one ample cheek. I managed to arrest this impulse but stroked her again. Her surface was absolutely even, there were no pimples or pocks or hairs to distract the sensation on my fingertips. My breath was hard and faltering, and my heart was racing.

I must have been caressing her in wonder for all of a minute when other senses broke through and alerted me to the fact that I was being watched. I suddenly registered the form in my periphery and turned to see her staring at me. My fingers jumped ashamed from Erato's bottom and I blushed for the first time in what must have been a lifetime. The watcher's expression was not one of scorn or censure, or even of mocking amusement. She just inspected me calmly, taking me in. I wanted to look her up and down, to see her body beneath the tight black clothes so similar to mine, but I just couldn't break her gaze.

Her mouth was wide and pouting, the top lip ever so slightly bee-stung under the dark red gloss. Her eyes were almond-shaped and as brown as mine, but set further apart. Her forehead was high beneath her fringe and her hair was sleek and straight, raven like my own, but probably dyed. Her skin was pale and flawless, her cheeks cut by a blush of applied red to show angular, high cheekbones. My first thought was that she was German, or maybe eastern European. But this frittered to inconsequence when my second thought pushed through: that she was the most beautiful thing that I had ever seen.

I could feel myself melting, my legs actually shaking as we regarded each other, some ten feet apart. Trepidation was alien ground for me – usually any girl I looked at for this length of time was already under my spell, whether gay or just curious. I tried to think of something to say, a plausible excuse for why I was stupidly stroking a statue's arse so lovingly. But my mouth was dry and frozen, and she did nothing to relieve my tension. She just stood, patiently and wordlessly waiting to reel me in. I recognised her technique for seduction so well: it was exactly the same as mine.

With my heart threatening to burst, I dragged my legs from their paralysis and took a step towards her. From out of nowhere a figure cut my vision and suddenly an elderly lady was there between us, addressing my girl. The blood hissed in my ears and muffled the old lady's question but I was still lurching forward, trying to divert my momentum away from them, too humiliated to stop and wait like a lost sheep and desperate now to just get away with as much dignity as I could muster. I could feel my face burning and as I passed them I felt her gaze still boring into me, tracing my departure.

I didn't want to walk away from her but I did. I was such a shaking mess that I had to go. I knew that she was still looking at me but I couldn't look back, not until I had reached the double doors to the stairs. I turned briefly and saw her speaking softly to the old woman. Then my eyes dropped to witness her round bottom sticking out against her leggings, and I gasped aloud. I needed to stay and absorb the wonderful sight but my foolish legs, unused to hurried flight, had already taken me out of the hall, and the doors were swinging back to close and hide her.

Her image wouldn't leave me. It made me so befuddled and lost me so much sleep it was almost a haunting. I spent hours bent over on my bed, my bare bottom reflected all around the room. I saw the curve of my cheeks and the dark split between them and wished my face could be just inches from it, absorbing its scent and beauty. I saw my tiny hole, hidden until I stuck my arse right out, a shy ring like an inward belly button with no trace of pucker, its little jet black opening at the heart. I watched engrossed as my wet finger slid slowly in and out while I longed for my bum to be hers.

I went back to the gallery every day for a week in the hope that she would be there, my stomach lurching with pangs of panic when it struck me that I had walked out on her and might never see her again. I tried at different times of the day. I made excuses to leave work to see if she might be there mid morning, or late afternoon. Every time I went I stood before beautiful Erato and looked at her gorgeous stone bum and dreamt of it as real flesh, the flesh of the girl I had left in the gallery.

And then, when my hopes had all but gone, she was there. I was once more forlornly stroking the statue and thinking of what might have been when I saw her from the corner of my eye. She had caught me fondling the inert marble once more and I should have whipped away my hands in embarrassment, but they stayed and continued their light caresses, even as I turned to her and met her gaze, seeing that same expressionless, wonderful face.

My body fizzed with instant adrenalin but I wasn't going to lose her this time. I kept my nerve and tried to take back some control, stroking Erato's backside with nail-tip brushes that would have electrified real skin. I could see her gaze fixed on my hands now. I lightly cupped and gently squeezed at each unyielding stone bun, feeling their coolness at my palms, praying for her warm softness instead. Then I sank to my knees, my face level with the marble bottom, not caring who saw me, as long as she did.

I held each cheek of the stone posterior as if gently spreading them, and then slowly leant forwards, parting my lips to let my tongue snake out to its fullest extent. The tip alighted at the lowest point of the statue's rear, where the gown covered her once more, the artists leaving only the tiniest hint of bulging lips between the thighs. I laid the flat of my tongue to this and lapped upwards, slowly and deliberately, tracing a wet line all the way up the cleft of Erato's peachy buttocks, right to the small of her back.

My head turned slightly as I licked, so that as my tongue finished its journey and remained stuck out and curled upwards at the tip, I was able to fix my gaze on her. I could see she was engrossed by my lewdness. Her mouth was slightly open and her bottom lip wet. Her eyes had a greater sparkle and seemed even darker brown than before. Her breath was sharp and erratic, and I knew that she was mine. I rose up again and turned to face her, my hands sliding off the statue, leaving poor Erato forgotten. Her expression was still blank but she had lost some of the composure and confidence of before. It was time for me to go in for the kill.

I gave her the slightest smile and then walked nonchalantly away, feeling her eyes drilling into me once more. As I neared the exit doors I turned, and with one curling finger, beckoned her to follow me. As I left I didn't look back: I knew she would come, and the gentle swish of the double doors some ten seconds later confirmed this. I heard the soft pad of her flat shoes on the stairs as I descended and made my way out into the street and towards my home, with her tailing some distance behind. I walked with as much composure as I could, having to check my speed to make sure she could trace my route and not lose sight of me.

I entered my apartment and left the door wide open, turning off in my hall and going straight down the long corridor to my bedroom. Once there, I stood in front of the bed facing back towards the entrance hall and removed my skirt, seeing my knickerless cunt and arse reflected all around the room. My nipples pushed at the thin wool of my black roll-neck jumper, but I kept this on, along with my fishnet stockings and black high-heels. I awaited her arrival with my hands on my hips and wearing the best expression of aloofness that I could muster.

I heard the soft scrape of her feet on the steps outside and then she was there in the hall, turning to see me and staring at the little slit of my hairless quim. She pushed the door shut and then reached behind her for the zip of her tight mini-skirt, letting it drop to reveal her wide, white thighs and tiny purple lace knickers. Her legs were bare and firm, even in her flat shoes, the calves slightly thick, which is just how I like them. She was breathing hard now, and sliding her panties down to reveal a neat, luscious puss, shaved bare and as smooth as my own.

She came down the passage towards me, our eyes locked and filled with desire for the combat of our passion. We were like two champions, neither yet defeated, both desperate to impose our will on the other – and one of us was destined to lose. She came to me and we embraced, our mouths open and hungry as they joined, our tongues darting out to dance and spar. We instantly grabbed each other's arses to hold us in, our bumpy pussy mounds pressing wetly together.

I couldn't believe how soft she felt in my hands. I had expected her to have firm cheeks considering their size and shape, but I was wrong. She was pliable enough to grab and squeeze and pinch, just as soft as me and maybe more. I let out an involuntary moan of pleasure as she yielded in my grip. I opened my eyes to see her reflection in the cheval-glass. She was almost as pale as Erato and every bit as flawless, but even bigger and shapelier. The heart of her buttocks where she was largest stuck out and filled my palms, yet even as she curved in towards her tuck I was still able to rummage down and gather handfuls.

How she did not droop or sag was a mystery, but she didn't. It was the perfect bottom, beyond even my highest expectations. I could hear my moans, almost like sobs against her lush mouth as I exalted in the sight of her backside. She was mirroring my actions, grabbing and squeezing at my arse and pulling the cheeks apart, making me feel cool air on my wetness. I shifted to the side so that our pussies clamped to each other's thighs, and I could feel my lips sliding in their own slickness as I ground against her and pressed my aching clit to her leg.

We rubbed against each other, kissed with wet urgency and fondled each other's bums. I wanted to take control but I couldn't bear to break the embrace. I felt her hand tap my arse in her excitement, a tentative slap with only her fingertips rather than her palm. I let it pass without even a sound of warning. Then she smacked me again, still only lightly but this time with her whole hand striking my bottom and creating an audible slap. No-one has ever dared smack me before. I was lost in this girl's beauty, hotter than ever and dying to either come or eat her up, but still I felt the burn of incredulity at her action.

I was a domineering figure though not a Domme, and have never used any kind of corporal punishment on any of my conquests, but in this case my reaction was immediate. I drew back my palm and gave her a hard warning smack that jiggled her right cheek and forced a squeal of surprise from her mouth and into mine. In the mirrors I could see my hand's white imprint in her flesh slowly turning a delicate pink. The thrill of slapping her exposed flesh went straight to my pussy and I leached even more juice onto her thigh.

I was confident I had tamed her and made her aware of who was in charge, but she was far from beaten yet. Instead of sinking further into me, she rammed her tongue with new vigour into my mouth, drew back her hand and planted a stinging slap onto my right buttock, causing me this time to squeal my shock. Before the pain had really registered I had reacted and sent her another smack, not caring if it hurt her now and glad to feel her bum cheek quivering under my fingers. She sucked in her breath, holding herself hard against me and bucking her hips to rub her clit in order to counter the pain. Then she lashed out again, and my mouth left hers as I yelled.

The battle for supremacy was now truly joined. We were panting and snarling at each other, our lips curled and wet. I spanked her hard and then she returned the favour. We pinched and gripped each other's backsides and then delivered our blows in turn, trying to out-hit the other and force a submission. I have never felt such pain. Each slap exploded across my arse and seared the skin. I could feel tears welling but I would not give up and neither would she.

I could feel her pressing into me, not just to appease her yearning clitoris but to force me off balance. I stood my ground and pushed back, and then on her next lunge I turned her as her weight came through and used her momentum to send her backwards to crash against my dressing table, sitting her against it momentarily. She was up quickly but not before I had seen and grabbed my flat-backed silver antique hairbrush. She snarled and grinned as she spanked my arse once more, feeling me jam into her with the pain, but I absorbed it, and then retaliated.

My blow was the hardest yet, courtesy of the added weight of the metal brush. Her eyes widened and her mouth dropped open to let out a high-pitched yell. She trembled as the hurt coursed through her, running up her body and as if trying to burst from her head, which in a form it did. With flaming eyes she gathered her fury and let it go in a shower of spit, right into my open mouth. She used my shock to impel me back across the floor towards the bed, a last-gasp attempt to get me over, but I regained my footing and stood firm. She had missed her chance so I took it, slapping her hard once more with the flat of the brush and spitting back into her mouth when it sprang open to let loose its cry.

I knew she was beaten now, I could feel her wilt, still desperately trying to calm the fire on her bum by rubbing her soaking fanny up and down my thigh. Even as she crushed my arse in her tight grip and pushed her spit-wet tongue back into my mouth I knew she was crying, and as she kissed me her tears ran onto my face. One more spank would have sealed her as mine and she knew it. She concentrated her dwindling energy on one final effort to force me over. My eyes were on her bum as her reflection danced from mirror to mirror. I felt her desperate slaps and saw my own spanked bottom in the glass. And that's when I flinched and allowed her to grab her chance.

The reddening of her pearly skin was acceptable and even turned me on, but it was the thickening of it that I couldn't countenance. I could feel my own growing thicker under the weight of her slaps, the skin almost shrinking as it pinked. I could bear it on my own bottom, but not on hers. Her bum had to be perfect. I wanted it soft and pale, to be squashed and spread on my face, to be worshipped and lapped and squeezed, not beaten and desecrated. So I simply gave up, and in a flash she was sitting on the edge of the bed with me pinned down over her knees.

She took off her flat shoe and beat me with it, all over my cheeks and thighs, down the backs of my legs and even on the soles of my feet, the slaps bursting all over me. I wriggled and screamed but let her hold me down throughout the blitz of torment. My bum cheeks were jumping apart and I knew that she would be able to see the wetness smeared up my crack and oozing onto her thighs. I didn't know whether to beg for mercy or scream out that I loved her. In the end I did neither, my eyes and nose running uncontrollably and my mouth too thick with saliva to do anything but moan.

Then the hurt stopped, and a new feeling spread through me, a blissful endorphin sea that lapped my entire body and made me crave her smacks, although they were barely discernable now. I climaxed over and over, my clit pressing against her leg as her shoe came down and crashed into me. I tried to open my legs, praying that the shoe would trace a path between my open buttocks and slap headlong into my dripping cunt. I felt the occasional sting on my lips but my big bum was too protective, and I knew that she would have to flip me over in order to give my pussy the spanking it needed.

She didn't oblige me, but I had come too many times now to care. She let me slide off her, leaving a trail of slickness down her legs as I collapsed at her feet. I was allowed almost no time to recover. She spread her legs wide, grabbed me by the hair and pushed my face into her delicious split. I lapped inside her for all I was worth, hoping she would be satisfied enough to want me there again. I spread her lips against my cheeks and coated my face in her sweet slick. I went to suck at her swollen button but she pushed me back down to suck her out, and put her fingers there instead, rubbing away beneath my nose.

My tongue was tired through kissing but I pressed on, plunging it inside her, desperate to be indispensable to her now and for ever. She started shaking. Her cries of pleasure broke into a silent scream and she came, squirting her velvet cream in a hot rush like urine into my mouth, filling me and making me swallow over and over. I was shaking still, and I loved her, totally. She spoke for the first time, in the accented English of an eastern European. She said:

'That is the only time you will ever spank me. If you ever want to see me again you must come to me as my slave. You are my bitch now. What are you?'

'A bitch,' I whispered. 'Your bitch.'

And so I am. And so I trail to the gallery day after day, hoping beyond hope that she will be there to take me, to let me surrender everything that I am and be hers completely. To let me feel again the exquisite thrill of hurt and humiliation and to worship her bottom in return. Nothing now matters in this world but her.

Paying For It
by Justine Elyot

He makes a living from spanking girls. Can you believe that? I told him it was money for old rope, but he said, 'Nah, I do spanking, not bondage.' Then told me to get out the strap for making such a disrespectful suggestion.

'What you don't understand, Kat,' he said, plying the leather and ignoring my gasps while I gripped the iron bedstead for dear life, 'is that spanking is not easy. It isn't just a case of throwing the lady over the lap and whaling away. There is finesse involved. Psychology.'

'Ouch!'

'Sensibility.'

'Ouch!'

'Sensitivity.'

'Ouch!'

'Good judgement.'

'Ouch!'

'Aesthetic refinement.'

'OUCH!'

'And maybe a soupçon of sadistic intent.'

The final stroke caught me at the top of my thighs and my resolve, along with my knees, buckled beneath it.

'OK, I'm sorry,' I panted, doubled over on the carpet. 'It's not easy. But please don't tell me it hurts you more than it hurts me.'

He chuckled softly behind me. 'No, I wouldn't go that far. Back up, Kat. Bending over the bed now, please.'

I pouted and made an authentic-sounding sob.

'It doesn't hurt me,' he said, once my upper body was pressed to the quilted eiderdown while my bottom, tight with the heat of the strapping, faced him at a jaunty angle. 'But I do maintain the requisite muscular strength. In my right arm in particular.'

I expected a smack just then, but I got something else: cold lubricant in that intimate pucker, and then he was easing one of his bigger-sized plugs into me, and I knew he was going to fuck me next, and I sighed, eyelids lowering in pleasurable anticipation.

But instead – and this was what convinced me that no ordinarily-wired man could do his job – he asked me if I'd ever been paddled with a plug in before.

Oh, the despair; the sweet, dizzying, dismaying, rapturous cruelty of it all.

The fucking came later, but I must make it clear that he rarely fucks the girls he spanks. Only, he tells me, the very naughtiest ones. The ones that really need it. Such as me.

'Do you ever get … you know … emotionally involved with your … clients?' I asked him afterwards, staring limply at his digital alarm clock, knowing he would probably have another girl to punish in about an hour.

'Of course,' he said seriously, then he reached over to ruffle my hair. 'With all of them. In a way.'

'Right.'

I showered and dressed and caught the bus home, grateful that there was standing room only, still feeling some of the residual heat my tights held into my thighs and bottom. I wished that the heat could last for ever.

We have been meeting regularly for six months now. I had split up with a boyfriend in a nasty way – all my fault – and had no heart for the dating game. I felt guilty and unworthy of all the nice men out there, who surely deserved a correspondingly nice girl. I was not nice. I had dark shadows inside me that kept escaping into my daily interactions. It was not fair to inflict that on anyone.

But I felt so guilty. I could not stop thinking about the way I treated my ex, and I could not stop fantasising about spanking,

76

and somewhere in the middle, the two obsessions collided and I found myself staring at a website advertising the services of 'Professor Strict':

I know your secret need for punishment, and I will cater to it, with all the necessary rigour.

He was probably a conman. Possibly even a rapist. Or a murderer. I read on.

Send me the details of your wrongdoings and I will formulate a suitable penalty. If you have a bad habit or recurrent fault you would like to work on, then we can establish a disciplinary programme, involving regular progress reports and motivational chastisements.

I felt prickly and tight-chested, my knickers incriminatingly damp. Even if he *was* a conman ... just an email wouldn't hurt, would it?

Several emails later, I rolled up at his door, dressed as instructed in a mini-kilt, white shirt, thigh-high socks and Mary Janes. I wondered if he would answer the door in a cloak and mortarboard. I rather hoped not.

And indeed he managed to swerve that particular cliché, even though he'd made me embrace it with my attire. The man who answered the door was younger than I expected – maybe about thirty – and I thought immediately that he was too handsome to be using all that fusty old schoolmasterish language. Even if I did find it hot. He wore a suit, which was ... reassuring in a way, but it was a sharply cut, trendy kind of suit and he had an open collar rather than a tie. And his smile was beatifically beautiful. He looked like a man I might eye up in a bar. And I was slightly alarmed that he might lack the natural authority for what I had in mind, especially when he said, warmly and without a trace of sternness, 'Ah, you must be Kat. Come in.'

His place was neat and redolent of modern bachelorhood. I had been expecting lots of chintz and brass, don't ask me why. He took my coat and offered me a seat on the leather sofa.

'Can I get you a drink? Sometimes a little Dutch courage goes a long way.' He half-winked at me.

I laughed nervously. 'Oh ... maybe a white wine. If you

have one.'

'Sure.'

Would I be expected to make conversation? I did not think I would be capable, but he eased me in with his pleasant, open manner and we found ourselves discussing work and traffic and the weather as if we were already friends.

'So how did you find me?' he asked, halfway through the glass, the change of tone so abrupt that I sloshed a little of the wine over the rim.

'Well … Google …' I said. Suddenly my breathing was not coming so easily and I wanted to fold my arms over my chest and look away from his eyes, which had been kind and were now piercing.

'Google, eh? I wonder what search term might have led to me?'

'Oh,' I laughed, very nervously. 'Something silly … and embarrassing.'

'Tell me.'

This wasn't light conversation any more. I felt as if I was in the witness box undergoing rigorous cross-examination. I bit my lip.

'When I ask you a question, young lady, I expect an answer.'

Oh, that did it. That opened the thigh-top floodgates all right, that 'young lady'. Even though I could not have been more than a couple of years younger than him.

'Well, I think it was … oh God, I can't believe I'm saying this …erm … "bad girls need a spanking".' I lifted my eyes to the ceiling in mortification.

'No, look at me. Good girl. That must have been difficult for you to say, but you said it all the same. I appreciate your honesty and courage.'

I basked in this stranger's approval, utterly transfixed by the effortless power he radiated. Had I really thought to question his authority? It seemed ridiculously blind of me now to have done so. I adjusted my frame of mental reference: quiet and low-key do not equate to easy-going and submissive.

'So you're a bad girl, are you?' he asked next, sipping at his drink.

'Sometimes.'

'You think you need a spanking?'

'That's, ah, why I'm here.'

He nodded, accepting my little hint of snark without rancour.

'Of course. It's why you're here. And this bad girl, Kat … is she bad a lot, or is this a one-off situation? Because I can deal with either scenario. A conscience-cleanser, so you can move forward with your life … or a more long-term mentorship arrangement. Which do you think would be most appropriate for you?'

Good question. 'I … well. I seem to never learn from my mistakes. I think I need something a little stronger than the possibility of everything going pear-shaped … to influence my decision-making. A deterrent. Stop me doing all the same things. Drinking too much and getting off with the wrong people. Slacking off at work and getting more and more disorganised. It's like, I can sort myself out for a few weeks, and then I start sliding again.'

The idea of this man being a mentor … a disciplinarian mentor … oh God. I was so wet now that I feared for the leather of the sofa. Would he spank me even harder if I messed up his furniture?

'Right,' he said, and he stood up, took off his suit jacket and rolled up his shirtsleeves. I forgot to breathe, my wine glass frozen in my hand, watching him like a tiny mouse in the sights of a raptor. 'If this goes well for you, then, Kat, perhaps we can come to a more formal arrangement. But first, I need you to put down that glass and fetch the straight-backed chair from the corner, please.'

My chest decompressed in an undignified rush. I rose on shaky legs and went to fetch the chair, which was plain old-fashioned wood with a very high back and no arms, in the Shaker style, I suppose, though I'm not sure that's still in fashion. I could imagine Professor Strict – or whatever his real name was – as the preacher of some old-time religion, thumping the Bible in a kitchen with a similar light oak finish.

Sending the girls outside to cut switches: oh yes, he had that look.

Shaker style was apt, because I was shaking, nay quaking, with the enormity of what I was doing. This was really happening. I could leave. I didn't have to go through with it.

But he took my elbow, firmly but not painfully, seated himself on the austere chair of chastisement, and pulled me down over his lap in such a seamless gesture that I almost didn't realise what he was doing. Talk about a shift in perspective. There, stomach pressed tightly to his expensively-trousered thighs, legs sloping down to the floor and head dangling perilously close to the shiny leather of his shoe, I truly felt the ignominy of my position. I was not even remotely in control of this situation, even though I was the 'client' and he the 'service provider'. It was such ... a relief. Yes. A relief. What happened next would not and should not be up to me. I wanted it to be up to him. And I knew he would not fail me.

'Do you think you'll be able to keep still? Or should I hold your wrists behind your back?'

'I really don't know. I've never ...'

'All right. We'll see how we get on.' One hand cupped the tartan seat of my skirt, tapping it lightly and experimentally. 'How's your pain threshold?'

'OK, I think.'

'If you get to the point where you really can't bear any more, you must tell me. Think of a word.'

My mind went blank. Think of a word? What sort of a word? Any old word?

'Or should I think of one for you?'

'Yes please.'

'OK, the word is Antidisestablishmentarianism. Got that?'

I giggled and squirmed in his lap. 'That's too long!' I objected.

'You had your chance. Right then. I hear you've been a bad girl, Kat, is that right?'

'Yes,' I muttered, glad that he could not see my flushed face.

'Didn't catch that, Kat,' he said, with a leisurely swipe of my behind that shocked more than it hurt. 'Was that Yes? Or was it Yes, sir? Which do you think is the right answer?'

'Yes, sir,' I squeaked.

'Better. So what do you think happens to bad girls, Kat? Bad girls who come to my home?'

'I think ... they get a spanking, sir.'

He rubbed my skirt over my bottom, the hem tickling my thigh so that I wriggled. 'Is this irritating you, Kat? Perhaps we should get it out of the way.' He raised the material to reveal my white cotton briefs, stretched tight over my vulnerable globes. 'That was the right answer, incidentally. Well done. Can't say it's going to spare you any of what's coming to you though. Speaking of which ...'

His hand raised the most resounding crack Oh, on the thin cotton his hand raised the most resounding crack, making me jerk and yelp in surprise. The fabric was barely any barrier at all to his painful purpose, and he rained down a few more, glorying in the crispness and efficiency of his technique, for I was already whimpering and trying to rearrange myself to a less wide-open position on his lap – which he was having none of, of course.

'You asked for this, Kat,' he said warningly. 'You know it's what you need. You shouldn't fight it, should you?'

'No, sir.'

'No, sir. That's right.' And his hand was being gentle now, rubbing at the site of the soreness, dissipating the sting. 'This'll help you take a longer spanking,' he told me, ruining my illusion that it was all out of the kindness of his heart. 'Short, sharp shocks are all very well, but I think a good, long session over my lap will be better for you.' And with that, he repeated the initial fusillade, peppering me with hard smacks until I tried to cover my backside and, sighing deeply, he was forced to hold my wrists in the small of my back.

He repeated the punishing process several times until I was no longer able to count, twisting like a tethered eel and failing in my original intention of savouring every moment so it would imprint itself indelibly on my memory. All I could think of was how it hurt and how I could minimise the hurting and how I somehow never wanted it to end all the same. I think I was supposed to be listening to what he was saying too, but his voice, though rather calming with its low, slightly northern, timbre, did not succeed in communicating its words to my brain.

Until he stopped and I flopped my head down from its tense upward crick and sighed.

'Think I've finished, do you?' he said. 'Have you been listening to a word I've said? Eh? What did I just say?'

'Oh … I don't know! I sort of lost consciousness a bit there,' I meeped apologetically.

'Well, it's an intense experience, Kat, but don't forget, the whole point is to learn from it. What have you learned so far?'

'That you have a hard hand.'

'Hmm. Well, that's true. I think you need to come up with a bit more than that though. Let's see if this will make any difference.'

'Oh God!' I spluttered as he began to peel the knickers down over my tingly-warm rear, tugging at them until they rested mid-thigh, exposing all my most hidden fleshy parts to close inspection.

'Let's get serious, shall we? You've been getting away with things for far too long. It's time for some consequences. Are you ready for the consequences?'

'Ah … I … think so.' A slap that must have printed the shape of his hand on my bottom descended. 'Ow!'

'I think so *what*?'

'I think so, *sir*.'

I've had many more spankings over his knee, or leaning over his table, or over pillows on his bed since then. Some have been by his hand, but these days he often moves on to something, as he would say, 'a little more salutary'. Perhaps a hairbrush or a belt or a long thin rod or a thing with lots of whippy strands. But that first occasion is the one that stands out, the one I often go back to in my sleeplessness. It is not so much the heavy hand falling on my bottom, or the humiliating nakedness, or the extensive and ear-burning lecture he delivered; it is more to do with the feeling of being cared for. I know that must sound insane. But afterwards, after he had straightened me up and pulled up my knickers and sat me down next to him on the sofa and stroked my hair and given me a tissue and made everything better again – that time was priceless and precious. And addictive.

I came back for more, and more, and more again. Twice a month, regularly as clockwork, I presented my backside for a blistering at his cruelly refined hands, and he never disappointed. On the second visit, he asked me if I wanted a little ... relief ... after my spanking, and I let him put the hand that had hurt me between my legs to wring pleasure from the pain. About a month later we started ending up in the bedroom – it seemed such a natural and logical extension of the unnatural and illogical way our interactions had begun. He cared for me, enough to see that I did not get away with being any less than I could be, and I loved him for that, and wanted to give the gift back to him.

And now, six months later, I am in line for promotion at work. I drink less, avoid dodgy people and situations, keep myself safe and clean and fresh. But there's only one problem – I don't want to get involved with anyone but him. Professor Strict. OK, that's not his real name. He is called Aidan.

I'm a fool for love, and there's no spanking hard enough to help me with that.

So I think this one will be our final session. I have to walk away before I fall apart. Only when I call to make the appointment, he says that he is shutting up shop.

'What do you mean? You don't want to spank girls for money any more? Are you mad? That's so many men's dream gig ... are you OK?'

'Fine,' he said with a slightly defensive laugh. 'Meet me for a drink. I'll tell you about it. Can you be in O'Malleys later on, about six?'

A drink! A proper social-type situation! As if we were friends, or something.

I hope he might at least offer me one final bottom-warming for the road, but when I see him in a corner booth, nursing a whisky with about half a polar ice cap in it, my heart jumps a little, then sinks. He looks so pensive.

I slip in opposite him with my wine.

'What's gone wrong, Aidan? Have you got RSI in your spanking arm or something? I wonder if Injury Lawyers 4U deal with that kind of thing ...'

His luscious lips curve upward in a faint smile. 'I doubt it,' he says. 'Anyway, my arm's fine. As you might get to find out for yourself, if you're lucky. Or unlucky, depending how you look at it.'

'So you're not quitting the scene then?' I grin, delighted, even though I know I had been planning to make this our last rendezvous.

'Oh, yeah, I'm not taking bookings any more.'

'Oh. So ...?'

'I don't need the money. My day job earns me more than enough.'

'Ah. OK. But ... didn't you enjoy it?'

The look he gives me turns the wine to fire, all the way from my throat to my stomach. 'You know I did. You know I do. But I don't want to be a gun for hire any more. I want an arse to call my own.'

The glass jerks in my hand and I slop wine over the table, as is my habit. I can't help barking with laughter at his turn of phrase.

'You mean ... a serious relationship? Of some kind.'

'Of some kind, yeah. Man, woman, kinky sex and, y'know, maybe even a bit of normal stuff thrown in on top. Like this. This is almost normal, isn't it? And it's OK. Don't you think?'

I do think. I think I don't even dare ask the next question. But I force it through.

'So ... do you have a candidate? Or are you going to start looking?'

'I have a candidate.' I feel sick. The wine is like prussic acid eating at my core. Why must he keep looking at me with those eyes? What does it mean?

'Oh,' is all I can say.

'Come on, Kat, put me out of my misery.'

84

The prussic acid is now gunpowder, setting off fireworks that shoot to the roots and tips of my being.

'Do you mean *me*?'

'Of course I mean you! I haven't spent the last six months shagging you just to bin you off because I don't want your money any more. God, what do you think of me?'

'What about the others though?'

'I didn't shag any of the others. Jesus. I'm not a fucking gigolo.'

'A non-fucking gigolo would be a bit pointless.'

'Don't, Kat. And that's exactly what I was – a non-fucking gigolo. Not that I think there's anything so wrong with that. But I want to move on now. With you, if you think your arse can take it.'

'I think it can.'

He smiles brilliantly enough to melt the last of the ice-cubes in his drink.

'That's a yes?'

'That's a yes.'

We seal the deal in the pub car park, over the low wall with my skirt up and my knickers down, his belt flying through the evening air, all invisible in the darkness but just close enough to the pub to add a hint of risk.

'You'd better get used to the idea of bending over at a moment's notice,' says Aidan, his arm beneath my ribcage, holding me against him, his other hand tugging at my hair so that his lips can reach my ear without hindrance. 'I'm a spontaneous kind of guy when I want to be.'

Afterwards, he sits me down on the hard brick so that I feel every tiny bruise and sore patch against my spontaneously-spanked bum, and he kisses me until I think I will fall backwards on to the tarmac.

'Are you sitting comfortably?' he whispers.

'No.'

'Good. Then we'll begin.'

It's All Jenna Jameson's Fault
by Cyanne

It's all Jenna Jameson's fault.

It was her book that gave me the idea.

The new club I was working at promised a shorter drive to work, an earlier finish, and access to the city's top earners as they entertained clients and were more than ready to splash their bonuses on having me rub myself all over them.

Happily for most of the girls, but sadly for my exhibitionistic self, the club was only licensed for topless dances, even in the VIP, where I had previously been able to go all out showing off my pussy and had climaxed on a customer's lap on more than one occasion.

I've been a lap dancer since I was 19 and have enjoyed every lip-licking, arse-shaking second off it. I've made some friends for life in those chilly dressing rooms as we safety pinned each other's costumes and straightened each other's hair. Most of us – whatever reasons we cite, when pressed by the occasional journalist passing through researching the new licensing laws, or filming the 'secret' world of the strip club for some voyeuristic mock-umentary for those who daren't step through the opaque doors and see for themselves – are there at least partly because we love the attention. Of course £600 in a night helps, as does the hours you can fit around studying for your masters, looking after the kids, or writing a book. But for many of us, we just like to be looked at. Did I say we? Obviously I meant *I*.

I've had a tendency towards exhibitionism from an early age. I first noticed men looking at me in my early teens and quickly became aware of the power this gave me. As a teenager my girlfriends and I would put on strip shows for each other and talk about what our stripper names would be, and what we would wear. At university we would study in the park and my friend Leah and I would deliberately try to distract the boys playing football by sneaking our legs further and further open as we lay on the grass. We'd compete with each other, squabbling over which one of us made the bloke do a double take and completely miss the ball, until we got so brazen that one of us would have a skirt on with no knickers, while the other had hot pants so tiny that our pussy lips would be poking out of one side. We'd wear bikinis and pretend to secretly unfasten each other's tops then feign embarrassment when we stood up and they fell off, showing our tits to the whole park. We'd get so horny that we'd fuck each other in our little single dorm beds. But we were straight at heart, so I'd be finger fucking her and telling her all about what a dirty little bitch she was showing her cunt to the footballers and how they were going to come in and fuck her one by one until she could hardly walk. Of course, when I saw the advert in the back of *The Stage* magazine for table dancers, it was her who came and auditioned with me and we learnt the strip club ropes together. Our two-girl dances were popular because the chemistry between us was real, and we'd push it as far as we could, sneaking our fingers inside each other's pussies where we knew the CCTV couldn't quite pick it up; some middle-aged man sat in front of us nearly coming in his pants.

I'd spent the last year working in Velvet, a slightly sleazy fully nude club, where I'd built myself up a group of regulars who not only got off on seeing my naked pussy but also on the fact that I just loved showing it to them. Fetishes and turn-ons are subtle, and it can take a while to hit the jackpot of finding someone with the same equal and opposite reactions, and that goes for sex workers' and their customers as much as any couple.

With one guy, I would whisper in his ear as I danced, telling him how wet I was, how I loved having a bare cunt in a roomful of men, knowing they all wanted it, but none of them could have it. Every word was true.

Stag parties would get wild. Girls would be putting on lesbian shows and getting fingered in front of everyone. About half the girls were escorting which was fine, but not something I ever went into myself. Showing off was my thing and I made quite enough money at it. The official story was that the owner had been offered a price he couldn't refuse to sell the old club to make way for a new cinema, but everyone knew it was on the verge of being closed down for pretty much being a brothel full of tax evaders.

Bikini was a whole other ball game. In theory a much better run club, with female management and bouncers that didn't look like East End gangsters. It had panic buttons, and strict policies on drunkenness and touching and knickers: they had to stay on. My first few weeks went by without a hitch but I was getting bored. Without being able to show off my pussy it was starting to feel like work. Before eleven we wore dresses and to assuage my boredom I took to slipping my knickers off in the changing room and walking to the bar at the other end of the club with nothing under my dress. I'd have a drink on a high stool and chat to a couple of customers and give them sneaky little glances at my pussy, before nipping back to put on a thong before I was due onstage.

For my birthday, Leah, now a happily married mum and a senior social worker, but still a filthy tart at heart, gave me Jenna Jameson's book *How to Make Love Like a Porn Star*. I laughed my way through Jenna's days as an underage Vegas stripper, remembering my own early career. She wrote all about working in a club where thongs had to stay on, and I found my hand wandering under the duvet as I read about how she used to wear a white thong and wet it before she danced so that the fabric would go see through and her pussy lips would be visible through it. I circled my clit gently, imagining the super-hot Jenna's pussy, just veiled by a slippery scrap of white mesh, and the look on the man's face as, instead of seeing the expected censored triangle, he sees everything, and it would be easy for him to imagine it was her making it wet.

Inevitably, the devil on my left shoulder got the better of the angel on my right, and less than a day later, I was risking my job, and risking some poor guy's entertainment licence, as I stole off into the club toilets and doused my white thong in water. I'd had a total wax, so the wet fabric clung nicely to my lips. I put my short, pleated skirt over the top. As I walked into the main room of the club I could feel my lips grinding against each other; whoever bought a dance off me was in for a filthy treat.

I walked straight over to a group of guys and picked out their obvious ring leader. I'd bring him to his knees. They all started to laugh and jeer at him as I took his hand and led him straight to the private booths. I whipped my top straight off and leaned over him, just brushing his cheek with my nipple and letting him smell my skin. He closed his eyes briefly. It's strange; so many men do that, when they're paying to look. I turned my back on him, ran my hands over my waist and hips, flipping up the edges of my skirt as I lowered myself onto his lap. I pressed my back against his chest and leaned my head back over his shoulder, lifting my breasts up to meet his gaze, and ground my arse into his groin. He was strong, muscular and smelt clean and well groomed. His hands never moved to touch me but his eyes lapped up every detail, a little smile creeping in. I could feel the fabric of the wet thong clinging to my lips, which were wet at the thought of giving him something he wouldn't be expecting. I lifted myself off his knee and swayed my hips as I inched my skirt down. I bent over completely in front of him and he audibly gasped. I indulged him, and myself, and stayed in that position a little longer, inching my legs apart to give him a good look. When I arched my back up and turned to face him he didn't know where to look first – at my pussy from the front, or at my face to figure out if I knew how much he'd just seen. His eyes darted all over me, hungry and pleasured, and settled on my gaze and I smiled at him. He knew, I knew. His eyes trailed over my breasts and down my stomach and settled on the tiny white triangle barely covering my pussy. I glanced down and suppressed a giggle; it was completely see-through. I got even wetter at the thought and felt like saying fuck it and rubbing my clit until I came on his lap. I've never seen a man look more engrossed. Even though there are hundreds of fully nude bars nowadays, there's something so much sexier about being just that little bit covered, about breaking the rules, about acting like it was accident.

As the song came to an end I leaned in and asked him if he wanted another dance, and he just smiled a lazy smile and handed me the dance vouchers. I liked him; he was confident. I got in a little bit closer, straddling one leg behind him then sinking onto his lap and I could feel he was hard. I couldn't help but rub my clit over his erection and we both moaned. By the time three songs were over, and I was £60 richer, I was so close to coming.

After that I was hooked. I wet my little white thong every night and even got more daring and wore crotchless panties a couple of times. I'd always thought they were cheesy, slutty garments but I found some in Ann Summers that were really plain and cute, with black satin edging and just a discreet slit that opened up as I bent over or opened my legs. I had to be careful to change before I went on stage as one spin around the pole as a manager walked past and I'd be rumbled. But I managed to keep my secret to myself and had a lot more fun as well as raking in the money.

One night I was wearing my crotchless panties under a tight black tube dress with no stockings and plain black heels. I was at the bar and was approached by a manager to say there were a couple of guys in the VIP who wanted me to sit with them. I fluffed my hair and went over. Two older business types were already drinking champagne and poured me a glass. We chatted for a while then they asked me to dance for them. I used the sofa opposite them to put on a bit of a show, reclining full length and running my hands up my legs and toying with my dress, just flashing a hint of nipple then smoothing it back up, turning myself on as much as them. I got down to my thong but kept my legs together, getting up on all fours and arching my back, letting my breasts hang down and knowing the curve of my arse looked gorgeous from the side. At the very end of the song I sat back on the sofa and spread my legs, feeling the thong part to show my pussy for just a second before I crossed my legs.

The businessmen didn't know what to think, and were exchanging furtive glances to confirm if they had just seen what they thought they'd just seen. I sat topless for a while, sipping my drink and enjoying the power my sexuality had over these strong characters, then wriggled back into my dress, telling them I would take it off again any time they wanted me to.

After I finished my hour in the VIP I was called into the manager's office. Normally all the girls went together to pay house fees after the club closed, but I thought nothing of it. Scott was duty manager that night; a man of few words, and a former doorman who'd worked his way up. He was sitting with his back to the door when I breezed in, high on money and power.

'Lacey …' he said with a strange half smile. 'I'm sorry to have to do this but I need to have a look at your costume.'

My heart leapt into my throat. I was rumbled. On the spot I decided to try and brazen it out.

'Oh, no problem,', I said. 'Do you want to go and see what I've got in my bag?'

'Not exactly.' His eyes darted to my middle. All the male staff were very careful not to seem sleazy or flirty. 'I need to look at what you're wearing now'.

Shit. I was definitely rumbled, but whether I could talk my way out of it was another thing.

'I think you know full well the club rules on dress. Your,' he faltered a little, 'your undergarments need to be opaque and with a string of at least an inch wide, and I don't think what you've been wearing tonight fits these rules. Moreover …' he was gaining power now. I was blushing. He stood up, 'I think you're a dirty little bitch and you're enjoying all of this.'.

He had me.

'Stand up and pull your dress up to the waist. I need to see these panties that have been causing such a stir'.

I felt like that stereotypical fantasy school girl getting told off for her skirt being above the knee. Except this was the adult version.

I rolled my tube dress up slowly. Damn my bodily responses: I was getting wetter because I was in trouble, and because my trouble-making pussy knew it was going to have another man's eyes on it. I stood in the middle of the office with my dress hitched up, feeling more exposed than I had all night. He walked around me, then behind me, and locked the door. I heard him fiddling with something, while he just left me standing there.

'Bend over.'

I had nothing to lean on so I reached for my ankles, straining against my high heels, knowing the panties would be splitting before his eyes.

I heard him draw breath.

'Turn around; I've got something to show you.'

I made to stand up and his palm landed on my back.

'I don't remember telling you to stand up.'

Mortified, in the most delicious way, and still bent double with my hands on my ankles, I shuffled my exposed pussy around the room in a circle. Until I came to face him, my eyes level with his knees.

'You could have got me in a lot of trouble tonight. Look at me when I'm speaking to you.'

I uncomfortably raised my head up to where he was tapping at the CCTV computer. 'So I'm going to show you what a filthy slut you look.'

The screen crackled to life and there I was, rolling around on the sofa in the VIP. I looked good, and I remembered the delicious feeling of the leather of the sofa, the soft fabric of my clothes slipping off, the look on the businessmen's faces as I showed them my cunt. The dance came to an end, and the on-screen me leaned back, topless and wanton, and opened my legs towards the men, and towards the camera I hadn't even known was there. He hit a button and the frame froze: my eyes were closed, I was leaning back, and an unmistakable hint of glistening pink was visible between the strands of my panties.

His hand glided over my buttocks, partly clad in the black mesh of the panties. His finger slid around just where the crotch started to split, just above my asshole. 'These are sexy. If I had a pussy like that I'd want to show it off as well. Doesn't change the fact that you've deliberately broken the rules though does it?'

His hand landed smack across my buttocks, making me jump. It stung, but I was getting wetter by the second.

I could hear a gaggle of girls just outside the office; I could hear one loud voice bitching about a regular client of hers, and a few high-pitched giggles. I silently begged them not to knock on the door. They passed by down the corridor.

'Look at yourself,', Scott was saying. 'Legs wide open, just feet away from those men. I can see how wet your cunt is on that film, you filthy ...' smack,. 'filthy ...' smack,. 'whore.'.

I was starting to get giddy with the dichotomous effects of pain, shame and excitement, and flashed back through the events that had led me to this point. All those years I'd stayed out of trouble dancing in a much sleazier club, and here I was bent over the desk in a respectable upmarket chain lap dancing club, with my pussy in my boss's face, getting spanked into a frenzy. I remembered the book. It's all Jenna Jameson's fault, I decided, and if I ever met her I would make sure she knew what she'd done.

His hand landing again shocked me out of my little aside. Harder this time, as he was getting into his stroke. 'You do realise you're actually dripping onto the floor? Those sorry excuses for panties can't even keep your pussy juice under control.'

I melted in the gorgeous shame as he bent me even further forward onto the desk, pushing my face closer to the frozen image of myself in quasi-orgasmic bliss showing off my pussy and lifting my arse up higher so he could get a better look at it in real life.

'You do realise I could post that on the internet don't you? After I've got all the doormen and bar staff in here for a good look. In fact, fuck the CCTV footage, I might call them all in here for a look at it in the flesh.'

He was playing with me; he knew exactly what he was doing. 'Please ...' I began, half playing along and half pleading that it had gone far enough. His big palm landed again, and then the back of his hand on the other side, and again, and again, until I cried out.

He was slowing down now, caressing my bum gently and I was desperate for him to touch my pussy. I pushed back even further towards his hand and he pulled away.

'I'm not going to fuck you,' he said, mock harshly. 'I don't go around breaking rules'.

'Please …' I started again, not even really sure what I was asking for. I wanted him to let me go, I wanted him to hit me again, I wanted him to fuck me. I didn't even know any more.

His finger trailed lightly down the split in the panties, grazing my ass and just touching my pussy and I moaned loudly. My whole body was alive, my nipples begging to be let out of the dress and not be ignored any more, and my cunt was so wet it felt like there was a piece of silk between me and his finger.

I tried to turn around to face him, wanting to get my dress off, and start fucking, but he pushed me back and a heavy smack landed again. He started a slow arrhythmic smacking again while his other hand probed the folds of my pussy. He found my clit and rubbed in little circles with his two fingers before dipping inside me. I tried to push back onto his hand, desperate to get those fingers further inside so I could ride his hand, but he pulled away and continued the infuriatingly gentle movements interspersed with occasional smacks. I lifted my head slightly to confront the image of myself, to remind me how I got here. I came hard looking at the filthy image of myself.

I turned round, sweaty, spent and red- faced, and he was already walking away and busying himself back at his desk.

'Scott …' I started.

'That will be all.' He said. 'But if I catch you doing anything like that again I'll …'

'Don't worry, you will.' I grinned, and he grinned back, before waving me out.

And I did. And he did. Talk about having your cake and eating it.

Spend or Save
by Heidi Champa

I clicked my key in the lock, making sure that I made as little noise as possible. I hadn't expected him to be home already, and I knew, if he caught me, I would be in big trouble. Peaking around the door, I heard the familiar drone of the television from the den. Creeping along the hallway, keeping my shopping bags still, I made it to the bedroom without him seeing.

I knew it was silly; sneaking around like a teenager. But, I also knew I was under strict orders not to buy any more shoes. Three new pairs now sat in front of me, next to two belts and a scarf I had splurged on that day. My resistance to the urge had been pathetic at best. Walking into that mall was a bad idea. I had let Becca talk me into a quick trip, just to browse. Somehow, I ended up the same place I always do. The shoe department. The one place I had promised Jake I would stay out of.

Since we had agreed we wanted to move into a house, and get out of our crappy apartment, we had both decided to cut back. Jake had sacrificed his yearly trip to the lake with his buddies, along with a new MP3 player for his car. And I was to give up shopping for shoes. At first, I had done very well. I managed to go a whole month and a half without even looking at a new pair. But the draw of a sample sale pushed me over the edge. I still remember the rush of walking around the aisles, finding those sling backs in the perfect shade of blue, in the perfect size. And half price. I was in heaven. Three hours and four pairs later, I knew I had officially fallen off the wagon.

I hadn't just broken my promise to Jake, I obliterated it. Shopping online at work was too easy, and the more I bought and got away with, the more I wanted. I had never been so obsessed with shoes until I wasn't allowed to have them. Now I could barely last a week without buying a pair, even if I didn't really want them. As soon as I knew Jake wasn't looking, I was buying. And the sick part was I couldn't even wear the shoes, for fear Jake would notice the new pair.

Once or twice I had managed to convince him that the brand new beauties on my feet were an old pair he had simply forgotten about. Since I own so many shoes it worked. But the rest of my collection shoes sat idle in a hiding place in my closet, waiting for the day when we could move, and my shopping ban would be lifted.

I heard him stirring in the other room, and I quickly threw the accessories back inside the bags and hid them under the bed. The bag had just made it out of sight when the door opened.

'What are you hiding in here for? I made dinner.' His smile was so sweet, so kind. I felt my stomach turn over with the thought of lying to him once again.

'Nothing. I was just going to get changed. I'll be right there.' He walked out leaving me to endure a fresh pall of guilt. Gingerly, I pulled a bag out from under the bed and opened a box. The purple Kenneth Cole's looked up at me fetchingly. I was soothed by their beauty, their intoxicating leather smell. They would look fabulous with my new black dress. Suddenly, my guilt was gone, and replaced by the warm feeling only new shoes can provide. Placing them back in banishment, I headed to the kitchen and my sweet, sweet man.

I knew I had to stop, had to rein myself in. Sooner or later, Jake was going to find out, and I knew I was going to be sorry then. I hadn't set out to hurt him, but when he found out (if he found out) what I had done, he would be hurt. I kept telling myself he would never have to know, as long as I stopped now, thinking I could hide what I already had. But, by this time, the whole top shelf of my closet and under the bed had been taken up by my clandestine purchases. I knew I was on the edge of being discovered.

Walking to the train station after work, I strode past the row of shops I see every day. Keeping my eyes forward, I tried to not notice the entire display of boots in the front window. I tried to untie the knot in my stomach as the black leather knee high boots called out to me from behind the glass. They sat proud on a pedestal, high above the other merely average boots. These boots were special.

I was fogging up the glass of the window. The boots seemed to be specially lit, shining in all their 40 per cent off glory.

Then my hand was on the door. Then I was inside.

I promised myself these would absolutely, definitely, without a doubt, be the very last pair of shoes I would buy for a long long time. The very last thing I would have to hide. The very, very last pair of boots I would ever need.

This time, when I went home, I didn't bother trying to hide anything. I walked straight into the bedroom, fearless. Jake had called; he was working late, so I would have plenty of time to enjoy my boots before they had to go into hiding with the others. I changed my clothes and poured a glass of wine. Pulling down the boxes and bags, I started putting on the shoes, admiring them one pair at a time. I had missed them all so much.

The last thing I did was slide the beautiful boots out of the box and slip them on. But as I stood in my underwear, staring into the closet, trying to find a prefect outfit to go with the boots, I heard the doorknob turn. My heart shot into my throat.

Jake walked into the room, his eyes wide with disbelief. All around me were shoes, and belts and new outfits too, all out of hiding, all exposed. Jake looked at me, and then the shoes, and back again at me. Finally, he found his voice. 'Would you like to tell me what the hell all this is? Where did it come from, Tara?'

I felt sick. The look on his face made me forget every good feeling buying the shoes had brought. I couldn't think of a single thing to say that would make it better. He walked towards the bed, surveying the damage. With Jake in the room and with my plunder all gathered in one place, the scale of what I had done surprised even me. His hand had settled on the Kenneth Cole shoes, the perfect purple ones.

'Answer me, Tara. Now!'

I swallowed. I had no defence. Especially after all he had given up for me.

'I'm so sorry Jake. I can't explain it. It's like an addiction. I don't know why I do it. I can't stop.'

Jake came towards me, still clutching the shoe in his hand. I had never seen him look so angry. He was always so sweet, so gentle. But that Jake had been replaced by a far more serious and pissed-off Jake. He grabbed my wrist and I was overcome by another shot of adrenalin. My hands started shaking uncontrollably.

'You're sorry. That is all you have to say. We agreed no more spending. I gave up my trip for you. For us. You couldn't give up some lousy shoes. God, Tara, this is crazy. I knew you were a shop-a-holic, but this is ridiculous. You were willing to lie to me, for this.' He shook the shoe in front of my face and then threw it back on the bed. His hand was still around my wrist.

'And, what do we have here?' He gestured to the boots on my feet. I had forgotten they were still on. 'Nice boots. Just get them today?'

I nodded, not knowing what else to do. 'Jake, let me try and explain.' But, before I could say another word, he pulled me towards the bed and turned me around to look at the huge pile of extravagances I had accumulated.

'So how long have you been lying to me, Tara? How long did you wait before you started buying stuff again?' He was behind me, digging his hand into my arm, his breath hot on my neck.

'Since March.'

He seemed unsurprised by my answer. I heard him sigh, and I waited for another rant, another onslaught about how terrible I was.

'What am I going to do with you, Tara? What are we going to do about all of this?' His tone wasn't angry anymore. That didn't surprise me either. Jake always had trouble staying mad at me, even when I did something really dumb.

I was surprised, however, by his mouth on my neck, gently biting my skin. My bra was soon on the floor, and I leaned back into him and let his hands roam over my body. Just as I relaxed into him and his teasing fingers on my nipples, he stopped. Suddenly, he had my wrists together in his hand, and pulled me down towards the footboard of the bed. I tried to break free, but he was too strong. Grabbing a scarf from the pile, he quickly knotted it around my hands and then to the metal frame. I pulled on my restraint, but it was too tight.

'This isn't funny, Jake. Let me go.'

He just smiled at me. I was bent at the waist; my face close to the mattress. 'Oh, I don't think so, honey. I think you need to be punished for what you did. For lying to me, for breaking my trust. What else am I supposed to do? You won't listen, and I can only think of one suitable course of action.'

He ran a hand over my back, before smacking my ass, lightly. The jolt of contact sent me forward; another surprise from my gentle boyfriend. He slapped again, just hard enough to let me know he was serious. Any thoughts I had about him joking left the room.

'Let's have a look at some of these shoes.' Weeding through the pile, he found the purple Kenneth Cole again. Holding it by the heel, he looked it over. 'Pretty. How much did they cost?' Before I could answer, he slapped the sole against my skin. Once, twice, three times more, the shoe hit my ass. I gasped, not so much from the pain, but from the whole situation. It was making me impossibly hot, something I had not expected.

'Three hundred.' With that answer, another three hits came down on my flesh. It hurt more than I expected, but each hit turned me on more than the last. I had never considered spanking before, because I never thought Jake would agree to it. This new side of Jake was having a huge effect on me. He put down the shoe, and reached for another from the stack. It was the black Jimmy Choo I had bought months before.

'What about this one? What did this set us back?' He ran the suede gently over my ass, now hot from the spanking. 'I don't remember. Maybe four hundred.' The words were just out of my mouth when the next barrage came. I lost count of how many times he spanked the beautiful shoe against my ass. Over and over I felt the sting on my skin, the small sole radiating pain out and over my whole body. My panties were soaked through, and I felt the sweat forming on my face. Jake stopped and stood behind me, admiring his work.

'You should see how red your ass is.' I jumped when I felt the palm of his hand. The gentle rubbing felt like sand paper, his touch not doing a thing to soothe me. Soon his fingers found their way to my pussy, and he teased me through the wet fabric. 'My, my. You must be enjoying yourself. Maybe you did all this on purpose, to finally get me to spank you. You could have just asked, you know.' He shucked off my thong, pulling it down over the soft leather of my new boots.

'These really are nice boots. Especially from this view. I think they were made for this.' His hands slid up my thighs, continuing upwards until they reached to my nipples, which were hard and aching for attention. Teasing me, I felt his hard cock through his pants, rubbing my raw bottom. But he didn't let it remain there for long. The spanking continued. Chanel, Manolo Blahnik, Christian Louboutin. They all had their turn on my searing, hot flesh.

Finally, he stopped torturing me, leaving the rest of the shoes in the mess around me. My wrists ached from the scarf, and I was desperate for him to fuck me. I whimpered as he walked around me, begging him to fuck me, to release the ache he started inside me. Just when I thought he was going to leave me there, his fingers slipped into my cunt, and with such ease. He leaned down and kissed my lips. His gentle side didn't stay for long, as he put his hand in my hair, gently pulling my head back. I couldn't take much more. I whimpered again as the pain shot straight to my pussy.

'Do you think you've learned your lesson yet?'

I nodded, pushing myself back onto his waiting fingers. I think, deep down, we both knew I would never reform.

'We'll see about that, won't we?' He groaned as he finally entered me with his hard cock. He fucked me slow, bumping

100

into my tender ass with each thrust. I murmured promises of willpower, self-control and no more shoes. But as my eyes scanned the bed, I realized there was a sale at Saks the following week.

After all, he hadn't said anything about purses, had he?

Red
by Charlotte Stein

He has absolutely no idea that I'm there, so it's not really a big deal that he drops his pants. He thinks he's all alone in the office and free to change into nice, comfy, after-work sort of clothes. No one is here to see that he's not wearing any underwear.

And certainly no one is here to see the flash of red, on his smooth golden ass.

At first I look away. Like I've seen something I shouldn't and I know it, instinctively. I don't mind staring at his bare butt, so much, but sneaking a peek at something secretive and strange, that's beyond the pale.

But then I want to be sure of what I've seen. I can still see that red mark, behind my eyes. I can see it when I sit back down at my desk, behind this cubicle wall. I need to have another look, before it becomes a trick of the light or something far more boring. Or becomes just, you know, not *that*.

But it *is* that. I peer back around the wall and laser in on where he's standing: by his desk, about six cubicles down. Just out in the open enough for me to spy him. And to spy what is definitely a red handprint, peeking out from beneath the completely inadequate cover of his shirt-tails.

Someone has spanked Blake Cooper's ass. His name is *Blake* and he drives a *Porsche* and he's the biggest most arrogant douchebag to ever walk the face of the earth, and yet someone has still spanked him. The evidence is right there, that blazing red mark like a scarlet letter. A scarlet letter written to me: *I have been punished, for being an immense douche*.

Once, I saw him wave his coffee cup at our boss, Mrs Henderson. If women turn him down, they're lesbians. He spends two hundred quid on a haircut, and then tells everyone in meetings, loudly.

And all the while someone's been spanking him, the fucking faker. It's all just a show, just a front, and he proves it when he turns around too suddenly, and catches me staring. All that expensive tanning drains out of his handsome face. He tries to put his jacket on, and instead jams his arm into a hole that isn't there.

Then he dashes off before I can expose further dents, in his asshole facade. Though for the life in me I can't think why you'd want the asshole to be your storefront, while the slap-happy slut lies locked in the closet.

I bet he doesn't think I'm going to follow him about, to see what he's up to. I bet the arrogance slips right back on, when his arse isn't on show. He can shrug it off, roll with it: so what if that little peon stared at him. What does she know about anything?

I know that everything here is grey, and I want red red red. I want to measure that handprint on his ass, and match it to his dirty co-conspirator. I want to see that slick exterior crumble and dissolve, leaving behind nothing. Nothing at all. He's never done anything to me, never said a word; in meetings, he looks right through me. But that's not the point, is it?

The point is that I can't stop thinking about him bent over something. Or maybe he doesn't bend at all. Maybe his partner in crime is really petite, and when he's standing his arse is at just the right level to catch a good swing from the shoulder.

The handprint looked quite small, so it's probably a woman. Maybe Connie, the head of accounting. She's small and strict and mean-eyed. I could imagine her smacking him and smacking him until his arse-cheeks grew hot and red, and then ordering him through some urgent fucking.

Get on top. Put it in. Move in time to the tapping of my fingernails, on this counter-top. Don't grunt, it makes you sound like a beast. Stop scrunching up your face, stop breathing hard. You're going to lose it, aren't you? I can feel that you're about to spurt, you disgusting animal. Go on, then. Go on.

I have no idea why thinking of Connie from accounting ordering Cooper about is turning me on. Though I guess my current state of arousal might have something to do with the following, the sneaking around, the anticipation of catching him again.

I think he might be anticipating it too. In the meeting after lunch, he's not looking through me any more. I can feel the absence of his absence, and his furtive, sweaty agitation. Even the boss notices it; she asks him if he's feeling like himself, today.

'Long night,' he says, and does the whole nine yards: winks, nudges, *hey fellas you know what I'm talking about, right?*

And it just so happens that I *do* know what you're talking about, Cooper. You're talking about how you lay in bed last night, staring up at the ceiling, gripped by the icy cold knowledge that one of your colleagues knows that in your spare time you like to bend over and just … take it.

And then maybe afterwards, when you're crying tears of shame and delicious agony, she (because his dirty co-conspirator has definitely now solidified into a she, in my feverish brain) takes pity on you, and licks cool stripes over the hot flesh of your perfect ass. Though of course it could be that she has no mercy at all and instead leaves you tied somewhere, with your ass burning and your cock stiffer than it's ever been.

The image of him squirming like a pinned bug is so clear in my mind, that briefly *I'm* the one who's embarrassed. I've never thought of Blake Cooper in anything resembling a sexual manner before, and yet here he is, naked from the waist down, bent and spread and humiliated, thick hard cock poking up at nothing. Begging for it, probably: *please, please fuck me. Please, suck me off. Anything, I'll do anything, just …*

I don't think I've ever been as turned on as I am right now, sat in this boring grey meeting with thoughts of Cooper's

104

potential antics running through my mind. Not even Ewan McGregor, fucking away in every film he's been in has ever gotten me to this point. I think I'm light-headed. I think I might be hallucinating.

Christ, I'd kill to know who gets to tug his leash! When he almost blunders right into me as we're leaving the meeting room, I come very close to letting him. He could crash into me and then I could slam him against a wall and …

But I don't need to do anything that insane, because it seems he did mean to sort of blunder into me. He uses it to slyly take my arm, and manoeuvre me down a hallway I didn't intend to take. Of course, if Blake Cooper had done such a thing before *what happened yesterday*, I'd have jumped away from him as though struck.

But things are different now. Now I'm laughing, and he's red-faced and grim. He pushes me into Gerald Farber's empty office in a way that suggests he's going to be the one in control, he's going to show me a thing or two.

Until he shuts the door behind us, and then he's just a wheedling, bargaining, guy-who's-into-some-kinky-spanking-fun. The transformation is astonishing, marvellous. He puts his hands together, like he's praying. His eyes are wild and desperate; his voice goes up and down like a rollercoaster.

'Scarlett, I'm asking you. No, I am *begging* you. From one trusted colleague and friend to another … please don't tell anyone about anything you may or may not have seen, some time yesterday.'

I almost feel bad for him. Or I would, if the heady thrill of having power over him wasn't going to my head as quickly as it had probably gone to Connie's, or Mrs Henderson's, or whoever it is that's giving him what he's so mysteriously embarrassed about.

Or not so mysteriously, all things considered. People might not see him as a potential youngest ever CEO of the company, if they knew he liked to bury his face in some Amazon's cunt, while she barked orders at him. *Harder, you little fucker. Harder, yes, God yes.*

My brain is rambling. I think I've been keeping my slap-happy slut in the closet too. Though, I've got to say, I think mine's more of a happy to slap slut, than happy to be slapped slut.

'I have pull in this place. If you keep this to yourself – and really, what did you see anyway? – I could set things up. In a year's time, you could be my executive assistant.'

I am currently occupying the exact same position he is, and in the last year my sales exceeded his by over thirty per cent. But I guess he's getting his second wind now. You know, the one that puffs him up to three times his actual size.

'I mean, come on. You don't want to tell anyone about this, right? I'm sure you do some kinky things, with your boyfriend. Even though you don't *have* a boyfriend. And you're not dating. In fact, I don't think I've ever seen you with *anybody*.'

He points his prayer hands at me.

'But I'm getting off target. You and me, we're cool, right? You're not going to tell anybody about this, and we'll just go on with our lives, like nothing ever happened. Right? Aces.'

He claps his hands together, smiling in that smug way of his, even if said smugness doesn't quite touch his darting, furtive eyes. He thinks he's got me down cold with that smooth salesman's patter, but his eyes still speak of his intense bowel-clenching fear.

I think it's this fear that stops him dead in his tracks, when I speak just as he's going for the door.

'What was it that happened, again, Coop?'

That's what his squash pallies call him, as they slap his back and coo over his car. Coop.

'I saw your … sunburned ass, correct? I mean, that's what it was. Sunburn. Right?'

He turns, throws up one hand. Blows out one of those blustery, *but of course* breaths.

'Exactly! We're on the same page.'

He even winks, and gives me the finger guns.

'The page where it looked like someone's handprint, on your bare ass. Right?'

His face collapses into the arms of desperate, again. But this time it's brought its friends. This time it's grim, and threatening. He leans in close, just so that I get the threatening, if slightly ludicrous, picture. He's just so sweaty and agitated.

'Listen, Scarlett. I could make life very difficult for you, here. Oh yeah, I can do that. I could destroy your career.'

'Are you sure? Because I hear that guys who like being spanked almost never get executive assistants.'

Truthfully, I'm sure people would actually think better of him, if they knew. I certainly do. But, oh, it's fun to watch him fall apart. He can be *my* executive assistant, little smug punk that he is.

He tries to laugh it off, but his laugh comes out higher than Joe Pasquale on helium.

'I do *not* like to be spanked, or humiliated, or dominated in any way, by anyone.'

I think I love him a little bit, for adding all those extra bits on without me having to ask.

'I bet you don't like having hot wax dripped on you while you're tied to a bed, either.'

'No, I definitely do *not* like that.' He pauses. The expression he then gives me is as delicious as it is amusing: it's greedy curiosity, plain as day.

'Why? Do *you* do that?'

'Do you *want* me to do that?'

The swagger in my voice. It's fan-fucking-tastic.

'Hey listen. I don't want to do anything with you,' he says, as though that's just the most hilarious idea in the world.

But I think he might actually be lying.

'Who is it?' I ask, and suddenly enough to catch him off guard. Of course, he acts like he doesn't know what I'm talking about. He tries to shrug it off. But what I say next has a different effect altogether. 'Tell me who it is, and I'll let you go.'

His electric blue eyes, perhaps the only truly sexy thing about him, snap to me. I think of mean Connie's hand descending, and have to squeeze my thighs together. I have to think of England. I think of the girl in the closet, raising her fist to smash at the door.

'I … no. I can't.'

There's no shrugging it off, now.

'Sure you can. It's easy. She won't mind, I'm sure. If anything, I've got to think she's proud of all the humble pie she's making you choke down.'

'You don't know the first thing about me.'

'Yeah, but I'm betting I know her.'

I could mean several things, saying that. I know it. But he homes in on exactly the right one, immediately. Which says something about him, I feel.

'You enjoying yourself, Scarlett? Feel good to humiliate me?'

I don't answer, but I'm sure he can read my response on my face.

'Maybe you want to get a little piece of what she's been getting. Teach me a lesson, huh?'

When he lunges forward and grabs a handful of my ass, I don't stop him. I let him push me back up against the only thing in the room: a big old desk that no-one wants to move. And all the while that hand stays tense and tight on my backside. He shoves himself hard against me, his face right in mine, though he no longer looks either panicked or threatening.

He looks like he's gagging for it, and is really, really angry about that fact. A combination that somehow bursts through me, tingling and delicious. He looks like he's on fire inside, and I don't mind that at all.

'Come on then, bitch,' he says. 'Show me who's boss.'

So I grab his ass right back. Right where the red was, hard enough to make his eyes go big and his breathing come fast and rough. He makes a sound of complaint, but then the sound is suddenly in my mouth, along with his tongue.

Of course, he's a good kisser. Even in the midst of trying to eat each other's faces off, he's good. Though I think, in part, it has something to do with all the noises he's making, like a rutting animal. And they vibrate right through me too. God it's good.

I smack my hand down on his ass, just to show him how good. Just so he'll choke out more groans and pants and even better: *you're not doing it hard enough.*

That's what he says to me, as he buries his face in my throat and kisses, kisses. His hand is tangled in my hair, and he's so close to me I can feel how feverish he is, even through our clothes.

'Harder,' he says, and I do it harder. I do it so hard that I clench in sympathy, thinking of how it must sting against his already sore flesh. And then I bite down on his earlobe, just for good measure. I get a handful of his goofy over-styled blond hair, and twist.

He makes the exact sound that my body is telling me to make. I think I almost come from the feeling of his hair in my fist, his entire body shivering against mine. It's like I've been drugged.

'Do it harder, goddammit!' he says. 'Where are you balls?'

He sounds so much like his usual self, it's hilarious. Captain of Industry, Blake Cooper, using his authoritative voice to get a woman to pull on his hair.

'You like having your hair pulled, you little bitch?' I ask, and he practically hiccups with glee.

'Of course I do, of course. Fuck, use me. Use me. Mess me up.'

I think it's love. We're soulmates, I swear to God.

He doesn't even flinch, when I shove him down over the desk. I guess he got all of the flinching out of the way, when Connie or Mrs Henderson or who-the-fuck-ever spanked him till he cried.

I think I'm going to spank him until he cries. I want to see tears squeeze out of his tight-shut eyes, but then he says *make me cry* so I've no idea what I want to do. It seems I don't have an original thought in my head – he's thought of them all first, for me.

And when I crack my hand down on that firm ass of his, oh when I give him what he deserves, hard and fast, I wish he'd told me about the thoughts I've been wanting to have, much earlier.

I think about the red, now marking his other cheek – courtesy of me. Not those other women. Me. He's moaning for me to do it harder, me to do it faster, he wants me to make it sting.

I'm surprised he doesn't have an instruction manual. He certainly sounds like one.

'No,' he pants, so hoarse and lust-shot that it sounds like another word entirely. 'No, flatten your hand out. Make it straight, then down — fuck!'

I think I got him right, that time. I know I got me right, because my palm is suddenly prickling hot and said heat spreads down and through my entire body, thick and delicious. My thighs squeeze together of their own accord; I crack my hand down again just to get that sizzling sting back.

'You like it,' he says, breathless but almost smug, and I do it again just to prove him wrong.

Only it's not proving him wrong, of course. It's making him right, the little shit. So I yank him up, and bark out:

'Get your fucking pants off.'

He moves five steps back as though I shot a gun at him. I've never seen a man go for his zipper as quick as he does.

'Yes ma– sir.' He stops, glances up at me. He looks harried and wild-eyed and, well, like a maniac, frankly. 'What do you want me to call you?'

I think of the handprint on his ass, now beside the one I've made. He *has* done this before, right? He's done this before, and I'm just the doe-eyed naïf. Right?

'Stop thinking about what to call me and drop your pants, you little punk.'

He drops them.

I think he has a right to be proud of what he's got. Much like the rest of him, his cock is extremely attractive. I think I actually ache to have it in me. I know that I feel suddenly empty and squirmy and I start picturing him on top of me, pounding away like a jackhammer.

But he doesn't need to know any of those things.

'Is that all you got?'

He actually glances down. It's definitely love.

'What exactly are you going to do with that pathetic thing, Cooper? I've fucked bigger pencils.'

'You've *fucked* a *pencil*?' He swallows. 'I'm going to pay for that, aren't I?'

He's going to pay for it by marrying me, tomorrow. Also, I think he might be doing it on purpose. I think he actually wants to say words like "I'm going to pay for that, aren't I".

'Get over here, pencil dick.'

He starts towards me, but I can see we're going to have many, many tutorials and Powerpoint meetings in the near future. Just to get him up to speed.

'Uh-uh,' I tell him, and to his credit he stops dead. I sit down on the desk, casual-like. 'I didn't say *walk* over here. On your knees.'

Blake Cooper has one amazing grin. It's wolfish and as broad as anything, it consumes his face.

So it's pretty obvious when he's trying to hold it down. He's busy trying, as he gets to his hands and knees.

'Crawl,' I say, and oh God he does. I almost tell him how utterly sexy he looks, prowling towards me over the crappy office carpet. Dear Lord, he deserves it. His shoulders roll. He smacks me with that smouldering, insane stare.

And then he gets to my dangling right leg, and wraps one arm around it, and kisses just below my knee in a way that ever-so-slightly suggests *bite*. You know, teeth scraping, that grin still in his eyes. Suddenly he's sliding the flat of his tongue up my inner thigh.

I'm really, really glad I didn't wear tights today. I'm also glad that he keeps right on meeting my gaze as he licks up and down, because there's something seriously lewd about that. Like he knows that I know where he's going with this.

But he still doesn't fucking go there. He keeps right on teasing and kind of pushing my skirt up a little and then not. Spreading his hands all over me in this aggressive Blake Cooper sort of way, and yet not *really* all over me.

And then he says, in between the tongue bath: 'Make me.'

It's almost like a goddamned stage whisper. You know, like: *line*. Even worse, it makes my heart beat faster. It makes me grab a handful of his hair and yank his head back.

'Oh yeah,' he says.

'Take off my knickers,' I tell him.

His hands fumble immediately beneath my skirt. It's hard for him, because I keep him looking at me: his electric blue eyes on my dark ones. But he manages it. He even manages to stuff my underwear into his pocket, before I force his face between my legs.

He shoves my skirt right up as he goes, hands braced firm and greedy on my thighs, my hips in the slots between his thumb and forefinger. And then his mouth on me, sloppy and eager.

Somehow, I had imagined Cooper would not be a good lover. A good kisser, maybe, to reel them in. But then he'd be the kind of guy who lay back and let you wait on him. The kind of guy who doesn't moan into your pussy, when you cream for him. The kind of guy who doesn't know where your clit is, or how to lick it hard and fast just right there, because he can tell where you like it. He's listening, for that little sound you make in the back of your throat. He can feel you, rocking against him when he hits it perfectly. Yeah, he didn't seem like that kind of guy.

But I guess you have to be, when you want to go into the service industry.

He's amazing. He only breaks focus when he twists his arm around so that he can get hold of my hand, and put it back on the back of his head. And when I clench my fist and pull the hair tight, he sucks my clit into his mouth until I'm screaming.

The door isn't locked, anyone could walk in. I don't care that I'm screaming. I don't. I come so hard I think I pull some of his hairs out. I squirm and my toes curl and I say his name in a completely non-sarcastic way: *Coop*, I say. *God, baby, don't stop*.

When I finally manage to release the death grip on his hair, he sits back on his heels. Mouth glistening, face flushed, looking real pleased with himself. But it's the first time I've ever seen him look pleased with himself without the smugness. It's an honest pleasure, half-cut with a kind of ruefulness.

I start tugging my skirt down.

'Well,' I say. 'I'd better get back to work.'

He just grins that wolfish grin. Shakes his head.

'I knew you'd be a bitch. I knew it. I knew it,' he says, and then his face smoothes out suddenly. It becomes something serious and intense. 'I knew you'd be incredible.'

I think that's when I know. I mean, I could have got it before: after all, you don't change your clothes right in the middle of an office, no matter how late it is. You just don't, and especially when you've got something you don't want anyone to see.

And then there's all that baiting he did, to piss me off. And the promptings. God, he's a manipulative little bastard.

'No-one spanked your ass, did they,' I say, and he has the grace to look embarrassed.

'I did it to myself. But it looked the part, right?'

The Corporal's Punishment
by Robin Moreton

Virginia, September, 1862

'What you did today was brave but foolhardy, soldier,' General Rufus K Slocum growled from behind his trestle war-table. To one side of the lantern-lit tent hung his sword in its scabbard and a daguerreotype of President Lincoln; on the other side was the furled Union flag.

Reluctant to make eye contact, Corporal Charley Compton stood to attention at the closed entrance flap and studied the superior officer's slightly ginger sideburns, which seemed to bristle. 'Yes, sir.' Charley's eyes lowered, staring at the cane on top of the outspread map. A wicked-looking cane.

Slocum's Union jacket was unbuttoned, revealing an opened sweat-stained shirt and curling chest hair. Shadows flitted across his handsome features, the light from the lantern flickering. He was rumoured to be in his thirties, but seemed older. Running a hand through his long unruly brown hair, Slocum barked, 'Look at me when I'm speaking!'

'Yes, sir,' Charley responded tremulously and their eyes met. The general had captivating periwinkle blue eyes, which, contrary to his tone, did not appear to contain any anger.

Getting to his feet, the general wrapped both hands round the cane. 'You defied my direct order, Corporal,' he said.

Charley blinked and quailed as if the general had used the cane. 'Yes, sir. I'll accept your punishment, sir.'

'Damned right you will!'

Charley's legs trembled. 'But I had to save Jimmy, my brother.'

'Aye, and you did. I've never seen anything like it! Your intemperate action was the catalyst, Corporal. If you hadn't risked your life by rushing forward to rescue your brother, the rest wouldn't have followed. Those damnable rebels didn't expect a charge, by God, but that's what they got – thanks to you disobeying my order!'

Charley's palms felt damp, clammy. 'I'm sorry, sir – for disobeying ...'

Slocum let out a mixture of a bark and a laugh then walked round the table and stood in front of Charley, one hand slapping the cane against his boot. The general was a good ten inches taller and smelled of cigar smoke, an avuncular aroma. 'How is your brother?'

'Thank you for asking, sir,' Charley replied, surprised at the change in the general's tone. 'Surgeon says he was lucky – if it had been an inch either way, the bullet would have – er – deprived him of his manhood, sir.'

The general grimaced. 'Aye, that's what I heard. Lucky fellow – to have such a brave sister.'

'Pardon, sir?'

Slocum looked askance at Charley, fingers stroking his chin. 'I was there while the surgeon operated on your brother. He was delirious. Thanked his sister, Charlotte. That's you, isn't it?'

Charley swallowed then nodded. Her mouth was too dry to answer.

'You realise I must punish you, don't you?'

Annoyed at feeling unsoldierly with tears welling at the corners of her eyes, Charley croaked, 'Yes, sir. I deserve to be punished – for disobeying your order.'

Gripping the cane, with his hands behind his back, he walked round Charley, and murmured, 'It's quite uncanny, quite strange ...'

But Charley deemed it prudent not to enquire further. She felt the tip of the cane slide down her straight back, pressing her threadbare shirt against her perspiring shoulder-blades.

'Drop your britches, soldier,' the general ordered.

She drew in a breath. This was so humiliating! Perhaps she

115

should turn and leave. He had no right – then she remembered her promise to Ma. 'I'll stick with Jimmy,' she'd said, not appreciating the subterfuges she would have to undergo to preserve her modesty and keep her secret. She was nineteen, older than Jimmy and therefore responsible for him.

'Corporal, I don't like to be kept waiting! My orders are to be acted upon immediately!'

Feeling her stomach swirling with unaccustomed sensations, she replied, 'Yes, sir, sorry, sir, at once.' Fingers fumbling, she unbuckled her belt and unbuttoned her trousers and pushed them down to knee-height. Even though she was wearing rough and itchy long-johns, she felt naked before him. Her face reddened with shame – and something else. What was it, though? Anticipation, daring, devilment?

The tip of the cane flicked the flap at the rear of her long-johns and sent an odd spasm through her loins. 'Sir?' she whispered.

'I used to chastise my late wife, soldier.'

'Yes, sir.' On impulse, she added, 'I'm sorry for your loss, General.'

'Aye. Thank you, Corporal. You know, I used to chastise her on her *bare* ass.'

Inwardly, Charley groaned, knowing and fearing what he was going to demand next.

'Bare yours, Corporal.'

Without replying, Charley reached behind her and unbuttoned the flap at her bottom; it dropped down and she was surprised to experience a flow of pleasure as she felt a draught of air on her exposed buttocks. It didn't seem possible, but her face was hotter still at this ignominy.

'Good. Obedience is very necessary – remember that, soldier.'

'Yes, sir. I'll do anything you require, General, just please don't muster me out,' she begged. 'I promised our parents I'd look after our Jimmy.'

'We'll see,' he said, 'though I don't make promises I can't keep. Now, bend yourself across my desk. But gently does it, I don't want this week's campaign torn.'

'Sir,' she whimpered, suddenly conscious that it would not only be her naked bottom visible to her superior officer. Obediently, Charley carefully leaned over the trestle table, her chest on top of the war map, offering up her white twin globes.

'Delightful. You shall get six strikes against you, soldier. Will you accept this punishment?'

'Yes, sir,' she replied weakly and bit her lip in anticipation of the pain. It was a long time since her father had laid into her with the strap, and not on bare flesh either; usually when she'd been defending weak-willed Jimmy.

The sudden stinging across both her buttocks made her gasp; it was so unexpected in its timing and sheer refined pain. She clenched her fists and tried to study the map, but all the words were upside down. Her head swam and she felt giddy. And that was only the first of six.

'Plead for another stroke, Corporal.'

Taking it as an order, Charley gritted her teeth and said, 'Please cane me again.'

'Politely,' he remonstrated and lashed out, hitting her left globe at an angle.

She winced and felt sure she could sense the welt already rising there. Her lower lip trembled and she bit it.

'That was an extra stroke, because you didn't address me correctly.'

'Sorry, General,' she whimpered. 'Please cane me again, General. I deserve it!'

'That's more like it!'

The next stroke caught her right buttock.

'Four to go!' the general explained, his voice taking on a thick throaty tone.

Charley closed her eyes, willing those incipient tears at the corners to dry up. She noticed that there was a surprisingly warm tingling around her bottom. It wasn't the heat of pain, though – she had her memories of her father's strap to compare. This was something quite alien to her experience.

The next strike caught her unawares; lower down, where the buttocks met the tops of her legs. It should have been uncomfortably painful, yet her body responded in an unlikely

117

manner. She sensed a warm moistness between her legs. It was a familiar sensation; she'd enjoyed Josh Trent's clumsy attentions in the barn those weeks before Jimmy was called up. But why on earth should the general's cane evoke such private and, she had to admit, quite exquisite, emotions? Right now, she wanted to hide, the shame of this was too much.

'Three to go, my dear!'

She nodded, and a pervasive longing for more threshed through her body. She felt her pelvis pressed against the table and her simple awareness of her sexuality spurred her on. Boldly, she said, 'Punish me, General, I deserve it!'

'As you wish!' The cane descended again and her entire lower regions felt on fire. At no time before had she experienced such longing.

'Two more, dearest corporal!' His words seemed thick with desire.

She arched her bottom towards him, wanting – no, needing – more. 'Cane me again, General, please!' she panted, her high cheekbones warm and flushed, as were the cheeks of her bottom.

A fiery inferno almost engulfed her inner being as the cane hit crosswise over all the other welts. She hissed and felt a slight leakage of desire dribble down her inner thighs. Where only seconds before she would have been mortified at her body's brazen response, now she was revelling in it. She moaned. 'Again, General, again!'

When it came, the stroke of the cane was almost tender, virtually kissing her flesh, the tip a mere whisker away from her aroused vulva. Shamelessly, she knew her whole body was straining and trembling with need.

Charley bit her tongue, aware that she must not ask for more, no matter how she desired it. Instinctively, she knew that it was not her place to ask for anything now. She must abase herself and willingly take the punishment.

When she felt the general's large hand brush across her inflamed buttocks, she flinched slightly and almost lost control, aching for release.

His demeanour and touch seemed gentle, in stark contrast to

moments ago when he had administered the punishment.

From somewhere he produced a salve and used his finger to tenderly trace it over the weals on her bottom. 'It is an old Indian remedy, from the aloe, they say,' he explained gently. The salve cooled the cane marks yet at the same time made her entire bottom and groin tingle quite pleasurably.

'It will heal you quickly,' he said.

Her voice was strangely velvety. 'I don't think you can heal me, General.'

He chuckled faintly. 'No, I suppose not. Once you have the taste for it, you cannot deny yourself.'

'No,' she purred, as two of his fingers slid down into her thoroughly wet and oozing slit. She moaned and squirmed on the table.

'I want you, Corporal,' he whispered in her ear, 'but just say the word and we will end it. And you can leave the Army.'

'Take me, General,' she breathed.

By now, his manhood had been released and she welcomed him into her moist cleft.

His hands gently held her shoulders as they began to thrust against each other.

Despite his earlier concerns about the fragility of the war-table, it withstood their considerable passion.

Two days later, Charley was again standing to attention in General Slocum's tent. 'Corporal, I find that your Commander has put you on a charge. Is this true?'

'Yes, General,' Charley replied.

Slocum detected an amused glint in her hazel eyes. Her hair was wheat-coloured, unkempt and covering her ears. The lantern light tended to accentuate the contours of her face, notably the high cheekbones and the upturned end of her nose. Her upper lip was quite thick and he found himself wanting to kiss her. 'What was the charge?'

'I deserted my post, General, and captured two rebs who were attempting to make off with our livestock, sir.'

Slocum stood and walked round his desk, eyeing her, tapping the cane against his boot. The closer he got, the more she reminded him of his late wife, Dora, who'd been taken away with the cholera, God bless her soul. 'Deserting your post. That's a serious charge, Corporal.'

'I appreciate that, sir.' She thrust out her chest proudly. 'I'm ready for any punishment, General.'

'Very well. Drop your britches.'

He was pleased to note that this time she had already divested herself of the undergarments. Now he was faced with her pale firm buttocks, each faintly blemished from the earlier punishment. He lowered the cane and walked towards her.

'Sir?' she queried, noticing he was standing by her side.

'Bend over the table, Corporal, just like before.'

'Yes, sir.' She leaned over the map and offered up her backside.

Forcefully, he slapped a hand down hard on the right cheek and she let out a half-gasp, half-grunt. He felt the sting of her flesh on his palm and noted the red hand-impression he'd left behind. 'This is just as pleasurable, but more intimate, don't you think, Corporal?'

'Yes, sir. It surprised me, though.'

'Well, you must be more careful and not make a habit of defying the orders of your superiors.' He slapped the other cheek and he was staring down at a matching pair of flushed globes.

She hissed then said, 'It's difficult, sir.'

'So I see,' he said and smacked her again and she moaned. 'You'll warm to the sensation faster at each occasion,' he advised her.

'I will, sir?'

'Indeed you will.'

'In that case, General, I fear I might shame myself should I ever mount a horse again!'

Letting out a great guffaw, he slapped her twice in rapid succession and she let out a squeal. She not only had spirit but a sense of humour. His whole body seemed to thrum with delight at the mere touch of her flesh. His passions had lain moribund since Dora's untimely death, yet now this corporal aroused them greatly.

Afterwards, they had only just managed to adjust their

clothing when Commander Henson called from outside the tent, 'I'm back to collect Corporal Compton, sir!'

'Very well, Commander, enter!' barked the general.

Turning to Charley, Slocum said, 'I trust you behave yourself in future. Otherwise, this could become a habit!'

'I'll do my best, sir!' she replied.

'I was lenient with the youngster, Commander, considering he captured two rebels.'

Commander Henson inclined his head and glanced briefly at Charley. 'My thoughts entirely, General.'

'Well, we have a tough fight tomorrow, so you'd best leave us and get some shut-eye.'

At the end of Charley's third visit for chastisement, Slocum gave her a shot of bourbon and she let its golden liquid warm her lips, lips that so recently had pleasured this great general sitting opposite.

Slocum sipped his drink. 'Commander Henson is no fool, Charley.'

'No, sir. I imagine he suspects something.'

'True. He dropped a couple of vague hints this evening over our meal. I took his meaning, anyway.'

'My Jimmy's getting a medical discharge tomorrow,' she added sadly.

'You seem upset about it?'

'I'm pleased for him, General. But I think my duty to my brother is done, sir. Now, you'll have to expose me and give me my discharge papers.'

'Aye, I suppose so.' He pursed his lips. 'I'd dearly love to keep you here with me, perhaps as my secretary ...'

'But I'd have to maintain my disguise as a man.' Her upturned nose twitched slightly. 'I don't know if I could.'

'No, your fears are correct. There'd be more talk. The men's morale would be affected, whatever they thought.' He sighed. 'Damn this war to Hell!' he growled and crashed the glass to the floor, where it shattered.

Boston, April, 1867

The servant shrieked as the silver salver fell out of her

121

hands and the three crystal brandy goblets shattered on the wooden floorboards. 'I'm sorry, general, sir!' she said, her voice trembling, her eyes brimming with tears.

The retired general gave her a dark look. 'Clear up the mess then send in Mrs Putnam!'

'Yes, sir, at once, sir!'

He watched her kneeling on the floor, gingerly picking up the glass shards. Her name was, if he recalled correctly, Enid. She was an attractive young woman, with an enticing behind. At one time he'd have enjoyed chastising her for causing the breakages. Mrs Putnam, the housekeeper, understood only too well. She continually employed pretty serving staff and even on one occasion had the temerity to guardedly suggest, 'You can chastise any of my girls, you know, sir. At any time. For even the slightest transgression.'

She'd been with the family for many years and knew everything. That should have made him feel uncomfortable, yet oddly it was strangely reassuring. The world had turned insane as a result of the War, but at least Mrs Putnam was one of life's certainties.

'You asked to see me, sir?' said Mrs Putnam, standing ramrod straight in her long black dress. Her face was stern, her eyes deep brown and solicitous.

'Yes, I think perhaps I need to refurbish the house.' He eyed the tremulous Enid who stood to one side of Mrs Putnam. 'I think we could start on the office. Clear it out.'

'The chastising room – oh, sorry, sir – the office, of course, sir. When should I arrange for the architect to assess the work?'

'Tomorrow would be –'

'Excuse me, General, sir,' the housemaid said at the doorway.

'What is it, Mildred?' Mrs Putnam enquired frostily.

Mildred curtseyed to the general. 'There's a lady at the front door, sir. Says she's your betrothed.' She screwed up her face in consternation.

'*What?*' barked the general.

Mildred backed away.

'Betrothed?' queried Mrs Putnam in a high-pitched voice.

'Ah, Rufus Konstantin Slocum, I've found you at last!' All eyes moved to the doorway where a radiant woman now stood. She wore a deep green silk dress with frills. A matching hat slanted to one side atop wheat-coloured hair done up in an attractive chignon. Her hazel eyes flashed mischievously and her small pert upturned nose twitched once.

'Corporal?'

She smiled, lips lightly painted red. Gliding across the floor, she offered a white-gloved hand.

'Charley, how'd you –?'

'I've been looking – or rather, aching – for you for a long time, sir,' she whispered.

As he took Charley's hand, he eyed Mrs Putnam. 'Ignore my request about the – the office. I think it is about to return to its old use once more.'

Leaning over the solid mahogany desk, her dress and petticoats pulled up around her waist and her lace bloomers encircling her ankles, Charley offered her bare buttocks. 'Sorry I took so long to find you, General.'

'These years have been empty without you in my life,' he said, 'and for that I must chastise you a great deal.'

'I expect nothing less, sir.'

'Very well, then,' he said and removed the tawse from a secret drawer under the bookcase.

'Chastise me, General. Please!'

And so he did, with great pleasure.

Historical note:

At least sixteen women are known to have enlisted in the Union Army, many to accompany their husbands, brothers or lovers. Most were discovered only when wounded or killed. Eight women were known to have enlisted in the Confederate Army.

The Happiest Days
by Amelia Thornton

The final bell resounded through the hallways, and the entire class erupted into their usual roar and disordered scrambling to get out of the room as quickly as possible, almost falling over each other in their desperation. I just sighed. I had long tried to get them to stay in their seats at the end of the lesson; tried to remind them that the bell was a signal for me, not them, and that I would dismiss the class when I felt it necessary. But it had become such a chore to repeatedly drum it into them, it seemed wiser just to leave it. None of the other staff seemed to bother anyway; often letting their pupils pretty much rule the lessons in the first place. So sticking to such a minor point so resolutely seemed only to serve to make life more difficult for myself.

Not that I was a soft touch, or anything like that. Oh, no. I knew full well they all hated me, all called me a bitch, all dreaded my lessons like a hole in the head, but I didn't care. All I had wanted when I first started teaching was to actually be the one guiding these young adults into their futures, giving them not only the knowledge to pass their exams with flying colours (despite knowing that physics was quite unlikely to be anyone's favourite subject), but also the knowledge of how to face life, how to be decent citizens of this society. Which was rather a lot harder than I'd thought it would be.

I picked up the heavy pile of books to mark over the weekend, slung my handbag over my shoulder, and headed out to the car park. With a little smile to myself, I thought about what was waiting at home for me; my one treat to make me forget all my responsibilities and authority for a little while and to just be myself. By the time I turned my car into the garage and bounded up the steps to the house, I was practically walking on air, my whole body tingling with excitement. I always got like this on a Friday.

The house seemed empty, just like it always did, and I dumped the books hurriedly on the kitchen worktop before racing up to the bedroom. There had been a bit of traffic on the way back, and I knew I was probably running a bit behind schedule, but didn't concern myself with actually checking the time or anything as sensible as that. No, there were more interesting things occupying my mind.

There, lying on my bed, was my smart pleated skirt, my neatly ironed blouse, my bottle green and navy striped tie. At the foot of my bed was a pair of sensible, flat Mary Janes, a pair of white kneesocks tucked into one of them, and a battered old leather satchel. It had taken us ages to find it on Ebay, since I'd insisted on only getting a genuine one, but it had been worth it. Things were just made to last back then. Leisurely I dressed myself, savouring the feeling of crisp cotton against my skin, the coolness as I pulled my fresh white knickers tautly over the cheeks of my bottom. I loved the way the skirt felt as it brushed against my bare thighs, just that little bit scratchy and uncomfortable, but like an old friend all the same. Pulling on my navy wool blazer from the wardrobe, I picked up my satchel and headed down the hallway.

As always, I knocked firmly and loudly upon the door when I reached it, waiting for the familiar sound of his voice, but it never came. Had he heard me? Was he in there? Just as I was raising my hand to knock again, his deep voice boomed out.

'Enter.'

Whenever I heard him speak like that, it instantly took me back to being the frightened meek little schoolgirl I never got the chance to be. My breath catching in my throat, I nervously pushed open the door and stepped inside, closing it behind me with a soft *click*. He was seated at his desk; an oppressive leather-topped one we had managed to save from an antiques auction, undoubtedly destined to have somebody's laptop perched upon it if we hadn't taken it away to restore it to its rightful purposes. He was writing something, completely ignoring me.

'In the corner, girl. Hands on your head.'

My hands clammy, I gently put my satchel down on the lone pupil's desk in the middle of the room and stood myself obediently in the corner, my eyes fixed on the intricately textured maroon of the wallpaper. I thought it was just going to be for a few minutes, but he left me there for what felt like eternity. I was starting to feel my arms go numb from being raised for so long, my fingers interlocked atop my neatly combed brown hair, and was just starting to shift my weight to my other foot, just a little, when he suddenly barked at me.

'Stand still, girl! Can't you follow a simple command? Come here!'

I felt the blood rush back to my arms as I dropped them to my sides and hurried over to his desk, where he was looking up at me with an expression of firm authority.

'Did I not summon you to be in my office at 5pm sharp, Smithson?'

'Yes, sir,' I managed to stammer, frantically calculating in my mind how long the traffic could possibly have held me up for.

'Are you aware of what the time is now?'

'No, sir.'

'Why not? Did you not think to make yourself aware of the hour before you dilly-dallied on your way to my office?'

'Well, no, sir, you see it was slightly out of my control in that –'

'Quiet! I don't want excuses from you, girl. The entire reason for you even being here in the first place is the abysmal state of the lines you last wrote for me, so I don't think you should be making things any worse for yourself than they already are. Do you?'

'No, sir,' I whispered, remembering ruefully the sight of him tearing up the 500 lines I had slaved over for him on account of their "downright sloppiness". I had spent several hours this week re-doing them, and desperately hoped they would be acceptable this time.

'Bring them to me,' he ordered, watching me as I scurried back to my satchel and removed my exercise book. Dutifully I handed it over to him, biting my lip as his eyes roamed over the pages upon pages of my neat, perfectly even script. How could he possibly find anything wrong with them this time?

'Hmm. Very good, Smithson. But do you recall why these lines were set?'

'Yes, sir, for using bad language last week, sir.'

I always felt that impositions for real-life misdemeanours were so much more effective than for imaginary ones. He always told me swearing was unladylike, and not becoming of a good girl like myself, though I just couldn't help it last week, and it had just slipped out of my mouth. I had certainly not sworn since then though, and even though it was hardly a schoolgirl mistake, it was most definitely one that needed accounting for.

'That's correct. I believe you will also recall I informed you that you would be punished for that this evening, Smithson. And I warned you not to be late. And yet you were late.'

I started to get a very dull, aching nervousness building in the pit of my stomach.

'Yes, I do remember that, sir. But you see it really wasn't my fault that –'

'Silence!' he interrupted, his voice shocking me. 'If I wanted to hear your *feeble* excuses, I would ask for them. As for your punishment, I had intended for it to be six strokes of the cane. But for your insolence, you will now have a dozen.'

I knew better than to protest, but inside my whole being was screaming *a dozen*! He had doubled it. It wasn't even my fault. I'm sure he could see the look of utter, silenced outrage on my face, as he just smirked at me, smug in the knowledge of how simple it was for him to increase the punishment he would give me, just like that.

'Bend over.'

My mouth dry with nervousness, I slowly reached down until my hands were tightly gripping my ankles and felt the cotton of my panties stretched taut across my bottom cheeks

127

beneath my skirt. I winced at the thought of the harsh flexible length of cane biting into my tender flesh. It never seemed to matter, how many times I had done this – how many repetitions of the endless game of us becoming these two other people, these two people insides ourselves – it still always frightened me when I thought about what was coming.

I stood there, presented to him, impossibly uncomfortable, while I heard his chair scrape back and his footsteps echoing across the floorboards. Five steps, that was all it took. Five steps from his desk, diagonally across the room, always perfectly evenly spaced, to the cupboard where he kept his canes. He would always take out each one, run his fingers along it, enjoying the sight of my body trembling as he *swished* it through the air, listening to the satisfying sound of it, longing for the cutting *crack* as it landed on my skin. I loved the ritualistic way he would do this; the way he would take each one out, line them up flat on his desk, survey them while he decided which one was most suitable to punish me with, yet I could never see which one it was. Sometimes, if he felt particularly nasty, he would tell me, tell me it was his thickest, hardest cane about to bring out bruises on my bottom; or if it was his thinnest, most flexible one, to slash across my thighs until they were covered with crisscrossing, burning lines. But he would always line them up first.

'Count them. And thank me.'

I swallowed hard, my fingers digging into the soft white cotton of my socks, wishing he had just told me to lean over his desk, so I could have something to hold onto, to support myself. Clearly, he was in no mood to do me any favours. Delicately, he tapped the cane against the scratchy wool of my skirt, lining it up before bringing his arm back and smacking it down with a brutal force. I felt like the breath was knocked out of me, my knees buckling, all of my concentration set on not crying out. The first one is always the one that gets me.

'One. Thank you, sir.'

'You moved, Smithson. You know the rules – if you move, you must take the stroke again, and I want to see those legs perfectly straight, do you hear me?'

128

Biting my lip, I fought back any semblance of an argument.

'Yes, sir. Thank you, sir.'

He brought the cane down again, even harder it felt, and it took all of my strength of will to stay in position, but I did it.

'One. Thank you, sir,' I managed to choke out. The next two felt just as hard, the fabric of my skirt offering little protection again the bite of the wood. But what little protection it did provide, I would soon appreciate its loss. I felt his hands pulling my skirt up, and tucking it over my back, before stroking my neat white cotton panties underneath. Without any warning taps, he whipped it back down against the tender flesh between my buttocks and the tops of my thighs. Lines of fire tore across my skin. I bit down hard on my lip to stifle the cry of pain.

'F-four. Thank you, sir.'

How could it only be four, and already hurt so much? The next two he landed in harsh, perfectly symmetrical lines across my cheeks, working his way upwards from that painful spot I hated so much.

I heard the clatter of his cane as he placed it back down on his desk.

'Good girl,' he murmured, his hands cool against my hot skin, gently stroking the neat lines he had left. Hooking his thumbs into the elastic of my panties, he slowly pulled them down to my mid-thighs, his fingers straying just briefly between my legs to feel the wetness already there. I had long ago stopped worrying about why punishment excited me so much, and decided just to accept it. It was moments like this that made me so glad.

'You certainly seem to be enjoying yourself, Smithson. Perhaps you would like a few more strokes. After your next half-dozen?'

'Oh please, sir, no, I'm really not! A dozen is really quite lot for me. Please don't give me any more.'

I felt his body coming up behind me, his erection straining through his suit trousers and pressing into my sore flesh.

'Perhaps I'll just have to think of something else to do with you instead, in that case,' he said slyly, before stepping back and picking up his cane again. I felt a shiver of excitement run through me as I thought about his cock pushing into me as he slapped his strong hands against the raised red marks he had left on my bottom, the thought of the pain and pleasure together making me even wetter. It was certainly worth enduring six more strokes for.

He knew this, of course, so decided to make the final six worth counting. Besides paying particular attention to the painful crease between my thighs and buttocks, he made sure the final three landed in quick succession in exactly the same spot, one on top of the other, making my head spin with the focus of staying still, every fibre of my being concentrated on taking my punishment as obediently as possible. I could feel tears pricking at my eyelids, building in my throat, just waiting to spill out, and I wanted to release them so much.

Without any warning, he then landed the cane firmly across the middle of my thighs, right above my panties, with such force it nearly knocked me forward, taking me by such an excruciating surprise as I had already counted my final stroke.

'Thirteen. Thank you. sir,' I said, gasping and feeling the first tear escaping from my eyes to roll down my cheek. My legs now burned as much as my bottom.

'Baker's dozen,' he said, and chuckled casually by way of an explanation, before strolling back to his seat, from where he could admire his handiwork. 'Stand up, and hold your skirt up for me,' he ordered, while one of his hands gently stroked the bulge in his trousers.

I could feel his gaze on me; the knowledge of him being turned on by punishing me only made me want him more. Tears streamed down my face. Crying after punishment always made me feel so relaxed, so at peace with myself.

'What a good girl you've been for me,' he said softly. He walked across to where I stood with my hands numb from gripping my ankles so tightly, my skirt bunched up in my hand, and my reddened bottom stinging fiercely. I looked up and into his eyes, my own still filled with tears. He smiled at me. 'A very good girl,' he repeated, brushing my tears away and gently kissing my forehead. 'So why don't you bend over my desk, Smithson, and show me how good you are?'

Feeling the familiar sparks of excitement darting though me, I positioned my body over the smooth, worn leather top of his desk; my bottom enticingly pushed upwards, showing him the beautiful red lines he had created, and the slippery wetness of my opening longing for his touch.

'Please, sir,' I whispered, fidgeting slightly against his desk, and wriggling my bottom in the way I knew would tempt him. 'Please?'

I heard the soft hiss of his zip being undone, the jangle of his belt buckle, his trousers falling to the floor. I could already picture his cock, firm and hard and thick, gripped tightly in his hand as he watched his eager little schoolgirl wife pleading for him. 'I want to be good for you, sir. Please let me be good for you?'

I knew he would be smiling now; walking towards me, his cock aching to push into me. I knew how much he wanted me like this.

'You have taken your punishment very well, Smithson. I'm pleased with you. You're always a good girl for me.' And with that, he was inside me, filling me with the thickness of his cock, making me gasp with the suddenness of it, the fullness of it, making me rock back onto him to feel him deeper inside me. Firmly, repeatedly, he smacked my sore bottom harder and harder, enjoying the sight of the redness spreading further across my skin, my gasps growing ever more intense as the sensation increased. Desperately, he pulled himself out of me, twisted my body round until I was on my back, my legs spread outwards, leaning myself back on my elbows to watch him as he pushed back into me. I scrambled to undo my school blouse and reveal the rosy peaks of my nipples to him.

Steadily he thrust inside me. His thumb and forefinger pulled hard on my nipples, making me moan as he twisted and tugged on them. My own fingers reached down to my clit as the dull ache of need built inside me. Feeling myself edging nearer and nearer to my peak, I pushed my knuckles hard against my clit, and began rubbing furiously in time to his pounding. I watched him as he fucked me. He wore his tweed suit; smart yet still that little bit mismatched, like any strict headmaster worth his salt should be, and smiling down at his well-disciplined schoolgirl as she brought herself off for him.

Panting, gasping, I felt myself climbing higher and higher until finally my entire body convulsed with waves of pleasure. His cock still pounded into me, the friction driving me insane until at last he exploded too.

He collapsed on top of me, our bodies clinging together on top of his desk, satiated at last. The sting of my caning began to return as the glow of orgasm faded.

Smiling, he kissed me. And disentangled himself from my limbs. He readjusted my school tie over my open blouse, making me giggle. I watched him dress himself again, admiring his broad shoulders and strong hands as he re-buckled his belt. I rubbed the raised lines on my bottom as I tugged my panties back up and over them. I then helped him to hang the canes back up in their rightful place, rearranged the desk and packed away my exercise book. Then I stood patiently, and waited to be dismissed. He sent me away to go and mark II B's stack of homework, while he disappeared downstairs to make dinner. Whoever said schooldays were the happiest of your life certainly had the right idea.

Pat-a-Cake
by Sandrine Lopez

Pat-a-cake, pat-a-cake, baker's man ...

Other girls thought I was immature, sticking with playground hand games until well into sixth form.

Bake me a cake as fast as you can ...

The truth was I had matured far faster than any of them. They just didn't know how.

Pat it and prick it and mark it with B ...

The hands are one of the most sensitive parts of the human body, with the exception of the erogenous zones. Pre-puberty, my hands were at the top end of that scale. As a baby, then young girl, I found sucking my thumb to be a real joy. Discovered all my fingers were equally wired, as were my palms.

Put it in the oven for baby and me!

Going through adolescence, they stayed at that peak. Not even my budding nipples, or my clit, or g-spot – once I got a handle on sex education and started reading girls' magazines – could hold a candle to my fingers and palms. If I played with myself, I got more from the touching, than being touched.

Of course there were the socially embarrassing consequences. When still young, playing Cat's Cradle with Granny was an exercise in bondage before I even knew what that meant. A simple handshake, especially a strong firm one from a guy, was like having him goose me. Washing my hands with liquid soap was a slippery, sensual, erotic island all of its own. Clapping at a gig or show was akin to having a quick frig. Well okay, perhaps that last one could go either way, especially for a singer or band you really, *really* liked.

When I started kissing boys, I'd always hold at least one of their hands, gripping it tightly until it almost hurt them. They had no idea my entwined fingers and our clasped palms, were giving me far more pleasure. Until one, Scott, took me by the wrist, ran his hot tongue up my palm and slid it between my fingers: up one side, down the other, up, down, sucking on them, until I almost passed out with ecstatic bliss. It gave a whole new meaning to finger fucking.

Scott stayed my boyfriend for a lot longer than most. I'd developed a playful slap across his face when being cheeky or boyish. That *really* turned me on. He kind of liked it too but one afternoon, it went too far. Lazing in the back garden with him and Mum, my summer-heated horny arousal turned heavy-handed, literally. When he made one of his jibes, I swung out too much, too fast, and unwittingly cracked him round the jaw. To me, it was rapturous, an orgasmic collision of my palm and fingers fully on his face. But …

Mum's head jerked up from her magazine at the gunshot-like sound, and looked at the sore red print of my hand across Scott's cheek. 'That hurt, didn't it?'

Tears actually welled up in poor Scott's shocked eyes. I covered my mouth with my hand, which still smarted sublimely, and my breath under it caused even more sensual stimulation. He nodded, and it was the beginning of the end for us. Even though I apologised again and again, he suspected – quite rightly – that I got something scarily pleasurable out of it.

Then I went to college and met Dylan. By this age, none of the other girls wanted to play hand games, having graduated to 'issues' and 'causes'. None shared the exquisite pleasure that palm-on-palm slapping gave me; almost climaxing on the rapidly racing rhythm of 'Pat-A-Cake', or 'Pretty Little Dutch Girl'. *Oh, go on, just one more,* I would have pleaded to school friends, until their arms were tired, while mine buzzed and tingled deliriously as only I could know.

Dylan was a bit left-of-centre, gothish, oddball, radical. K-i-n-k-y, the other girl students would mouth, mime and point behind his back. If they knew my way of pleasure, they may have said the same about me. I wasn't sure exactly how k-i-n-k-y he was until out of the blue, possibly having been rejected by all the others, he asked me down the pub for a drink. Nothing ventured, the saying goes …

After the usual alcohol-fuelled foreplay, I found he was a reasonable kisser. But he held hands like he *meant* it, as we virtually arm-wrestled under the pub table. God, this guy was good. My wrist ached but his grip was a vice. My palm pressed like never before, my fingers felt every sensation fiercely and fully with a cap 'F'. I don't know what signals he got from that, but it wasn't long before we fell into his bed.

I wasn't a virgin, though my idea of sex was more obviously touchy-feely, foreplay and finger orientated. The best compromise so far with guys had been handjobs, because I got to feel a cock where I was most responsive; the subtle tremors and powerful judders as he came between my palms was beyond anything I'd experience if he were just plainly, *essence a la vanilla*, inside me. To hold it, grip it, jerk it off until my fingers were covered in his hot clingy cum was orgasm to me. Then I'd lick it off them, sucking and slurping round my acutely keen knuckles, sensually savouring his sticky spunk. Sometimes the guy would lick and suck it from my palms and fingers too, which multiplied my pleasures.

Dylan was as forceful with his fucking as he was with his hand-play. I would entwine my fingers with his, and let him hold me down as he pounded around inside my twat with hammerish abandon. He got the wrong idea, changing to my wrists, until I managed to wrap our hands together again. The difference between hands and wrists may not have seemed much to him, but to me it was like any other girl having her cunt or g-spot just missed, or like a guy shagging her thigh or muff instead of where it counted.

As he came, his fingers closed into mine. My fingers were almost crushed in climax, my palms pure with pleasure as my hands were pressed into the sheets. Tears streamed from my eyes as our nails dug into backs of each other's hands. Tears of pain but also of joy; the most delightful, enjoyous, hand hump ever.

'Sorry, did I hurt you?' he asked after, wiping my tears, stroking my face.

I caressed his face as well, my extremities glowing post-orgasmically, and even more delicate now and feeling the prickle of his stubble, every hair, each pore of his skin, 'No.' Meaning *yes*, but in the most wonderful way imaginable.

Dylan needed a pee, so as he scampered off naked to his loo. I lay on my front, crossed arms under rested chin, letting them smart nicely in post-fuck bliss. I must have started to doze off dreamily, relishing the impression of the strength of his own hands against mine, grappling and grinding, when he woke me with a slap across my bare bum cheek.

Ouch!

The temptation was there to start the face-slappy thing, but remembering what happened with Scott I thought better of it, for now.

'You like that?' he enquired.

Well, no actually, since he asked. But I was slightly jealous, wondering how much his hand felt doing that. I rolled on my back, pulled him onto the bed beside me, deciding a bit of give and take was needed here.

'Maybe,' I purred. I rolled him on to his front, knelt up, and spanked him hard across his firm butt. Hand to hand had this hardness, the bones underneath making things somewhat brutal. But this was unique: the solid curvy flab of his arse under my palm, and the slap shockwaving out like ripples in jelly. A bouncy waterbed which the sensitivity of my palm and fingers found astonishingly sensual. Having brought my hand sharply away, I now returned it to soothe the carpet cover of fluffy hairs. Tender under my touch. More so with the brand new, bright red mark of my hand shining on it.

'Mmm,' Dylan hummed appreciatively. He *liked* it. *Really loved it*. Perhaps this was what the girls meant by k-i-n-k-y.

Now I'm no dominatrix, and I'd hardly call Dylan submissive, but for us this slightly sado-masochistic approach could have mutual benefits. The physical side of our relationship ramped up dramatically. Naked, I sat in the small

of his bare back and started with my old 'Pat-A-Cake' game.
But it wasn't quite the same; it was way too girly for him. Then
he dug through his CDs and found one he thought might work.
And to the neo-tribal tunes of an obscure Euro grunge band he
followed, I got into the rhythm and slapped away with my head
tossing back and forth wildly, energetically spanking out their
beats on his bum like it was a pair of bongo drums.

Whacka slappa whakka spankity spank spank!

Until he got close to the edge and I jumped off, rolled him
over and wanked him until he came in my sore, sensitive hands
like a sexy soap dispenser.

Adopting our position again, I piled a dollop of cum on each
cheek and *spanked that spunk* under each palm. Well, it was
more like a *splat!* Little white globs splashed everywhere. I
massaged the rest into his fuzzy skin like balm, and squished it
through my fingers as if I was rubbing shampoo through my
hair. Then off-on with the slap beat until he came again, and
again, and my hands had their own raw orgasm. By the time
we'd finished, his arse was an abstracted criss-cross pattern of
red finger marks and purply blue bruises, highlighted with
small sparkly white pearls of semen. I'd like clothes with that
design on, and I took some digi-cam pics for a friend on the
textiles course to oblige. Spank fash', FTW.

How Dylan could still sit through classes I don't know.
Mind you, typing up my essays I was suffering quite a bit too.
If he was mincing when walking, I was doing the keyboarding
equivalent. My arms ached from all the spanking, and it
percolated through the rest of me in a giddy haze of delightful
discomfort. I wore the glazed smirk of someone high on
blissing out. My friends must have thought I was on drugs or
something, and blamed Dylan.

But masochists have their limits, even Dylan, bless his poor
bruised bum. Soon, lying on his front was all he could do in
bed; wiggling his agonised arse at me, the *tease!* I was always
tempted to let my horny hands have him, and to spank him
until he begged for mercy. But I'm not one to inflict pain by
choice, simply by need.

Arms dropping off or no, there was one evening when I was

there and needy. And Dylan could tell. Was there anywhere else he could be spanked perhaps? He lay on his side and looked at me beside him; naked, full of anticipation and expectation.

D.I.Y.?' he suggested. Frigging doesn't really do it for me, not in the sense I suspect he means.

Dylan indicated I should sit up against the pillow, heft my thighs up and pin my legs under my knees with my forearms. Then he drew the flat of his hand back and …

Thwack!

Right across my pussy, over my clit. Now that should *really* have hurt. But compared to my hands, I'm not quite as sensitive down there. There's a vague memory of seeing girls slapping their bits, probably in a porn film an ex had. It hadn't really clicked before, but it did then. Thighs spread, knees lowered, I raised my hand and watched Dylan for a reaction. He nodded, like he now understood what turned me on, and brought my own hand down hard, flat, slap, *spank*, on my exposed pussy.

That sharp contact – the spark of pangs – flatlined to an awakening throb. Up my arm, inside my gut too. I responded to myself better than him doing that.

Because it was *my* erogenous zones nerves connecting and exciting all my other senses; a domino reaction. Gentle fiddling hadn't done it until then, like that; the aftermath of all that spanking.

And so I lay there, propped up, spanking my pussy as powerfully and passionately as I could into the purest of pleasures, complementing the heavenly hurt of my exhausted hands.

But when my arms got tired, Dylan took turns – well it gave his battered bum a rest – and I found that wasn't so bad either. I could even get to like that too, and then let him fuck me the old fashioned way, later …

Smarting and aches are joy for me and you!

138

Reading Between the Lines
by Izzie French

Relieved, Sophia closed the bookshop. Her heels clicked loudly as she walked to the back of the shop, and headed upstairs. The morning had been quiet, the silence broken only once by a disorientated tourist. The Internet was knocking her trade. She needed lunch and a little light relief. Slipping the key from under the edge of the carpet, Sophia unlocked the room above the shop. The walls were lined with books of a different nature to those lining the shelves downstairs. No textbooks aimed at students from the university here. No, this room housed her late father's collection of erotica.

Sophia gulped a sandwich and reached for a book. An old favourite: *Fanny Hill*. Settling herself in the ancient leather swivel armchair, she flicked to the chapter in which Fanny and Charles fuck for the first time. That always pleased her. Wriggling, Sophia hoisted her skirt up over her hips. It was a tight fit. Nominally demure, Sophia dressed to please herself. The more discerning customer might be intrigued by the hip-skimming pencil skirt; the wide patent belt, cinched in to accentuate her waist; the white shirt, long-sleeved, crisply ironed, top three buttons open, hint of a lace bra underneath. Her hair was tied up into a slick pony tail, and she just wore a smudge of mascara and a slick of lip gloss. Superficially simple. She had created a carefully controlled image. The fully trained eye would know she wore stockings, notice that the balconette bra just skimmed her nipples, and would imagine her panties were silk. They could only begin to guess what pleased her, though. She smiled at the stupidity of those who surreptitiously watched Sophia in the fish-eyed mirror. Didn't they realise that she could see them open their flies, pull on their cocks for a couple of minutes, leaving without purchasing anything? But then it would surprise even the savvy to be told that Sophia loved being watched. And watching in return.

Sophia's chair faced the window. She kept the wooden blinds half open, the room carefully lit with table lamps. The rear of her shop faced university buildings, inhabited by at least one academic with a penchant for wanking in full view of her room.

Sophia flung her legs over either arm of the chair, expertly holding *Fanny Hill* open at the relevant spot. Her right hand rubbed over her mound; encased today in a tiny black g-string. This week she was shaven. She tucked her index finger under her g-string, running it over her smooth pussy. A tingling sensation pulsed through her. The smoothness was worth it then. No pain no gain. She kept her touch light – fingering along her lips, savouring the moistness – then parting them with expert fingers. Her clit was waiting for her touch. She shuffled her arse forward a little.

A shadow passed across the window directly opposite. He was in his room. Probably finished a tutorial in which he creamed over some pretty young undergraduate. Sophia remembered those days well. Dirty bastard. He had his back to her, but, by the speed and action of his right arm, she knew exactly what he was doing. And at that rate he would finish long before her.

She circled her clit, increasing the pressure; dropped the book to the floor, threw her head back and closed her eyes. With her left hand she began to open her cunt, the moistness easing her passage. She felt a squeeze around her fingers. A good sign she was well on her way. On days like this she wished for more hands. Her breasts were crying out for attention; her nipples erect, pushing against her bra, begging to be touched and sucked. As her orgasm threatened to overwhelm her she opened her eyes. The academic had turned to face her. She could see him clearly through the slats, and she suspected his view was clear too. She thought he'd come; he still held his cock, but his movements were slow and lazy, as though he was reluctant to get back to his routine. As she met his gaze she came. Juices flowed over her hand as her cunt tensed and relaxed, finally subsiding as she reduced the pressure and speed of her fingers on her clit, just tweaking the last few quivers of her climax from herself.

She loved this time, in this room. It was her secret pleasure. Still stroking her clit she delved into her memories, reluctant to stop altogether for now, like her anonymous academic.

One of the joys of working in a bookshop in a university town was the steady flow of pretty men. One Saturday, five or six years ago, she'd spotted a beautiful blond man browsing in the economics section. Her cunt tensed as he flicked his long hair back from his forehead. His T-shirt was tight, his jeans hung low on his waist, and he rested his hips against the shelf. Gay or straight she wondered? Not that it mattered. He was out of bounds. She didn't fuck students. Too inexperienced, despite their cockiness. Not that this promise was easy to keep. She thought he was either a mature student, or post-grad, in his mid-twenties. About her age. It was hard not to wonder what he looked like unclothed. He was slim built, and would be lithe no doubt, with little body hair. Taut buttocks, an average-sized cock, she imagined. Then, as she watched, she saw him tuck a textbook underneath his t-shirt, and head for the door.

'Hey,' she called, moving quickly. She was used to attempted theft. Making it to the door before him, she quickly turned the key, barring his way.

'You've no right to stop me leaving,' he protested, attempting to cover the book with crossed arms.

'I've every right. You've stolen from me.'

He shrugged, pulled the book from its hiding place and handed it to her, offering a glimpse of a flat stomach and dark pubic hair disappearing into his jeans.

'Join me upstairs, please.' Her polite words belied her firm tone. He hesitated, then followed her.

'You're not going to call the police, are you?'

Sophia enjoyed the sound of his pleading. She almost felt

141

sorry for him. She didn't reply. He followed her into her room. Stopping, she turned to face him.

'Theft is a serious matter.'

'I'm sorry. And you've got your book back. What more do you expect?'

Sophia knew she needed to tread carefully. He was beginning to sound belligerent. Probably needed to get back for a lecture. There was little she could do to stop him leaving. And now she had her book back it would only be her word against his.

'I expect you to accept your punishment. Like a man.'

'Of course I will. Bring it on.'

His tone had changed. He was sounding curious now. His stance had changed too. He'd drawn himself up, placed his hands on his hips, as though he was going to resist her in some way. Which she wouldn't allow. He might not come from the elite, like so many in this city, but he was certainly upper middle-class. His accent and demeanour gave him away. He had confidence, insouciance; an attitude to life that said he was in control, the world was at his feet. She was surprised at how relaxed he seemed, despite his dilemma. Usually she came up against more resistance. Sophia was beginning to have fun. She pulled up a chair, and sat down. He glanced around. There was no seat for him, and she could see he felt at a disadvantage.

'So, you understand why I need to punish you?'

He shrugged his shoulders. Not willing to divulge everything then. Sophia's stockings swished as she crossed her legs. His gaze was fixed on them. Her stockings were sheer. Silky. Of the highest quality. Though the business was beginning to show signs of trouble even then, Sophia was reluctant to cut costs on what she purported to be essentials. She guessed he was mentally undressing her. He licked his upper lip, unhooked his arms and ran his hand over the front of his jeans. She could detect a bulge.

'I can offer you a choice.' She pointed to a corner of the room. He raised his eyebrows, opening his eyes in surprise. He was shockable then. He turned back to her.

'Not much of a choice.'

'Thieves can't really be choosers.'

'I guess it'll be the crop, then.'

'Good choice.'

Sophia collected an item from a bookshelf. He watched her, still apparently unperturbed.

'Beautiful, isn't it,' she whispered, stroking the crop against the palm of her hand. He nodded. It was. Sophia had crafted it herself from leather and deep red silk velvet, carefully plaiting the two fabrics together, leaving several inches at the end loose. Some of the loose ends had tiny knots in them. The softness of the velvet complemented the harder, rougher leather, although both were of the highest quality.

'Hold out your hand.'

He obeyed her. He thinks this is it, Sophia thought. And he doesn't know whether to be relieved or disappointed. She placed the crop in his upturned hand. No doubt he was attempting to distract himself; thinking of England, maybe.

'Try it.'

He grasped the handle and stroked the velvet and leather tip across the palm of his other hand. He handled it with respect. This was going to work. Then he turned to her and touched the tip to her face. She could have relinquished power to him at that moment. Hitched up her skirt, bent over the chair and offered him her bare arse, allowing him to spank her senseless. But she managed to draw herself back, regain control. The punishment was for him. He had attempted to steal from her. She would teach him a lesson.

'Over there.'

She nodded in the direction of a ladder resting against one of the book-lined walls. She was entirely in control. She could do what she wanted with him.

He turned his back to her and made his way over to the ladder, resting against it, his hands holding on to some upper rungs. She approached him, glancing at a long bevelled mirror that leant against the wall opposite him. He would be able to see his reflection throughout his punishment, and she would be able to watch herself too.

She stood behind him, stroking the crop against the palm of

her right hand. His breathing was deep and slow. She stroked his clothed back and legs with the crop.

'Time to undress,' she whispered to him. He gave a small nod of assent. Placing the crop on the floor, she reached round, unbuckled his belt and unbuttoned his jeans. His breath was more ragged now. She dragged his jeans and boxers over his hips, pushing them to his ankles. His arse was exposed to her. It was smooth and tight. She took some deep breaths. It was important for her to stay disciplined; keep her eye on the task in hand. His thighs were firm, tanned. She wanted to run her hands over his arse, then her tongue; insinuate it between his cheeks, find his arsehole, plunge inside him. Cup his balls in her hands. Tug on his cock. But she wouldn't, not now. She had a task to carry out. Picking up the crop she ran it over his arse and down the back of his thighs. She knew exactly how this felt. What sensations it would be inducing in him. She was no stranger to the crop. He shuddered. She could see his cock was beginning to harden and rise. Time for her to begin. She stood back slightly and raised her hand, then allowed the crop to fall, softly the first time, across his arse. He remained completely still, obviously determined to show no emotion. Neither fear, nor pleasure or pain. The second blow was less soft. He braced himself slightly. She was displeased to see him glance over his shoulder and smile.

'What is it? Six of the best?'

He took his right hand away from the ladder, and placed it on his cock; beginning to wank.

'Hand away, now.' Her voice was firm. This wasn't allowed. She went over to her desk, opened a drawer and took out three pieces of black silk. Two ties and a blindfold. He shrugged as she approached. She held his arms above his head, attaching them to upper rungs of the ladder. Now he couldn't reach his cock. Then she placed the blindfold around his eyes, knotting it carefully behind his head, tugging it back slightly as she finished.

'That will teach you to play with your cock.'

'Will you play with it for me, then?'

'Silence. Otherwise you will be gagged too. And be still.'

She raised the crop and slapped him. Harder this time, imagining how his arse cheeks would throb, stinging with well-deserved pain. The tiny knots had begun to leave their mark. His skin was now covered with tiny red lines. Sophia couldn't resist dropping the crop to her side, licking her finger and tracing it along the lines. He winced. And moaned, throwing his head back, his mouth open, his tongue flicking across his cherry-red lips. She slapped him again, making new marks. She felt intensely euphoric. The power she was wielding over a beautiful man was making her cunt drip with desire. Knickerless today, her juices begin to run down her thighs. It was all she could to do prevent herself hitching her skirt and pulling the crop between her thighs, soaking up her juices, caressing her clit until she came. Quickly and hard. But then she would be powerless, no longer in charge of his destiny. And that was what she was trying to demonstrate. That she could suppress her own desires, despite extreme provocation. She stepped back, dizzy with desire.

'You still there?'

His voice was calm. He was made of strong stuff. She admired him for showing no fear. Enjoying himself, in fact. His cock was hard again. Bobbing in front of him each time she slapped him. She moved up close to him, and knelt behind him.

'So you are still there.' She was sure she could detect a smile in his voice.

'I am. You've done well.'

She reached forward and licked the stripes she'd inflicted. He sighed. His skin tasted sweet. She pushed the fingers of her left hand between his arse cheeks, accepting that he had earned the right to be pleasured. She reached for his cock with her right hand, and began to stroke him, slowly but firmly. Her index finger pushed its way into his arse. He gasped. She licked, sucked and bit his arse cheeks, adding more marks to those already there. She soon sensed his balls tensing, his orgasm close.

'Faster, please.'

Now she was willing to obey his request. She untied his

restraints, turned him round and took his cock in her mouth. Her lips caressed him, sucking and licking.

'Fuck, you're good,' he groaned. His come spurted into her mouth, and she swallowed with pleasure. Once his climax was complete she pulled his boxers and jeans up over his still firm cock.

'Go now.'

'But you haven't ...'

His voice trailed away as he watched her take the crop again. He knew what she was about to do, and he hesitated. She wasn't going to allow him to watch, or be involved. He couldn't see her release, her pleasure. That might demonstrate weakness, a lack of control. And re-living the last hour would ensure she and the crop would be able to give her the orgasm of a lifetime.

'Good to see you again.'

Sophia started as a strong male voice broke into her reverie. Re-living the memory of the beautiful blond had ensured her second climax of her lunch break. A man stood to one side of her chair, deep in the shadows. She recognized him, despite the fact six years had passed. His hair still flopped over his forehead, but he was dressed less casually this time: open-necked shirt, jacket, dark jeans. He looked every inch the businessman. Sophia still had her fingers buried in her cunt, when he walked, uninvited, into her room. Her private space. She refused to remove it just for him. She was relishing the final few spasms of her orgasm.

'What the fuck are you doing here?' At last she pulled her fingers out, and licked them.

'The front door was open. Rather lax of you. Don't worry I locked it behind me. Anyone could have come in and ransacked the place.'

'A minor slip. No more,' she replied.

She spun her chair around to face him. It was the first time he'd seen her pussy of course. Last time their intimacy had been of a different nature entirely. She wondered if he liked what he saw. Smooth, plump and moist. She could feel a familiar tingle build up again.

'I have a proposition for you.'

'Indeed?'

Sophia began to unbutton her blouse. Her breasts deserved some attention now. They'd been neglected.

'A business proposition.'

'How disappointing.'

She was encircling each nipple with her fingers, through her satin bra, rubbing the fabric against them, ensuring they were swollen and responsive.

'Stop and listen, Sophia.'

His voice was sounding irritated; but she still gave him a wry smile. His erection was impossible to hide.

'It's common knowledge you're in trouble. I want to help.'

'Are you some kind of Victorian benefactor? Helping damsels in distress?'

She failed to keep the sarcasm from her voice. There was sure to be some kind of payback required. She tugged her bra down, allowing her breasts to spill over the top. They were full, but firm. Her nipples dark and erect. She twisted them, sending shots of pain and desire through her body.

'It would be a business arrangement. There's quite a market for printed pornography, still.' He glanced around the room.

'I can understand that,' Sophia smiled. 'There's nothing I like more than hard copy porn in one hand, the other buried deep in my cunt.'

He was looking exasperated.

'Liquidize 10% of the books in this room, set up a nice little Internet site to get rid of your surplus stock downstairs, and you would be back in the black.'

'Well, sir, I'm not sure I can be bothered. I am so tempted to let the place go to rack and ruin.' Her voice was lazy, drawling. She massaged her breasts now. Pummelling them hard. Pinching her skin. She knew she would leave marks, like tiny love bites. She was flaunting them, for his benefit. She tore her blouse apart, sending tiny pearl buttons skittering across the wooden floor; then flicked her front opening bra apart. Her legs were still spread. His eyes darted between her breasts and her pussy.

'I don't even know your name.'

He stepped towards her.

'If you allow the contents of this room to remain shut up, not turn a profit for you, you are one stupid bitch. My name is Josh Walker, for the record.'

'Well, Mr Josh Walker. The twenty-first century seems to be passing me by.'

He grabbed her wrists. It was her turn to raise her eyebrows.

'How masterful.'

'Quiet.'

In a deft movement he took her by the waist and flipped her over, her legs hanging over the side of the chair, her face buried in the leather seat. She felt his hands push their way up the back of her thighs, hook into her stocking tops and tear them away. Then he dragged her skirt over her hips, ripping the zip apart as he did so. She was naked from the waist down now, but for her high-heeled pumps and her garter belt, her arse exposed to him. She estimated her cunt was just at the right height to match his cock; if that was what he intended. She hoped it was. This felt delicious. She felt completely at his mercy.

He moved across the room. She knew what he was doing. He was right behind her again in an instant; breathing fast. Angry and turned on. Just how she liked her men. She sensed the crop being raised high and hanging there, momentarily. She held her breath, her eyes tight shut in anticipation. Then she felt it *thwack* against her skin, the tiny knots she'd so carefully hand-crafted causing her to squirm with the sweetest mix of pain and pleasure she'd ever experienced. She knew this was enhanced by the hand that helped deliver the blow. She reached round to touch her arse cheeks, to intensify the sensation.

'Don't touch,' he whispered, delivering another blow just as she'd pulled her hand away. She groaned, lifted her arse higher and spread her legs. Another blow followed soon. She wanted to reach down and touch her cunt, which was aching with desire, but she knew he wouldn't allow that.

'Learning your lesson?' He raised his hand to deliver more

delicious torment, striking her again. Her buttocks were hot, burning. Her cunt was throbbing, begging for attention. She hoped he wouldn't ignore that very essence of her. She nodded. She had dreamt of this day for the last six years. Out of the corner of her eye she saw him lay the crop on the floor. She hoped it wasn't over. That he wouldn't just leave. But then she heard a tiny metallic sound. She was quite certain he was unbuckling his belt. She buried her face into the leather, smiling. Moments later she felt his hands all over her arse, slapping, pummelling the already tender flesh. She writhed against the chair, making contact with her clit. Her capacity for satisfaction was huge today. She felt him part her cheeks, his cock push at her lips, beginning to part them, then pull away slightly, teasing her. She moaned.

'Something you want, Sophia?'

She shook her head slightly; quite sure if she nodded he wouldn't give her what she knew they both wanted. Then she felt his cock, so hard and thick, push further into her this time. She felt herself spasm around him; wanting to draw him right into her, for him to impale her, fuck her completely senseless. But he moved slowly, his passage eased by her copious juices. She felt his hands on her hips as his desire began to overcome his willingness to torment her, and he began to thrust harder. She reached down and parted her lips, bringing her clit into immediate contact with the leather. She felt his right hand on her arse again, and smiled; hoping she knew what was coming next. He parted her arse cheeks, and encircled her arsehole with a finger, before insinuating his way in. She gasped with pleasure; feeling satisfyingly full, her climax building to a peak as he thudded into her cunt and arse. The lines left by the crop stung each time his body made contact; the sweetest of stings. Moments later she relinquished herself to her orgasm, tightening and squeezing round his cock, as he shot his come deep inside her. Her third orgasm of the day was by far the most intense. He soon pulled out of her, and she stood to face him.

'So, Mr Josh Walker, satisfied?'

He nodded. Sophia knew, despite his apparent mastery of

her; that she was still in complete control. That she was tormenting him; had pushed him to this. She had known from that day six years ago that he would be back. That he was promising to be her saviour came as a surprise. But Sophia would accept his offer. Although she suspected it might be like making a pact with the devil.

Spanker's Justice
by Aishling Morgan

Olivia Fielding risked a glance to one side. Five young ladies stood to attention, each in her neat khaki uniform, the peaks of their caps and the points of their polished black shoes making two straight lines towards a blank magnolia-painted wall. Slightly to one side a window opened onto the straight paths and green-painted Nissan huts of Rushmoor Camp. The sky was clear, with a light breeze making the flag flutter and sending golden brown leaves tumbling along the ground. Olivia knew what had to be done, but found herself wishing that she was outside instead of lined up with her fellow ATS educational officers.

She didn't feel like an officer, but very small and very guilty like a suspect; the others looked as if they felt the same.

Each girl, blonde or brunette, had her hair bound up into a tight bun beneath her service cap and her eyes fixed at a point in space just above the head of the single, very different woman who faced them. This was Senior Commander Buchanan, whose harsh features and elongated, bony body had earned her the nickname of "the Hatchet". The name also suited her character, and her voice, which was both hard and sharp.

'Your purpose in being here,' she was saying, 'is to make up for those regrettable shortcomings in basic education that are so common among our troops, notably those conscripted and now ready for demobilization. Reading, writing and arithmetic, Ladies, not going to the cinema, not visiting public houses and most definitely not this.'

She stopped abruptly, and as she did so she pushed at an object on her desk, not with her finger but with a pen. The object was a small, square box of thin cardboard, once red and white, now smeared with mud but not so dirty that Olivia was unable to read the legend printed in bold, flowing letters "Lucky Dips" and below that two words that explained Major Buchanan's disgust, "Prophylactic Condoms".

'American,' the Hatchet continued, as if that in itself were enough to condemn whoever had brought the packet onto the base. 'An empty packet. Originally it contained three items, which would seem to imply that one of you, or just possibly more, has ... eyes front, Subaltern Fielding!'

Olivia snapped back to full attention, the blood rushing to her face in a hot flush that spread slowly down to her chest and belly, leaving her stomach in a tight knot and her fingers trembling. There were rumours about Senior Commander Buchanan, nasty rumours. Two girls had been transferred abroad, suddenly and without explanation; both Chief Volunteers and both exceptionally pretty. Then there had been Susan Pirbright, a Volunteer from Cheltenham so shy she barely seemed able to lift her eyes from the ground, also very pretty, with exceptionally long legs and a bottom as round as a ball. Susan had been hauled up in front of the Senior Commander for no apparent reason, and she'd been very reluctant to make use of the bathhouse that evening too. But when ordered, in no uncertain terms, to get stripped off, she'd revealed rear cheeks with a distinctly pink flush. Later, Olivia had spoken to Susan.

'... gross irresponsibility from persons who should be setting an example,' the Hatchet was saying. 'Whoever is responsible will therefore step forward, this moment.'

The knot in Olivia's stomach tightened. Dizzy, her heart pounding and her cheeks burning, hardly knowing what she was doing, she took a step to the front. The girl to her left gave a faint gasp; maybe from shock but maybe from amusement. Then there was silence. Olivia stood stock still, her gaze fixed firmly to the front, but already hazy with the tears gathering in her eyes. She knew what the other girls were thinking, their disbelief compounded with disgust, but perhaps there was also a little envy and certainly a secret delight in Olivia's downfall. Not that it mattered. What mattered was the reaction of Senior Commander Buchanan, who made no effort to conceal the doubt in her voice as she went on.

'You, Subaltern Fielding?'

Olivia managed to speak. 'Yes, ma'am.'

The sound of her own voice, so weak, so pathetic, released the first of the heavy tears that had been building in the corners of her eyes. She blinked, desperate to conceal the fact that she was crying. But it did no good, merely nudging a second tear free so that two moist streaks decorated her cheeks as the sharp voice continued.

'I am astonished. Very well, the rest of you may leave.'

The other girls filed out. Olivia stood rigidly to attention, trying desperately not to snivel, but the tears now rolled freely down her cheeks. Even as the door closed behind the last of the girls, Senior Commander Buchanan began to speak once more. 'Yes, I am astonished. In fact, amazed might be the more suitable word. And yet they do say it's often the quiet ones. So, what is to be done with you?'

She stopped, her hand moving to the point of her chin as she regarded Olivia, who had given up trying not to cry. Her make-up now ran in black lines down her face, and her nose wrinkled as she struggled to avoid adding the shame of a snotty nose to her already agonised feelings. It was getting hard to breathe as well, her chest heaving and her uniform suddenly tight across her breasts, while for some hideously embarrassing reason her nipples had begun to grow stiff. The Hatchet sat back, making a steeple of her fingers as she carried on.

'A large fine? Pointless. Your dear daddy would simply pay. Demotion? Why bother, when you'll be demobbed in a few months anyway. A spell in the glasshouse? I dare say that would teach you a lesson, but still … perhaps we should just shave your head? I believe that's traditional for little sluts who can't keep their drawers up for five minutes at a time.'

The Hatchet smiled, as if she had made a joke. Olivia found her mouth twitching into a smile, a smile forced by the Senior

Commander's strength of will and her own inability to resist. Again there was a pause and Olivia found herself imagining how it would be to have her head shaved. It would be public, outdoors, with a ring of grinning squaddies and sneering girls watching her. They'd probably have a couple of beefy corporals to hold her in case she struggled. But she wouldn't. She'd sit in meek acceptance of her fate, as the barber scraped away the pretty blonde curls she'd been so proud of all her life, leaving her as bald as an egg, her disgrace on show to the world. Senior Commander Buchanan was still smiling, but her hawk face now expressed more cruelty than amusement, as if she were able to read Olivia's mind. She nodded.

'Yes. That would be suitable, but perhaps there is another way, an unofficial way. Perhaps, Subaltern Fielding ... Olivia, we should take into account the fact of your behaviour and punish you accordingly. Do you think it suitable for an officer in the Auxiliary Territorial Service to be consorting with other ranks in such a disgusting fashion?'

'No, ma'am,' Olivia managed, her voice a barely audible croak.

The Hatchet lifted her chin a trifle. 'I beg your pardon?'

'No, ma'am,' Olivia repeated as the hot tears once more began to course down her cheeks.

'No,' the Hatchet echoed. 'It is not suitable behaviour for an officer, nor for a young lady, especially a young lady of such high birth. Indeed, I believe you are, technically, Lady Olivia Fielding?'

'Yes, ma'am.'

'Yes, you are, aren't you? You are the daughter of an earl. An earl who also happens to hold a post in His Majesty's Government. And what do you think the Earl will say when he learns about your behaviour?'

Olivia had gone cold inside, and although her mouth opened, no words came out; the thought of her father being told about the incident was simply too much to bear. The Senior Commander's smirk grew broader, and crueller.

'I imagine he will be very cross indeed,' she went on, 'very, very cross. Perhaps, when you're sent home in disgrace, he'll put you across his knee and smack your naughty bottom?'

Olivia went scarlet; a blush so hot it covered not only her face but her neck and chest, making her now painfully stiff nipples prickle with sweat. The Hatchet saw and gave a brief, harsh chuckle, then continued.

'Yes, I think he might very well do that, Olivia. He might very well put you across his knee and smack your naughty bottom. Spank you, Olivia, that's what he'd do, like the little brat you are. In fact, given the way you have behaved, and that you have forfeited any right to be treated like a lady, I imagine that he might even roll up your skirt and slip before he spanked you. Maybe he'd even take down your drawers and spank your bare bottom. How would you like that, Olivia? How would you like your bare bottom spanked?'

Quite unable to speak, Olivia gave a frantic shake of her head. Every single word had been spoken slowly and with obvious relish, leaving no doubt at all of the Senior Commander's intention, and the implication of her final question. It wasn't her father's knee Olivia would be going over, and it wasn't her father who would be spanking her bare bottom. The Hatchet spoke again.

'Yes, I think we understand each other. Put the blinds down, Olivia, and lock the door.'

Olivia obeyed, mechanically doing as she was told despite her raging emotions. With the door locked she clipped the heavy blackout blinds into place, save for the last two fastenings, leaving the room full of a dim golden light. As she worked, Senior Commander Buchanan had pushed back her chair, leaving her positioned well back from the desk, with her long, bony legs making a lap. Olivia swallowed hard as she came back to attention in front of the desk. Nothing more needed to be said. She was going to be spanked, and she was going to be spanked bare bottom; just as Susan Pirbright had been spanked, in that same office, and also bare bottom.

'Very good,' the Hatchet remarked. 'What an obedient girl you are. I wonder, did your boyfriend simply tell you to pop your knickers off and spread your legs? No, at the very least he'd have had those fat titties out of your blouse. Yes, I imagine he would have done.'

Olivia gave a single, feeble nod.

'I see. And did he have you strip, or was this sordid liaison outdoors? More a case of titties out, skirt up and knickers down, I imagine? Perhaps he even had you from behind? Yes, that's it, isn't it? You pressed up against a wall, I suppose, with your bottom stuck out and his hands all over those fat titties while he had you? You're a disgrace to the uniform, Fielding. Aren't you ashamed of yourself?'

All Olivia could manage in response was yet another weak nod. It was true, her shame burning in her head for what she'd already done, but far more for what was about to happen to her. The reference to her breasts had struck home too. She had always struggled between embarrassment and pride for their size. While it was impossible not to feel secretly pleased by the envy of other girls, being so busty was extremely awkward at times; no matter how she dressed everybody's attention seemed to go straight to her chest. That included Senior Commander Buchanan, who was now admiring the twin bulges that strained out the front of Olivia's uniform jacket.

'Undo your jacket.'

It was an order. Olivia felt a fresh blush start to creep up her face, making her cheeks grow hot, and hotter still as she realised that Senior Commander wasn't going to be content with dishing out a bare bottom spanking, appalling though that was. Olivia was to be humiliated first, in ways that were quite unnecessary for her to be effectively punished.

With trembling fingers Olivia unfastened the buttons of her uniform jacket, allowing it to open across her chest. As she came back to attention the sides opened further still, just far enough to expose the twin bumps where her erect nipples pushed out the material of her blouse. Senior Commander Buchanan gave a knowing chuckle.

'Now your blouse.'

Olivia obeyed, unable to stop herself but barely able to fumble open the first and highest of her buttons. Her tie got in the way and she was forced to loosen the knot before the button would come loose. The Hatchet watched, patient, amused, her eyes flicking across Olivia's chest. Button after button popped open to reveal first smooth, pale flesh and then the cotton lace trim of Olivia's brassiere. Two more buttons and her blouse was wide open, her breasts cupped in white, feeling impossible large and prominent, each straining nipple an added embarrassment. Two more and the top of her girdle was showing, along with a slice of soft, pink tummy flesh and her belly button. For the last two she had to tug her blouse out of her skirt, leaving her feeling scruffy and intensely vulnerable. She closed her eyes, wondering if the display she was making of herself would be sufficient to satisfy Senior Commander Buchanan's cruel lust, but very sure it wouldn't. Sure enough, the next command was exactly what she'd been expecting.

'Now your brassiere.'

Olivia's hand went to the catch immediately. A moment wrestling with the taught elastic and one obstinate hook among the four and she felt the weight of her breasts loll forward in her brassiere, giving her an acute pang of shame for their size and weight. Wishing earnestly that she was even a little bit smaller, she took hold of the undersides of the cups and tugged them up, spilling out her breasts, plump and pink and bare, her nipples pointing ever so slightly skywards. She knew she made a ridiculous sight, with the two fat globes sticking out with her tie hanging down between them, all framed in dishevelled cloth, and yet she also knew that compared with what was about to happen to her the exposure of her breasts was a only a minor indignity.

She was left for a full minute, standing to attention with her naked breasts thrust out. Her eyes were fixed straight ahead, but she could clearly see the clock on the wall above the Senior Commander's desk. Each second seemed to last an eternity, with her feelings building to a peak so strong that she came to the edge of breaking before the order she expected finally came.

'That will do, I think. Now come over my knee.'

Again Olivia obeyed without hesitation, walking around the desk and draping herself into that awful stance, across another woman's lap: her hands and feet braced on the ground, head down and bottom up, spanking position. That was bad enough, but to have her breasts dangling heavy and naked under her chest added a whole new dimension to her shame. Yet a faint doubt remained in her head, that she would be spanked on the seat of her uniform skirt, at least to begin with. Senior Commander Buchan's hands went straight to the hem, tugging it up past Olivia's knees as she spoke once more.

'Let's have this up then, shall we? Lift your body.'

Olivia went up on her toes, her eyes tight shut as her skirt was hauled unceremoniously up her thighs and over her bottom. Her slip came with it, exposing the broad white seat of her knickers; big, comfortable, modest knickers that encased the whole of her bottom and sported no more than a half-inch wide trim of the same cotton lace that decorated her brassiere for vanity. The Hatchet took hold of the waistband immediately and Olivia braced herself for the final indignity of having her knickers pulled down and her bottom laid bare. Only for the motion to stop. She was held, the waistband of her knickers lifted and just a little way down, exposing the gentle V at the top of her bottom crease but no more.

'Or perhaps,' said the Senior Commander, 'Miss Olivia would like to keep her knickers up for her spanking?

There was no mistaking the taunting tone of the Hatchet's voice. Olivia made a face, reluctant to play the humiliating game because she knew full well that whatever she said her knickers would come down in the end. Not to answer would certainly mean a harder, longer spanking to punish her defiance, yet she bit her lip, determined not to speak until the harsh voice came again.

'Well, would Miss Olivia like to keep her knickers up for her spanking? Would she? Answer me!'

Olivia broke, unable to resist the tone of command in her tormentor's voice. 'Yes!'

The Hatchet seemed to be struggling not to laugh as she went on. 'Is that yes, Miss Olivia would like to keep her knickers up for her spanking because she's embarrassed to show her bare bottom? Or is that yes, Miss Olivia would like her knickers pulled down because she knows she doesn't deserve to keep them up and ought to be spanked bare bottom?'

'Knickers up, please, ma'am,' Olivia sobbed.

'I beg your pardon?'

'I … I'd like to keep my knickers up, please, ma'am!'

'I beg your pardon? Repeat what I said, Olivia, and I might just be merciful.'

'I … I mean, Miss Olivia would like to keep her knickers up, please, Ma'am!'

'I beg your pardon? Repeat what I said, Olivia.'

'Please, Ma'am!'

'Repeat what I said, Olivia.'

Olivia broke once more, the words spilling from her mouth in a torrent. 'Oh please … Miss Olivia would like to keep her knickers up for her spanking because she's embarrassed to show her bare bottom. Please don't pull my knickers down, ma'am, please … please …'

Her words gave way to a gasp as the grip on her knickers tightened, leaving her mouth agape and her eyes wide, as slowly but surely they were peeled down over her bottom. She felt every instant and every inch of her exposure, from the moment her hips and the small of her back came bare, through the unveiling of her cheeks, to the finally ghastly indignity of having her upper thighs and the pouted rear lips of her private parts put on show. Only when Olivia's bottom was fully bare did the Hatchet speak again.

'No, Olivia, that is not the right answer, as I suspect you are perfectly well aware. The right answer, and the one you should have given, is that you know naughty girls don't deserve to keep their knickers up when they're spanked. Why should you be an exception?'

Olivia didn't answer. The words had been accompanied by smacks to her now naked cheeks and the spanking had begun. It was not hard, but the simple fact of lying across the stern woman's lap and having her bare bottom spanked was enough to render her incapable of speech. She hung her head, the tears streaming down her face and splashing on the wooden floorboards beneath her, overwhelmed by her own feelings for what was happening to her.

It rapidly grew worse. After perhaps a minute of applying gentle smacks to Olivia's quivering bottom, Senior Commander Buchanan made a slight adjustment to the position of her knee. Olivia found her bottom lifted higher still, to make her cheeks part and to add the display of her anus to her woes. Worse still, as the spanking began once more, harder now, she found herself unable to prevent the little puckered hole from opening and closing to the rhythm of the smacks. It was an exhibition at once unspeakably lewd and hideously shameful, and yet there was nothing she could do either to close her cheeks or prevent the winking of her anus, or her other bodily reactions.

The smacks were getting harder, stinging her flesh to make her kick her feet and toss her head. Little cries began to escape her mouth, sobs and gasps of pain and misery, pleas for mercy and desperate, pointless apologies. She knew none of it would do any good, yet that didn't stop her, her pride quite broken as she whimpered and babbled. The spanking grew harder still, now delivered full across Olivia's cheeks to make her bottom wobble and set her breasts bouncing and jiggling beneath her chest. She'd begun to grow warm too, adding the fresh humiliation of wet privates to her suffering. The Hatchet gave a chuckle, rich with contempt and amusement, then tightened her grip around Olivia's waist.

'So it's like that, is it?' she laughed. 'You can't help yourself, can you? Even when you're having your bottom smacked you react like the dirty little tart you are! Oh I do hope you're ashamed of yourself, Miss Olivia, I really do!'

Olivia was too far gone to even attempt an answer. The spanking had now grown furiously hard, making it impossible for her to control herself at all. Her head was tossing frantically back and forth, shaking her hair and making her breasts jump and slap together. Her hips were bucking up and down to the rhythm of the smacks, making her cheeks open and close repeatedly to show off the pulsing ring of her anus and the wet smudge of her cunt. Her legs were pumping in her knickers, so hard that one shoe had flown off, nearly hitting the Hatchet, who promptly adjusted her grip.

The spanking stopped. Two quick motions and Olivia was trapped between her tormentor's knees, her bottom still the highest part of her body, her cheeks still well spread, but her legs now firmly trapped in place. Her knickers were adjusted, tugged further down to make sure she was left with absolutely no modesty whatsoever. But as she braced herself for a fresh assault on her now blazing bottom the Hatchet spoke once more. 'American nylons, I do believe. And the prophylactics were American too, weren't they? What have you been up to, Olivia?'

As she spoke she had traced a slow line up the seam of Olivia's stocking to where a low swell of flesh bulged over the top, which she began to tickle. Olivia gasped, then began to giggle, unable to stop her reaction. Her thighs began to kick again, her bottom to jiggle and spread, once more showing off her anus to her tormentor. The Hatchet chuckled, now sounding thoroughly pleased with herself as she continued her exploration of Olivia's flesh; tickling, then beginning to stroke the hot skin of the well spanked cheeks.

'What have you been up to?' she repeated. 'Trading favours with United States servicemen, I imagine? You are a dark horse, aren't you? Our own boys and the Yanks too, and all the while I thought you were such a sweet little thing. What does it cost, for a pair of nylons? Do you have to take them in your hand? Do you have to suck their cocks? Or do you have to go all the way, knickers off and legs apart to fuck like the dirty little tart you are!'

The last few words had been accompanied by hard smacks to Olivia's bottom and the spanking had begun once more. Now it was mercilessly hard, while having her legs trapped made it impossible to dispel the pain. She began to squeal and writhe in the Hatchet's grip, but that only made it worse, the smacks raining down on Olivia's dancing bottom until she felt sure she would faint, and all the while that same, harsh voice mocking her.

'How does it feel, Olivia, with a man's cock in your mouth while you suck it for a pair of nylons? How does it feel to be a whore, Olivia, because that's what you are.'

Olivia broke completely. 'No! I didn't! I'm not a whore, I'm not! I bought them, that's all! I … I'm not a whore!'

Again the spanking stopped.

'Hush,' Senior Commander Buchanan said, her voice suddenly soft, and as she went on she had moved her hand from Olivia's bottom and began to stroke her hair. 'I know you're not a whore, darling, and I know you never did any of those beastly things. You wouldn't do that, would you? Oh no, not an invert like you. You just wanted your little bottom smacked, didn't you?'

Olivia didn't answer immediately, but allowed herself to be eased gently to her knees. Kneeling to the woman who was now tugging up her own skirt, Olivia stuck out her hot bottom, let her hand slip between her legs, licked her lips in happy anticipation for what she was about to be made to do, and then nodded. Senior Commander Buchanan lifted herself in her chair, slipped her drawers down and off, then made herself comfortable once more, now with her naked sex on offer to Olivia's tongue. She spoke again. 'Before you get to work, darling. You do know how that packet came to be in the ATS officers quarters, don't you?'

'No.'

'I put it there.'

From Wanting to Wanton
by Laurel Aspen

Luke looking up at the modest brass nameplate: The Worth Collection of English Literature. This Victorian temple to learning and enlightenment would have stood out in any small provincial town. Here, in a side street in the heart of the City of London, dominated by even grander institutions, it became architecturally anonymous.

Pushing open the heavy oak doors Luke stepped into a surprisingly light atrium where a slender woman stood behind a polished wooden counter. Her dowdy dress sense belied her years; early 20s, he guessed. And probably a very pretty girl if she gave herself half a chance, but not so eye-catching without make-up, or jewellery or a discernible sense of style to provide a hint of the personality within.

He introduced himself. 'I'm researching some material for a book, I've got a letter here permitting me access to the library for six months to –'

'You're Mr Forbes. Luke Forbes?'

'Yes that's right.' Luke gave his most winning smile. Establishing a rapport with librarians was vital in his experience; getting them on-side could save hours of tedious research.

'The trustees told me you were coming. I'm Rose Hall, the senior librarian.'

Luke looked around the lofty reading room where rays of weak wintry sunshine illuminated the lofty bookcases. 'I can imagine it's often pretty quiet in here.'

Rose frowned. 'Not many people know of the Worth

Collection, even though we're almost as old as the British Library. So many investigations are done on the Internet these days. Recycling others' opinions and not bothering to go to the original sources. In my opinion.'

'You're quite right. I'm here to do some proper delving, though, so I'll be grateful for your expertise. Do you work here full-time?'

'Not enough visitors. Just Monday to Thursday mornings. The rest of the time I'm finishing a PHD thesis on late twentieth-century female fiction. What are you researching?'

'Erotic writing. Especially that written by and for women. It's become quite fashionable in the last couple of decades.'

Rose blushed. 'Not really an area I've paid much attention to. Are you writing a book?'

'Yes. On how erotica reflects, or even affects, modern sexuality. It started out as a newspaper article for one of the Sunday lifestyle sections, but was so well received a publisher commissioned it. Has to be finished quickly though before people's attention moves on.'

'Oh so it's not academic work?'

'Does something have to be academic to be of worth?' There was an edge to his tone.

'No of course not.' To cover her embarrassment, Rose turned around and led Luke towards the books.

Nice chassis, trim little figure, probably shapely legs under those thick tights; it occurred to him that young Ms Rose might present a pleasant challenge. Not quite Professor Higgins and Eliza Dolittle, but if he could just draw her out a little the results might prove rewarding.

Perhaps, Rose tried to convince herself later that day, sampling contemporary women's erotica might help restart her stalled thesis. Albeit embarrassed, she made the appropriate purchases.

A few erotic short collections later, it had become clear to Rose that these titillating tales were underpinned by certain prominent and reoccurring themes. Dominant men and submissive women for example; and such stories often involved an element of dressing up. Despite Rose's lack of dress sense, the idea of exchanging her serviceable white, with a tint of grey, M&S undies for some racier lingerie slowly took root. She wondered, having never ever tried, what it might be like to wear stockings; certainly if these stories were accurate, they invariably seemed to push all the requisite male buttons. Increasingly enthralled by this strange new world of sartorial and sexual possibility, Rose read on voraciously. Stories about spanking were guaranteed to hit the spot, dampening her knickers and sending her fingers surreptitiously down between her thighs to bring urgently required relief. Far from being epistles of brute sadism, as she'd previously believed, CP fiction, as she now understood it to be called, was a far subtler *mélange* of literary arousal.

Unbeknown to her, though Luke also enjoyed the genre, he'd been fortunate enough to have already enjoyed a couple of long-term CP relationships.

'Fancy a coffee?' Rose asked him midway through the third week of his attendance. It'd taken her that long to pluck up the courage to attempt anything more than professional or a merely mundane interaction.

'Sure,' answered Luke readily, and over cups of cappuccino it became clear Rose was more than just curious about him.

'How's the research going?' She asked, nervous.

'Good. Quicker than I expected.'

'Oh.' Rose couldn't keep the tone of disappointment from her voice. The faster he worked the quicker Luke would be gone. There was obviously no time to lose. 'I've been looking at some of the books you've finished with. Thought they might be useful for my own studies. But tell me, do you find them arousing?' Rose flushed at her own boldness.

'Sometimes.' Luke was disarmingly frank. 'I'm only human, how about you?'

Involuntarily Rose reddened. 'Certain themes seem to be ubiquitous,' she said, evasively.

'Such as?'

'Well.' Rose had entered uncharted territory. 'It's interesting how clothes are always used to accentuate a female character's sexuality. To proffer her body as an offering.

Stockings and high heels for example.'

'Many women wear them as a matter of routine. Look at the average City office.'

'You know, I've never worn them. In academia women have made a virtue out of dressing down. But I can see it might be fun to dress up. Perhaps erotic clothes could enable less brave souls to feel uninhibited. And in the spanking stories there's always an element of sexual coercion: he is completely in charge, she is forced to submit and so is absolved of guilt and responsibility, as a result, for what follows.' Aware she had now given voice to feelings she'd not really thought through enough, and in a somewhat awkward academic fashion, her discourse promptly stalled. They hadn't, she was suddenly acutely aware, even been discussing spanking. It had just crept in.

'Why not test the idea,' suggested Luke. 'Isn't that how you scholarly types are meant to proceed?'

'What me?' Rose laughed. 'You're not serious.'

But on the walk back to the library Rose glowed with pleasure.

Walking alongside her in companionable silence Luke's own thoughts were definitely not innocent. With a little more effort, and a little less Oxfam she could make something of herself. *But don't get rid of the glasses because actually they're very sexy.*

Two days later Rose spent her lunch hour browsing shoe shops, and eventually emerged with a pair of sleek black court shoes with high heels.

Walking in them was tricky, so she practised assiduously, enjoying the way they thrust her shoulders back and made the most of a not very big bosom, and tensed her calves, and pushed her small, firm buttocks into a whole new prominence. In fact, Rose began a plan to startle Luke with a new and sophisticated image. She'd wear the shoes with a knee-length black skirt, sheer pale tights and a crisp white blouse. Let her hair down too and put some lipstick on. She was determined to be the equal of any modern girl.

166

But to her chagrin Luke didn't appear to notice her new attire. They exchanged the standard pleasantries and he got down to work.

Rose was furious and out the corner of his eye Luke watched her angrily pacing up and down, her heels clicking out an angry percussive accompaniment to her mood. Of course he'd clocked the transformation, but saw no need to let Rose know. Not yet anyway.

Damn him. He will notice me.

Grabbing a couple of seldom requested volumes, she pushed a stepladder into position, immediately adjacent to Luke. As if the tomes need returning on the uppermost shelf, she climbed high, and the tapered toes of Rose's new fuck-me footwear searched for grip on the worn wooden steps. Not completely unknown to her, each time she raised a knee, her skirt exposed a sinuous nylon-covered thigh and one of her delectably taut buttocks.

'Very nice,' observed Luke, laconically. 'Is this a new you?'

'Possibly.'

'So you're emulating a femme fatale? And trying to distract me from my labours, for which sin I shall have to take you to task.'

A thrill, part fear, part excitement, surged through her. 'How so?' Her voice was small, almost a croak.

'By spanking the bottom you've so obligingly revealed'.

'And if I refuse.'

'You won't, because it was you who bought the subject up. And you were right in your textual analysis of CP literature. The essential element is coercion, so whatever happens next, you're not to blame. Now, come here.'

Rose descended, unable to take her eyes from his face. She teetered towards him. And soon found herself face-down, over his knees, with her fingers and toes touching the worn wooden boards, and her bottom raised enticingly. Tingling with anticipation, every muscle in her body tense, she gritted her teeth, held her breath and waited.

And waited.

Not until she relaxed did his palm descend, and as each slap came into contact with Rose's tightly skirted rear, a satisfying crack echoed around the hallowed walls. After an initial volley Luke paused. Rose had no words to describe the rush of unfamiliar emotions coursing through her and stayed silent. But not for long. Feeling his hand grasp the hem of her skirt she anticipated Luke's intention and immediately protested. But then regretted her outburst, as an admonitory slap to the back of each of her thighs stung like fury.

Luke expertly pulled the skirt to her waist, exposing a most beautiful bottom, barely covered by skimpy white briefs and every spanker's sworn enemy, tights. He spanked harder and her alluringly firm cheeks juddered most pleasingly. Rose was breathing heavily, squirming her hips on his lap in response to what he knew were contradictory feelings of pain and arousal.

He stopped a second time, and adroitly tugged her knickers and tights down and around her knees. Resting his hand on Rose's lightly toasted rear, he felt the silky skin glowing hot beneath his tender touch.

Rose mewed and sighed as his fingers caressed her, teasing and squeezing her labia. She squirmed and she squealed with delight at the delicious torment. One finger, two fingers, slid effortlessly into her honeyed vagina and pistoned insistently, in and out, while his other hand returned to chastising her rear end. The combination of the two sensations was irresistible. Rose could not help herself. She came hard.

Dazed and smiling, endorphin-stoned, her gaze unfocused, it took five hazy minutes before she'd recovered enough to stand upright.

Luke murmured something to her: 'Prior appointment. Must go.' Rose doesn't take in most of what he says. But he smiles at her and promises to return the following day.

Rose spent a restless night; appalled by her wanton reaction to Luke's spanking, yet thrilled by her belated discovery of hitherto unimagined sexual pleasures. Elated and emboldened she decided to again push the boundaries of her new relationship.

As promised, Luke returned to the library the following day, but acted as if nothing had ever happened between them, and promptly got down to work.

Undeterred, with her own research to pursue, she cornered him, pressed her hot little body against him. Luke felt her braless nipples harden through her thin T-shirt; could feel her firm stomach, naked under the crop top. Ducking down, Rose freed his half erect penis and took it into her mouth.

She'd never attempted a BJ before, but she had always been a good student and had read enough about oral sex since meeting Luke, her enthusiasm quickly took him to the brink. 'Rose, I'm …' he gasped in warning.

It was, she reckoned, less messy to simply suck and swallow. And besides, what better right of passage to becoming a new woman?

She looked up at him, smiling in triumph, as a thin trickle of come ran down her chin.

'This is for distracting me,' Luke said through gritted teeth.

And Rose was thrust face-down over the counter. Feet barely touching the floor, her baggy combat trousers were tugged down to her ankles. Hands pinned into the small of her back, she was held helpless, as Luke doubled the worn leather of his belt, then raised his hand high.

A flash of pain seared her naked rump; a sensation far removed from the previous day's more sensual spanking. This was punishment pure and simple, yet for Rose its erotic effect was every bit as potent as the day before.

Six livid wheals decorated her jiggling bottom before Luke tossed the belt to one side. Tears filled her eyes. And when he pulled her tiny thong to one side, her sex was every bit as wet as her teary face. As he grasped her hips, Rose pushed herself up and back on to her toes, expectant, eager for more. Until a knock at the door broke them apart.

Luke didn't visit the library the following day but sent an email. He would be in on Monday, he informed her; the day when his work at the Worth would be complete. 'But there was,' he wrote, 'unfinished business between them which he intended to resolve.' And Rose should therefore 'dress accordingly and be in a suitable frame of mind.'

That weekend Rose took another shopping trip on which she purchased a dress in a 50s style, high-heeled sandals, and finally, with an insouciance she couldn't have imagined a couple of months previously, a pair of sheer black stockings and a matching suspender belt.

Back at her flat she could scarcely believe her own transformation; from drab librarian to chic attractive femme; and from wanting to wanton.

'You like?' enquired Rose mischievously, when Luke arrived at the library. She's never held this much sway over a man before, let alone had the self-assurance to use it.

'Yes, very much,' Luke said. He carried a long canvas bag under one arm.

'Then let's lock the front door and adjourn to my office,' said the newly confident Rose.

'Now,' she enquired, once they were ensconced inside. 'About this unfinished business?' Her glasses slipped down her nose and she peered over the top.

Without taking his eyes from her, he reached out and gently grasped one of her breasts. Squeezed the firm flesh and felt her nipples stiffen in response. Slowly, he raised the hem of her dress; over nylon-clad knees, up shapely thighs, and onward, past the dark welt of her stocking top to the enticing nexus where her legs and torso met. 'You appear to have forgotten your knickers,' he said.

'I didn't forget anything.'

'Aren't you taking a risk?'

'I hope so.'

The CLOSED sign went up. Heavy doors were firmly locked against the world. The answer-phone was switched on. High windows and thick walls would ensure they were neither seen nor heard.

'I think you know what the resolution of our unfinished

170

business will involve,' said Luke. From his bag, he produced a cane and theatrically swished it though the air.

Rose nodded a mute assent.

'There's no need for preliminaries.' Luke's strong hands clasped her shoulders and guided Rose carefully, but insistently, to her desk. She allowed him to position her; upper body bent forward until she lay prone along the smoothly polished wooden surface. She reached out and grasped the sides.

Luke's hands grasped each of her slender ankles, tugged her feet wide apart, then lifted her dress to her waist.

She tensed her calves, pushed herself up slightly on to her toes and locked her knees. The stance pushed her buttocks out and upward in silent invitation. Luke tapped the tip of the cane lightly against her two perfectly proffered cheeks. Rose screwed her eyes shut. And the first stroke of cane fell to become a thin line of fire across the crest of both buttocks. She gasped. A second stroke followed. Then a third. Rose wriggled on the tabletop, struggling to endure the increasing smart.

But the area of tenderness only increased as three more strokes followed; each applied with precision, none overlapping. She'd taken the *sixer* well, she knew; no hollering, no tears. Instead, she'd somehow channelled the tremendous discomfort inwards. And it was as if the heat from her buttocks had suffused to her sex, which had flooded.

'There'll be a further six,' announced Luke.

Rose haughtily tossed her head. 'I can take it.'

'Can you indeed.'

He employed a wrist-driven action, making full use of the rod's pliable qualities to whip the perfectly curved outline of Rose's posterior.

Her jaw set in determination, Rose gritted her teeth, determined not to cry out. The cane cuts were even harder this time and fell lower, slicing cruelly across the tender junction where her thighs and buttocks merged. Rose's feet kicked out in involuntary response, as the pain rapidly accumulated into a persistent, throbbing smart.

Eventually Luke stopped.

'You really laid those on hard.' Rose struggled to maintain her self-control. 'My arse feels as if it's on fire.'

'Don't pretend you didn't deserve it, or crave it. But you may stand up now.'

'No.'

'What do you mean, no?'

'You may be ready to stop, but I'm not.'

'Rose. Look over your shoulder at the indisputable evidence of a soundly caned rear end.'

Rose obliged, craning back to peer at her pertly presented posterior. 'You're right. It's deeply marked. And it hurts like hell, but I need more.'

'Well, you asked for it.' Inevitably this time the strokes started to intersect, causing Rose intense suffering. And when Luke halted for the third time, 18 strokes had been delivered cold

But Rose has yet to shed a tear. True, her eyes were wet, her face creased with the effort of enduring the intense discomfort of a thoroughly beaten bottom. But Rose steadfastly retained her punishment position. Luke rested the rattan's tip at the apex of her thighs, observing tangible evidence of arousal to which she gave a low moan of pleasure.

'One for every year of my life, please,' she declared resolutely.

Rose was 24; another six strokes to go. 'Very well, it's your choice.' Luke raised the rod and Rose thrusts out her red-striped rear.

At the finish, every inch of Rose's perfect bottom had been thrashed scarlet, and she was finally reduced to tears: 'I think I deserve my reward now,' she whimpered, smiling through her tears.

'Ever been taken from behind before?' Luke asked, scarcely able to comprehend such a feat of endurance, and such an appetite for depravity in one so young and inexperienced.

'In my bum? Will it hurt?' Rose is wary but doesn't demure, a fact Luke gratefully files away for future experimentation.

'From, not *in*, silly,' Luke reassured her.

172

'In that case no, but I'm about to be aren't I?' Rose's tone was unashamedly lascivious.

Luke guided the tip of his cock into her wet sex. Her bottom cheeks glowed hot and her stockings rubbed against his thighs. Clasping her small tits, Luke slid right into her depths.

She wanted the moment to last for ever and pondered how to prolong the bliss. 'Turn me around.'

'What? Your sore bum on that hard desk. It'll hurt,' he warned.

'I'm too turned on to care. Besides I think it'll add to the sensation.'

So Luke did and they were both proven right. Her cheeks smarted, but the pain simply spurred Rose on.

'Do it!' she cried out, losing herself, taking her pleasure roughly and joyously. And as she came so hard, Rose had few doubts that she could keep Luke and be exactly what she wanted, simply by choosing to submit.

Butt in a Sling
by Landon Dixon

'You get me those LCVP's pronto, Sergeant! Or, by God, I'll have your butt in a sling!'

'Trouble, General Williams?' Imee Aquino politely asked, strolling into the map- and memorabilia-cluttered office just as red-faced Warren Williams was in the process of slamming down the phone.

'Damn NCO's couldn't run a rotary club back home, let alone a goddamn pacific war!' His bony face softened, as he watched Imee strut across the office and, drop a teletype message into the basket on the desk.

The twenty-year-old Filipina was tiny and her taut, tawny-skinned body topped by cupcake breasts jiggled deliciously when she walked. Her face was an almond-coloured oval, lusciously punctuated by plush, red-lipsticked lips and huge, brown, liquid eyes. Her jet-black tresses were pulled back from her pretty face and secured by a red, white, and blue ribbon, and her hair shone under the bright lights, like the velvety skin of her slender legs and arms on display in a short-skirted, dark-blue polka dot dress.

The girl had taken to all things American, but especially the silver screen, and today was her Joan Crawford in 'Hollywood Canteen' look.

'Get me the Tarawa invasion plans!' Warren barked. He leaned back in the bamboo rocking chair that had somehow survived the hasty and perilous evacuation from Corregidor to Australia, and hooked one tan khaki leg over the other, admiring the view of the Islands.

She batted her long black lashes and rolled her eyes, said, 'But, General, the Tarawa invasion was a year ago – don't you remember?'

'Damn it all, girl, do as I say!'

Imee shrugged and turned and walked away from the desk in her polished black heels.

And Warren just about had a conniption. Because the skirt of the girl's dress was pinned up at the back, exposing her bare, brown, bountiful buttocks. Which were bolstered up even more extravagantly plump and juicy by her pulled-down panties; the panties bunched into a thin, white cotton line just below the bottom of her overflowing butt cheeks. They rippled and shivered and shuddered wickedly as she strolled over to the row of filing cabinets in the corner.

Watching the cheeky young woman squat down in front of the bottom drawer of a filing cabinet, Warren almost swallowed his tongue.. Her buttocks hung out like sun-ripened, sun-browned melons from the slender vine of her body, supported and buttressed by that tight line of panty.

He gulped. 'Wh-wh-what's th-th-the m-m-meaning of this!?' He stuttered whenever he got flustered. Staring into those fantastically fleshy orbs, gleaming like copper moons under the office lights. , his face and body flooded with more heat than even the brutal Brisbane summer could generate,. 'Y-y-you c-c-can't be d-d-dressed like that! By God, M-M-MacArthur himself might come by any moment!'

Imee slowly straightened up, lithe as a panther. She turned her head, but not her body. 'Why, whatever's the matter, General?' She placed her hands on her hips and pulled her best Betty Grable pose, times ten.

'By God, I'll t-t-teach you something about Army discipline, young lady!' Warren bellowed, untangling his long legs and jumping to his feet.

He stalked over to the ass-blessed girl, and clapped a hand to her cheek. Then the other one: gripping, squeezing, plying the thick hot firm flesh; his cock tenting his pants like a relocation camp. He smacked the right cheek, the left, watching and feeling the heavy butt flesh reverberate all through his surging body and mind.

Imee pursed her glossy lips and mewled, 'Oooh!' Her brown eyes gleamed. Her bouncy, butt-mounded body tingled all over – especially in the hand-warmed caboose. 'An army travels on its ass, doesn't it, General?' she said, Mae West sarcastically. 'Especially the brasshats.'

Warren grunted, clutching the girl's heated, impudent rump in his sweaty hands, his wire-rimmed glasses fogging up like Manila Bay. Her body shivered through her cheeks into his hands and throughout his wiry frame.

He reluctantly released her buttocks and grabbed her little hand and dragged her over to the chair. He dropped down into the rocker, then pulled the sassy, assy Filipina over his knobbly knees. He raised his right hand in warning, and she twisted her head around to glare at him, to dare him. And he fired an opening shot, smacking the girl's gloriously bulging behind.

'Mmmm, I thought you'd never get around to doing that,' she murmured, a la Barbara Stanwyck in *Ball of Fire*.

Warren spanked her again, and again. And again. Smacking her joyfully jumping cheeks over and over, his bony pale hand forming a stunning contrast with her lush, brown hills; e. Each cushiony touch of the succulent flesh sending thrills racing up his arm and into his groin.

Imee's quivering buttocks blushed not a bit, easily absorbing the impact of the blows; the sharp whack of burning hand on brimming ass echoing throughout the stifling office. 'Maybe I should call in the Marines, soldier-boy,' she taunted, a snarl curling her lips like Ida Lupino's in '*High Sierra*'.

'Y-y-you asked for it!' Warren spluttered. He picked a corncob pipe up off the desk and cracked it across Imee's brazen bottom.

The MacArthur mouthpiece was no match for this taut resistance. It broke apart like the Imperial fleet at Midway.

Warren tossed the stem aside, and picked up a pointer; whapped the rubber-tipped bamboo down on Imee's bum. Her cheeks and body jumped, and she moaned. He struck her repeatedly, lashing her swollen ass with the slender stick, making some small impression on her butt and one large

176

impression on her twat.

He raised his arm up to the ceiling fan, crashed the stick down on her bottom. And it splintered apart like the pipe.

'Damn it all!' Warren thundered, throwing the mortally wounded pointer to the floor. He ran a shaking hand through his shock of blonde hair, desperately thinking. Her over-endowed derriere stared up at him – demanded more.

Then he snapped his fingers, and leaned over the hard-breathing honey and felt around under the desk. Found the polished, knobbly walking stick and pulled it out. It was the spitting, preening image of the one Mac sometimes used.

With a righteous glint in his blue eyes, Warren rolled Imee off his knees and pulled her over to the 'strategy table', where the big, laminated map of the Pacific theatre was laid out. He positioned the girl's hands on the edge of the table and her legs slightly apart, so that she was bent forward, her smooth-skinned, spongy bottom showing. Then he pulled back the walking stick and turned it into a whacking stick, letting fly, smacking her plush bum with a resounding splash.

Miniature aircraft carriers and battleships went sailing, the heavy impact rattling the girl and the table. She bit her lip and whimpered, this stick actually leaving a mark on her seat, and soul.

Warren whaled her flagrant rear-end, blow after blow whistling in and thudding against ass, scrambling Allied strategy and shivering Imee's buttocks. She gasped, vibrated, her bloated butt cheeks taking on a life of their own; a trembly anticipation of a blow, then a fleshy embracing of it, sucking in the savage slash. Repeatedly, the knotted wood sunk into her stinging cheek-meat and set it to a gyration, raising a white-hot, red flush that fanned all through the girl's shimmering body.

Warren brutally caned her vibrant bottom. Before finally pausing, gasping for breath. He shoved his misted glasses up the slippery slope of his nose, his uniform soaked through with the sweat of exertion, his cock a hard, throbbing thing like the red neon lights in Manila's hoochie-coochie district. 'H-h-had enough?' he rasped.

Imee jerkily turned her head, her arms and legs and buttocks quivering wildly. Black mascara streaked her face; her brown eyes were shining pools of needful lust. 'Fuck me, GI!' she hissed. 'Now that you've warmed me up, fuck me in the ass with your big stick!' It was all nasty little Imee now, the glitzy Hollywood impersonations gone.

Warren dropped the knotted maple and his khaki trousers as fast as Zeroes dropped out of the sky during the Battle of the Coral Sea. He pulled his boner out of his skivvies, as Imee reached back and pulled her battered butt cheeks apart.

Warren glanced from the girl's tiny auburn pucker to his mushroomed purple hood and pulsing length of vein-ribboned pipe. He licked his lips, and swallowed. This looked tougher than an amphibious landing at night.

Imee dove a hand in between her legs and rubbed her pussy. Then smeared her bumhole with the hot, slick girl-juice. 'You do it, too,' she instructed.

Warren reached down between her slender, shaking legs and rubbed the damp, springy fur of her pussy. He gasped at the depth of her wetness, the soft, slippery feel of her private lips. Then he greased up his cock with the heated moisture, her juices on his prick making his knees buckle.

Gun loaded and lubed – check. Cheeks spread and open – check. Commence invasive action.

Warren steered his arrow-straight cock towards Imee's anxiously awaiting bumhole. He groaned when his cap bumped browneye, moaned when he pressed forward and she pressed back and his hood popped through and his shaft sunk home.

'Christ, yeah!' He plunged deep into Imee's hot, tight chute.

'Kristo, si!' she cried, wallowing in the wicked feel of Warren's hard cock stuffing full her pulsating ass.

He gripped her hand-spanning hips and pumped his narrow hips, sliding his iron dong back and forth in her gripping ass. She dug her red-varnished fingernails into Sumatra on one side of the map and the Hawaiian islands on the other. Up on her tip-toes, surging with pleasure with each penetrating thrust of his cock in her chute.

Warren started churning his hips, really pounding Imee's big butt with his battering-ram dick. He groaned, and she moaned, the room and body temperatures soaring, sweat flying, the frenzied smack-smack-smack of corded thighs striking cushiony ass, rattling off the picture-laden walls of the sex-funked office. Warren's knuckles went white on the girl's glistening brown skin, digging his nails into her soft flesh and pistoning his cock to the flapping balls inside her anus, over and over and over.

Imee took it and loved it, whimpering, shuddering, Warren pumped her full of a languid, liquid heat that flooded her to the sexual core. She tore a hand off the rocking tabletop and plunged it down and onto her pussy. When her fingertips touched her puffy clit it triggered a chain-reaction, an orgasmic explosion.

'O-Day!' Warren wailed, going off full-cocked in the girl's sucking bum. He jerked around on her rippling rear-end like a rutting Sherman tank, blasting off cap after cap of fiery jizz.

As Imee danced around on the end of his spurting prick, feeling his heated splashes, hot, humid ecstasy washed over her like high tide on an island beach.

'I don't have time for any air raid preparedness plans right now!' Brigadier-General Donald McDougall bellowed out in the hallway. 'Mac's expecting me for pinochle and brandy in the Officers' Club at eight!'

The weary sergeant just shook his head. General MacArthur had returned to the Philippines, as promised, four weeks ago. Slightly in the rear of an invasion force that Brigadier-General McDougall had been deliberately left out of. The tropical heat, apparently, having fried the one-star general's brain in his steel helmet some time earlier.

Warren and Imee heard the voices and hastily retreated from their advanced anal positions, Warren just making it into the outer-office in one clothed piece as his boss marched through the door. 'Evening, General,' he snapped, saluting the older man.

'At ease, Private Williams,' the General snorted, briefly eyeing his aide's damp, beet-red face. He sniffed at the strange scent in the air, then dismissed it as enemy propaganda. 'Get me the Tokyo Bay weather reports! I'm meeting Mac for whiskey and shuffleboard on the deck of the USS *Missouri* there in the morning. And I want to know if I should bring my rain slickers.'

He strode into his inner-office, a broad grin breaking over his sun-weathered face as he spotted Imee bent over the strategy table, straightening things up. He watched the girl's swaying, undulating rump and licked his chapped lips, his glassy grey eyes beaming. Then he humped up behind her and grabbed onto her plump, squeezable butt cheeks, and squeezed.

'What the hell!?' he roared, his young secretary's bum hot to his lecherous touch.

Imee giggled, as the General hoisted the hem of her dress and took a look, eyeing with astonishment the extent of her and Warren's brutal lovemaking.

'Wh-what's happened here!?' he sputtered, furious that someone had mustered on his parade ground. He'd plied Imee's ribald cheeks many times before, and had planned on launching his own anal invasion in only a matter of days. And now he'd been left behind on this one, as well. It was too much.

'By God, I'm going to get to the bottom of this!' he ranted, looking wild-eyed from Imee's blistered bum to the broken corncob and pointer lying on his desk. 'Someone's butt is going to be in a sling over this one!'

Warren grinned in the outer-office, fingering the General's recently received transfer orders. The old man was finally, mercifully, being sent home to his wife and his rotary club. Leaving the young Private free to pursue his back-end courtship of the bottom-beautiful Imee Aquino.

There was only room for one MacArthur in this man's army, after all.

Spanked by my own Step-daughter
by Teresa Joseph

The moment that I first started falling for Roger, I knew that I'd be living a cliché.

After all, he was forty-seven years old and I had only just turned twenty-two. So of course, it would be obvious to everyone that he was having a '*Mid-Life Crisis*', divorcing his wife and shacking up with a Bimbo who was less than half his age. But in reality, however, it was love at first sight, and I know that I will love him until I die.

As a matter of fact, even Roger's ex-wife saw how happy we both were together and wished us all the very best for the future. After all, she had only really married him in the first place because he had got her pregnant. So, in many ways, the divorce had been a fresh start for both of them and a real chance to finally be happy.

However, this cliché that I was living would never really be complete without the presence of a grown-up daughter from Roger's first marriage, banging on about the fact that her new *mother* was almost the same age as her. And yes, it turned out that Stacey was only a couple of months younger than I was.

Far from hating Roger for leaving her real mother though or resenting her new step-mother in any way, I'm pleased to say that Stacey was incredibly devoted to her father. In fact, they both even lived in the same apartment building so that they could spend a little time together each week.

From the moment that I first moved in with Roger after the wedding, my step-daughter made it absolutely clear: anything that made her dad feel happy would make her happy in turn.

And likewise, anything that made him feel *un*-happy would provoke a swift and proportional response. But although I just smiled and nodded, believing that these were only empty words, I received my first taste of what was to come the next day when Stacey saw me borrowing some cash from Roger's wallet.

'Did you ask him?' She demanded as she closed the door behind her.

I shook my head and shrugged my shoulders. I always borrowed money from my husband's wallet, just as he sometimes borrowed it from my purse.

The next thing I knew, though, I was sucking air through my teeth as Stacey suddenly smacked me on the thigh. It was a hot summer's day and I was only wearing a short skirt. But before I even had a chance to ask her what the hell she thought she was doing, she smacked me again as she told me off as if I were a naughty little child.

'What if Dad needs that money to pay for something?' she snapped angrily. 'What if he gets there and finds that he's short because you *borrowed* it without asking?'

By this point, half a dozen sore, rosy-pink handprints were forming along the sides of my thighs. All I had to do to stop her was to simply walk away, or even just cover myself with my hands. In fact, I knew that I could have eased the pain at any moment, simply by reaching down and rubbing my thighs. But instead, I just stood there with my hands up under my chin, dancing from one foot to the other as I winced with pain and waited for her to smack me again.

I apologised to her for taking the money and promised that I would *never* touch her dad's wallet without asking. Then, after Stacey had left, I pulled my knickers down and started fingering my pussy; actually feeling disappointed that she hadn't spanked my naked rump.

I've spent much of the last five years trying to understand it. But to this day, I still can't explain why.

I actually get off on being spanked by my own step-daughter, and I honestly don't believe that there's a real or a tangible reason.

Out of sheer curiosity, a few weeks later I even visited a visited a woman who spanked *Naughty Girls* for a living, just to see if she could turn me on as well.

When I arrived, I paid her for a full hour. But as it turned out though, I left after five minutes because I *really* wanted to punch her in the face.

When she smacked my thighs, I pulled away and told her to get off me. And when she started *telling me off*, and treating me like a child, I knew that I'd have to leave right away because I was practically fuming with rage. But the next day ironically when Stacey demanded to know what I'd been doing, annoyed about the fact that Roger had been really worried about me, my pussy tingled as my step-daughter quickly dragged me down over her knee, pulled off my knickers and began furiously spanking my bare behind.

It stung like hell, but I didn't try to resist. I didn't even try to cover myself.

Instead, I crossed my ankles as tightly as I could, just to keep myself from kicking or trying to escape.

I bit my tongue and held my hands together until my knuckles literally turned white. And as Stacey rhythmically spanked my bottom bright pink with the flat of her hand, I felt a wonderful orgasm building deep inside my pussy, being stoked by the burning agony in my rump.

I held my breath until my face was probably the same colour as my flaming cheeks.

When Stacey's hand got sore, I squealed with pleasure as she started using the sole of her flat shoe instead. And obviously mistaking the meaning of my outburst, she told me that I deserved it as she doubled the pace.

Less than two minutes later, I howled and squealed with pleasure as I climaxed and gold stars flashed in front of my eyes.

Of course, Stacey must have thought that I'd been keeping quiet because I was trying to be stubborn and defiant, refusing to give her the satisfaction of hearing me cry out or beg her to stop. So now of course, since I had finally 'broken down and started bawling,' she just kept going to make certain that I had learned my lesson once and for all.

Even though I'd already climaxed and the sore burning was almost unbearable, I didn't beg the woman to stop, and I still didn't try to move.

In fact, in the end, I believe that it's the sweet humiliation of being punished by my own step-daughter which makes me so eagerly submissive. The perverted shame of being spanked by a woman who's younger than me, even if it's only by a couple of months, and who, at least according to tradition, should be laying across *my* knee.

In fact, I can even remember experiencing the same sensations back when I was still at school. Because every day when she was standing behind me in the lunch queue, a girl named Donna (who must have been at least a couple of years younger than I was), would suddenly begin smacking the backs of my thighs.

Once again, I never moved or tried to complain, and I *certainly* didn't try to cover myself. Instead, I just kept shuffling forward as each girl ahead of me reached the lunch counter. And holding my hands very firmly in my lap as the sore pink handprints began to throb, I bit my tongue and held my breath as the tears streamed down my cheeks.

I would even try to time entering the lunch queue so that Donna was standing behind me every day. And a couple of times in my final year, I even got into trouble for wearing skirts that were *far* too short, longing to give Donna the opportunity to spank the tops of my thighs as well. But, in spite of all my uncertainty, after countless sleepless nights, I am absolutely certain of one thing.

I love Roger. I may love being spanked by his daughter, but that's got nothing to do with why I married him. I'm not merely using Roger so that I can be with her. And, as evidence of this, I know for a fact that if I ever cheated on my husband, his daughter would go absolutely ballistic and beat my backside until I couldn't sit down for a year. But even though the thought of this may sometimes turn me on, I could never possibly bring myself to hurt the man I love.

Besides, Stacey's punishment for my *minor misdemeanours*

was more than enough to satisfy my craving; smacking my thighs if I ever needlessly insulted Roger during an argument, and spanking my backside a delightful shade of pink whenever I stayed out without calling.

To be honest, most of the offences themselves were so trivial that I can't even remember why my step-daughter was so angry with me. But the idea and the memory of the spankings themselves endured; if I close my eyes when I'm fingering my pussy and wish that she is spanking me right there, I can almost seem to relive every single sharp and biting stroke.

Of course, a couple of the *crimes* that I've committed in the last five years have really stuck in my mind, mostly because the punishment itself was so deliciously unique. And from all of these memories, the one I'd really like to share was the time that Stacey caught me borrowing money from Roger's wallet again.

In spite of my step-daughter's warning, I'd seen a beautifully ornate, brown calfskin belt which I simply *had* to have. But by a cruel (or perhaps even a fortunate) twist of fate, this was the last day of the sale. I wouldn't get paid until the next day, and by then it would be too late.

I remember taking my time as I picked up my husband's wallet, almost begging for his daughter to suddenly walk through the door.

When she finally did, I almost let out a squeal of delight as she caught me red-handed, holding £100 cash in one hand and her dad's wallet in the other. I felt a tingle in my pussy as I struggled to explain myself, going on and on about the gorgeous belt which would make my whole life complete. She decided that if I loved belts so much, then I should have one across my rump.

As luck would have it, I was already wearing skin-tight jeans with a leather belt that day. And ordering me to take them off, she folded the belt into a fairly painful and erotic-looking strap.

Standing there in nothing but my white ankle-socks and my T-shirt, feeling my own pussy growing wetter by the second as

I waited for my step-daughter to begin, without thinking, I laced my fingers together and rested my hands on top of my head.

Of course, Stacey honestly didn't even seem to even notice. But as far as I was concerned, my posture really underlined the fact that I was desperate for my *punishment* to begin. And sure enough, when she started lashing the sides of my thighs, I physically needed to bite my tongue to keep myself from begging for more.

For more than ten minutes as I just stood there in the middle of the room, bolt upright and clenching my hands on top of my head, my step-daughter circled around and around, lashing every exposed millimetre of my thighs.

My face was red as I clenched my teeth and the tears were literally streaming down my cheeks. Every vicious whack across the front of my thighs was soon followed by another along the side. And this in turn always curled around to sting the front as well. An equally vicious whack then landed across the back of my thighs, and then another along the other side.

Starting up near my rump, Stacey methodically worked her way down to the very top of my knees. Working clockwise for five minutes before circling the other way, she made certain that every inch of my skin was swollen and blazing red; covered with angry purple welts that were left by the edges of the belt. And having long since climaxed and started howling like a baby, still standing bolt upright and never even considering that I could just simply run away, when Stacey ordered me to touch my toes, I obeyed without a single moment's thought. Following that, I spent another ten minutes howling as my step-daughter belted my naked peaches black and blue. Or to be more accurate, a deep, blazing shade of crimson, criss-crossed with the same angry purple welts that now covered my thighs.

After giving me the money to buy the calfskin belt from her own purse, she told me that I could expect exactly the same thing if she ever caught me '*stealing*' again.

Have any of you ever tried wearing skin-tight jeans over sore and inflamed thighs? The denim feels like sandpaper, aggravating the burning welts whenever you try to move. Indeed, I was still in tears when I went out to buy the belt in question. And when I tried to force myself to sit down and cross my legs, I almost screamed as the course thick material dug even further into my flesh.

After receiving a belting like that from Stacey, it would only be a matter of time before Roger would notice the marks. And even if I'd tried to hide them and had worn loose trousers 24-hours a day, he was also bound to notice how much I was wincing whenever I tried to sit down.

After all, a blushing pink bottom might only require a couple hours to recover, but the angry purple welts on my bottom and thighs took several *weeks* to heal. And when he asked me what on earth had happened as he rubbed some cooling cream into my skin, I felt myself coming as I explained how his daughter had been spanking me every week for several years.

Roger was aghast, but the truth was that the shame of it was actually turning me on. It seemed that I'd been longing to receive these angry purple marks for quite a while; the evidence that would finally force me to confess my humiliating secret.

'I was such a *naughty* girl,' I said, panting, as I longed to feel my husband's cock inside me. 'I tried to borrow some of your money without asking, and Stacey punished me really hard.'

Roger couldn't understand why I'd enjoyed it so much. But in the end, he honestly didn't have to. Being beaten by my own step-daughter like this had made me ecstatically happy, and the *shame* of admitting it to my husband was making me feel as horny as hell. So begging him to 'cuddle me better' as I spread my legs and lay down on the bed. Actually getting off on the slow throbbing pain that was burning in my bottom and my thighs, I actually squealed when my welts began to sting as we had the most wonderful sex of our marriage.

Sadly, that was the only time that my step-daughter has ever *really* punished me. And although she gives me an over-the-knee spanking a couple of times a month, she's expecting her first baby in November, and I don't think she'll have much time for me after that.

As weird as it may sound, however, now that Stacey's had an ultrasound and is positive she's having a daughter, I finger my pussy whenever I imagine turning forty-seven myself. And as I bring myself to climax, I can almost feel my naked rump being belted by my twenty-year-old step-granddaughter, because she's caught me taking money from her grandfather's wallet, just like her mother before her.

Hot Enough for June
by Philip Kemp

Very quietly and carefully, June turned the key in the lock. Mark always slept like a log – so if only she could creep in and get herself into bed, he'd never know what time she got in. Always assuming – she offered up a silent prayer – that he was asleep.

No such luck. Even before she'd closed the door behind her she heard Mark's voice from the lighted living room. 'June? That you?'

She turned, putting on her most innocent expression as Mark appeared in the doorway. 'Oh hi, honey! What're you doing still up?'

The look on her boyfriend's face was a mixture of concern and anger. 'You OK, baby? Where on earth have you been? Don't you know it's nearly three o'clock?'

Something told June she could be in even more trouble than she thought. This might need some serious cajoling. Putting her arms round Mark's neck, she offered him her cutest smile. 'Oh honey, I'm sorry. You know how it is when us girls get together. The time just went. I never noticed.'

'You've been at the restaurant with Cathy and Sue, all this time?'

'Why sure, honey, I told you that's what we were doing.'

Unwinding June's arms from round his neck, Mark took a step back. Anger was now definitely the expression that was winning out. Lightly and delicately, a few butterflies started performing a stately dance in June's tummy. 'June, that restaurant closes at midnight. I called them at 12.30. The staff were just heading home.'

She gulped. 'Oh, er. Yeah, well, we went on somewhere. Just for a bit.'

'Somewhere, just for a bit?' Mark repeated grimly. Taking her hand, he led her towards the living-room. 'Come in here, young lady. I think we need to talk.'

'Oh honey, it's awfully late,' she protested, trying to resist. There was something about the phrase "young lady" that made her feel strangely apprehensive. 'Can't it wait till the morning?'

'No, it can't. And tomorrow's Saturday. Or rather, today is. Plenty of time to sleep in, if we want to. Or for anything else that needs doing.'

Normally, the prospect of a long lazy Saturday morning in bed with her boyfriend would have filled June with delighted anticipation. She and Mark had only been living together a couple of months, and their love-life was still firing on all cylinders. But it crossed her mind that for once Mark – this new, grim, rather scary Mark – might have other ideas which might not prove quite so alluring.

In the living room Mark sat down on the couch, motioning June to sit opposite him. 'OK, my girl,' he said, 'time for some straight answers. Just where did you go after the restaurant?'

'Oh, just to a bar, honey. It was no big deal, honest.'

'No big deal, huh? June, you told me you'd be home well before twelve. Didn't you think I'd worry? Didn't it occur to you I'd be phoning round, frantically trying to find out where you were? Calling the hospital, even. Did you never even think of calling me? I tried your cellphone. But it's switched off.'

'Oh honey, I'm so sorry!' exclaimed June, genuinely meaning it. She went to give Mark a hug, but he held her off.

'No, stay where you are, June. I know you, and you're damn good at being all sweet and cute and loving, and getting round me that way. Well, not this time, my girl. Straight answers, I said. You went to a bar. Which one? And the truth, now.' he added, seeing June hesitate. 'Remember, I can always check up if I have to.'

'We, we went to Smokey Joe's,' June stammered.

Mark gazed at her, appalled. 'Smokey Joe's! That dive?'

'Oh, it's not that bad, honey, honest! Cathy knows one of the guys that work there. And people were pretty friendly. Let us play pool and everything.'

'Oh yeah, I just bet they did.' Involuntarily, his mind's eye conjured up a picture of his cutely curvy girlfriend leaning over a pool table in her form-hugging jeans, while the crowd of drunks and deadbeats that frequented Smokey Joe's feasted their eyes on her temptingly rounded rear end. 'I bet they just loved that. Three attractive young women, on their own, way past midnight. I'm amazed you three didn't get yourselves raped in the parking lot.'

'Oh, Mark honey,' wheedled June in her most melting tones, 'we were just fine. But it's so sweet of you to worry about me. And I'm really sorry I forgot to let you know.'

Again she went to hug him, and this time he didn't push her away. But as they kissed he suddenly froze and held her at arm's length. 'June, have you been drinking?' As she dropped her eyes he held her by the chin and lifted her face, obliging her to meet his gaze. 'The truth, now, young lady. Have you?'

'Er, well. I just had one …'

'One?'

'Well, maybe two …'

The look in his eyes was now sheer anger. 'On top of all this, you were drink-driving?' Mark's jaw tightened. 'OK, Mary June Macarthur. That's it. You are in deep trouble, young lady. Stand up.'

Nervously, June obeyed. There seemed to be a lot more of the butterflies, and now they were dancing a tango. Mark's use of her full name sounded decidedly ominous. 'Mark, what are you …?'

'Going to do? Something that should have been done a long time ago, my girl. I'm going to put you across my knee, take down your panties and give you a damn good spanking on your bare bottom. Now get those jeans down!'

'A *spanking*? But, but you can't. I mean, I'm 22. I'm much too old to be spanked!'

'Think so, do you? Well, young lady, this is where you

191

learn different. No girl is *ever* too old for a good spanking, and certainly not you. Now if those jeans aren't down in five seconds …'

Reluctantly, June started to undo her belt. 'But Mark, I'm not a little girl any more. No one's spanked me since I was ten!'

'Haven't they now? Well, maybe that's just the trouble! Your mom and dad are lovely people, but you twist them round your little finger and they let you get away with murder. If you'd spent a bit more time across your dad's knee as a teenager, maybe you wouldn't be in so much trouble now. As it is, my sweet, welcome to catch-up time!'

Reaching out, Mark pulled June's jeans down to her knees, then taking her by the hand drew her down across his lap so that the upper part of her body rested on the couch, with the plump curves of her bottom uppermost and perfectly positioned for his hand.

June's mind was in a turmoil. Part of her accepted that a good sound spanking was the least she deserved for the way she'd behaved this evening; and besides, she couldn't deny that there was something rather exciting about this new, masterful side to her boyfriend. But at the same time it was humiliating that she, an adult, an intelligent young woman, should be treated like this. And if the look on Mark's face was anything to go by, this was going to be no lenient spanking. A tingle of alarm quivered though her upturned bottom-cheeks; alarm that intensified when she felt his hands at her waist, and realised that her panties were being deftly lowered.

'Oh no, Mark, please!' she begged. Twisting round on his lap she gazed imploringly at him, her blue eyes filling with tears. 'I'm so sorry. Really I am! I'll never do it again, I promise! Please don't do this to me!'

Mark laughed scornfully. 'Oh come on, honey. This is me, remember? How often have I seen you pull this tearful, penitent act on traffic cops and people like that? Then two minutes later you're laughing at them for having been such suckers. Well, young lady, you're not suckering me.'

'Oh but please, Mark. At least not on the bare! It'll hurt.

192

And it's so embarrassing!'

'These little panties wouldn't be much protection, honey,' retorted Mark. 'As for embarrassing, that goes with the territory, wouldn't you say? In any case, I promised you a bare-bottom spanking, and that's just what you're going to get!' So saying, he drew down the skimpy garment till it dangled around her thighs, well clear of the target area.

And as target areas went, this one was a peach. Mark had often admired the shapely contours of his girlfriend's rear. And more than once, in her more wilful moments, his palm had itched to administer the treatment those ripe curves so temptingly invited. But now, as he prepared to give the sweet, spoilt girl the first real spanking of her life, he was struck as never before by what a superb bottom she had. Pale, full and beautifully rounded, the girlish mounds positively cried out to be spanked – long, lovingly and often. Enchanted, he stroked the cool globes, squeezing them gently. They felt deliciously soft, trembling at his touch as if anticipating the punishment they'd soon be enduring.

'You know, June,' he said, 'you've got a gorgeous bottom. Really beautiful. Only one thing wrong with it. It hasn't been spanked anywhere nearly enough. But that, young lady, is something I intend to put right. From now on you can count on getting this treatment whenever you deserve it. Starting right now.'

'Oh!' cried June as, out of the corner of her eye, she glimpsed Mark raising his right hand high in the air. The next second –

Smack.

'Ow!' she yelped, as much from surprise as from pain. Never would she have guessed just how sharply a hard male hand can sting a soft, unprotected female bottom.

Smack.

'Ow!' A second swat, just as hard, connected with her other cheek. Mark paused to admire the two pink hand-prints now adorning the pale mounds, then settled down to spanking her hard and steadily, smacking now left, now right, and taking care to cover the whole expanse of her ripe rearward curves.

After only a few spanks, a warm pink blush suffused the pretty bottom-cheeks, deepening steadily to a rich glowing red. With each spank June gasped and squealed, kicking and wriggling frantically. But Mark had her in a secure hold, and there was no escape for the increasingly penitent young woman.

'Ow!' she wailed. 'Oh, Mark, no more, please! It hurts, it really hurts!'

'You bet it does, honey,' retorted Mark pitilessly, as his hand continued to rise and fall. 'It's a spanking, remember? They're meant to hurt!'

There was another reason for June's discomfort. It was humiliating enough, in all conscience, for a bright, independent-minded 22-year-old to be turned over her boyfriend's knee and soundly smacked on her bare bottom like a naughty child. But even as the heat built up in her spanked rear end, she was embarrassingly aware that adjacent parts of her anatomy were also becoming heated. Her spanking was stinging like hell, worse than anything she'd ever known, but at the same time, she couldn't help realising, it was turning her on.

'Oh please stop, honey,' she implored tearfully. 'That's enough! Oh! Ow! I'm sorry. I'm really so, so sorry!'

'Are you, June?' asked Mark, pausing. 'I wonder. Are you sorry for what you did. Or just sorry because you're getting spanked for it? Do you know what you're being spanked for?'

'For drinking and driving?'

'Oh no, not yet. We haven't even got to that yet. This is for being so selfish and thoughtless. For staying out way past the time you said, and not letting me know. And then trying to lie about it when you got home.' He leaned over and stroked her hair. 'And also, honey, you're being spanked because I love you and care about you, and couldn't bear it if anything bad happened to you. So next time you're tempted to act so irresponsibly, I want you to remember two things: first, that I love you, and second, just what it feels like to be put over my knee and spanked good and hard on your bare bottom.'

He caressed the roseate curves. 'Your bottom's a lovely colour, my sweet. All hot and blushing. Makes it look even more beautiful. But it's going to be a whole lot redder before we're through here tonight.' He helped her up off his lap. 'OK, young lady, that's it for this stage. Now go into the bedroom and fetch me the hairbrush. The black one with a handle.'

June pouted tearfully, stamping her foot. 'That's not fair. Not the hairbrush. It'll be agony!'

'Oh, like my hand wasn't?' asked Mark, grinning. Reaching out, he landed a swat on June's burning rear that made her yip. 'Go get me that brush if you know what's good for you, my girl. If I have to fetch it, you'll be even sorrier. And no, you needn't pull up your jeans and panties. Take 'em right off!'

Resentfully, June stepped out of her jeans and panties and stomped off to the bedroom. Mark watched her go, relishing the sight of her rosy spanked cheeks peeking pertly out beneath her T-shirt, jiggling charmingly as she walked. She looked so adorable that he was tempted to follow her into the bedroom to cuddle and soothe her and make love to her. Quite apart from anything else, spanking his pretty girlfriend on her bare bottom was proving to be a highly erotic experience, and he had a rampant hard-on. But he repressed the impulse. Time enough for that when this sweet, spoilt girl had thoroughly learned her lesson.

In the bedroom, June couldn't resist checking her rear end in the mirror. 'Wow.' She gingerly stroked her fiery bottom-cheeks. The mirror also revealed a telltale gleam of moisture between her legs. How could something that hurt so much be such a turn-on, she wondered in bewilderment.

'June! Get that brush here now!' came Mark's voice from the living-room. This was a whole new side to her boyfriend, a man usually so gentle and easy-going. She ought to resent it, she knew, but somehow she was finding it exciting. Scary, sure, but exciting.

She trotted back into the living-room and held the brush out to Mark, pouting imploringly. 'Please, honey. Not too hard,' she begged.

'No harder than you deserve, my girl,' came the inexorable response. 'OK, back across my knee with you.'

Reluctantly, June let herself be drawn back down into prime

spanking position. Mark stroked the bristle side of the brush across her glowing curves a few times, making her wriggle, then turned it over and rubbed the wooden side over the same area. It felt cool against June's hot, spanked rear, but very soon, she reflected apprehensively, it would feel anything but.

'OK, my girl,' said Mark, 'the hand-spanking was for being thoughtless and selfish and not telling me where you were. The hairbrush is for going to that crummy dive and putting yourself in danger with all those lowlifes.'

'And – and the drink-driving?' she asked nervously.

'We'll get to that.'

Yikes, she thought. And then 'Yikes!' she yelped out loud, as the hairbrush landed with a sharp crack on the already tender and ultra-sensitive curve of her right cheek. The hand-spanks, she now realised, had been mere love-taps in comparison with the brush's burning kiss. 'Oh stop, honey, please. It hurts! It hurts!' There was nothing phoney about June's tears now. After only a dozen swats with the brush she was crying for real, with helpless convulsive sobs.

Yet strangely enough the pain of the spanking wasn't the main reason she was crying, although that was the catalyst that was allowing the tears to flow. As her spanking continued June found herself experiencing a strange mix of emotions – uppermost among them a sense of release. For the first time since infancy she had totally ceded control to another person. In allowing Mark to spank her – for she hadn't physically resisted him at all – she had handed over responsibility, giving him all her trust. In return she felt deeply loved, cared for and protected, even while the stinging spanks rained down on her blazing bottom, and this confused medley of emotions found vent in a flood of tears.

Hearing his girlfriend's sobs, and recognising how different this was from the easy tears she could call on to manipulate situations to her advantage, Mark was tempted to stop spanking her. But it was vital, he felt, that her lesson should be well and truly learnt, and that this spanking should be one she'd never forget. So, hardening his heart, he brought the brush down a few dozen more times on her scarlet, squirming cheeks, paying particular attention to the sensitive sit-spot: that delectable under-curve where bottom meets thigh.

To June, gasping and wailing, it seemed as if her bottom was on fire and swollen to twice its regular size. But at last Mark paused, and stroked the fiery mounds. 'OK, honey,' he said gently, 'we're nearly there. Up you get.'

Awkwardly she rose and stood tearfully rubbing her burning rear. 'Nearly there?' she gulped. 'Oh, Mark, haven't I been spanked enough yet?'

Mark stood up and hugged her. 'Not quite, honey,' he said. 'There's still that drink-driving to take care of, remember? Now just lie over the arm of the couch like a good girl, with your bottom nice and high. You're going to get two dozen good licks with the belt.'

'No,' said June, but her voice was mostly just breath and all her independent willpower seemed to have deserted her. Obediently she draped herself over the couch's padded arm, buried her face in the cushions and awaited her fate. There came to her ears a swishing noise which, she realised, must be Mark drawing his belt through the loops of his jeans. The sound was intensely scary, yet strangely thrilling.

How sweet she looked lying there so submissively, Mark thought, her plump round bottom upraised and defenceless, its vivid blush contrasting exquisitely with the whiteness of her back and thighs. Never had she looked more feminine, nor more adorable. But at the same time her well-spanked cheeks presented an irresistible target. Doubling the belt in his grip, he took careful aim.

Thwap.

'Ah!' yelped June, as the supple leather lit a trail of fire across her already blazing rear end. And she continued to yelp and squirm as the belt descended two dozen times in all, deepening the blush on her bouncing flesh-cushions. The pain was intense, but at the same time it seemed to lift her and take her to some place she'd never been before. She hardly registered when Mark stopped spanking her, but lay shuddering and whimpering, lost in the turmoil of her senses.

Gently Mark lifted her from the couch and hugged her

closely in his arms. 'It's OK, honey,' he murmured, stroking her incandescent rear cheeks. 'It's all over now. You've had your spanking and you took it very well. You're a sweet lovely girl and I love you very much.'

Lifting her tear-stained face June kissed him passionately, pressing her body against his. 'I love you too,' she whispered tremulously, 'and I promise I'll never do anything so silly again.' Mark kissed her back, letting his hand stray down between her legs. Her cleft was dripping wet, and at his touch she moaned deep inside her throat. 'Oh please, yes, come inside me now,' she murmured urgently. 'But I'm too sore to lie on my back.'

So moments later June once again found herself bent over the couch, her blushing rearward curves presented to her lover as he drove deep into her from behind, feeling the heat of her well-spanked bottom against his belly until, within seconds, they exploded together in a gasping, simultaneous climax.

Later still they lay closely entwined in bed together, drifting into warm post-coital slumber. June's bottom was still very sore, but she was aware that the sting had transmuted itself into a deep radiant glow that was much closer to pleasure than to pain. She felt cleansed, released, and very much loved and cared for.

'Mark?' she murmured.

'Yes?'

'You remember what you said, about how from now on you'd spank me whenever I deserved it?'

'Yes.'

'Did you mean it?'

'Course I did. Why?'

'Well, I was just wondering. If it wasn't always quite so hard, would it *only* be when I deserved it?'

More Spanking Titles from Xcite Books

9781905170937 £7.99

9781906125837 £7.99

9781906125899 £7.99

9781906373702 £7.99

First Spankings – True Spanking Initiations
By Peter Birch

Accounts of real spankings given to real women! From the occasional bit of fun to tales from the most dedicated enthusiasts, the detailed stories include well know names from the genre of spanking erotica, many personal friends of the author, and confessions from around the world. It's an enthusiast's book, no question, but if you're curious about what really makes the kinky girls tick, then this is a must for any erotica shelf.

Peter Birch has been spanking girls for thirty years now, and has collected stories from the thirties to the noughties. This is the very first encyclopaedic erotica collection of erotic punishment given by boys to girls, and given by girls to girls, even in public. And one thing is guaranteed: every single confession is a genuine account of a woman's first experience going over the knee.

ISBN 9781907016271 £7.99

203